IMMIGRANTS OF TIME

IMMIGRANTS OF TIME

A GREAT DAY TO BE ALIVE

ISBN: 978-1-7360516-0-3

Library of Congress Control Number: 2020922203

Any references to historical events, real people, or real places are used fictitiously. Names, characters, and places are products of the author's imagination. Any resemblance to actual persons, living or dead, or actual events is purely coincidental.

Printed by A.G. Torres in the United States of America.

First printing edition 2021.

I dedicate this novel to my family of predominantly Native American descent who immigrated to this country in search of a better future for themselves and their children.

CONTENTS

CHAPTER 1 – WAKING UP AT LAST

The star-filled night sky was accompanied by the Milky Way acting as an arrow pointing west. Fleeing the violence and escalating severity of hurricanes on the East Coast, Sebastian drove his family across the forested canyon highway. West was going to be their new home. Although it was night, his six-year-old son was wide awake, despite the advice given to him to get some sleep. He tugged on his serape scarf while exploring the cosmos. His eyes were glued to the sky, as this was his first time seeing such a celestial body drawn out on the dark canvas. He had only ever known the electric lights of New York City. In the passenger seat sat Sebastian's partner, the mother of his child. The couple being around age thirty. The baseball cap on her head casted a silhouette over her eyes as she snuck glances at him and their child through the car's rear-view mirrors. Her wide pink smile gave away that she too was excited for the fact that her family was finally moving towards a better life.

"Looks like we're going to be celebrating New Year's Eve on the West Coast for the first time," she said.

"2042 here we come," Sebastian said smiling with his eyes still on the road. "For the first time we're also going to be celebrating Cinco de Mayo, Mother's Day, Father's Day, Fourth of July, Día de los Muertos and much more on the West Coast."

Sebastian gripped the wheel tighter. He began shifting his eyes from the road to the stars.

"Hey, do you want to get some rest? I can take over the wheel."

"No. No, I'm fine. Really. I am."

Sebastian let out silent breaths until he regained his focus. He did not want to let go of the wheel. He enjoyed driving in a quiet night when the stars were visible.

1

Since he was last a soldier of the global war currently engulfing the planet, the stars had always cast a warm energizing spell on him much more than what the sun did for many people. He did not know why but it did. He was in a good mood, made clear by their continued conversation, but the war was soon on his mind. He tried to stay cheerful but suddenly fell into a flashback and lost control of the wheel. The screeching of the tires sliding off the road were paralleled by screams inside the vehicle until a crash into a tree down the hill was the last sound heard in that dead-silent forest.

**

A man in his early twenties opened his eyes for the first time in who knew how long. He lay on the hospital bed, surrounded by human-shaped robots. Their silver-and-gold metallic bodies were so shiny that the little amount of light in the room that bounced off their bodies rivaled the sun. He grabbed the top of his short black hair, as if that could stop the pounding in his head. He gazed down at his amber-skinned hands, and then at his feet. One of the robots poked the man with a needle, starting from his toes and ending with his head, provoking every imaginable reflex possible.

"Hey, where am I?" the man asked, irritated by the pokes. "Who are you? What's going on?"

The robots in the dimly lit room remained silent. He began to sweat profusely. He couldn't remember anything, not even his name. His heart pounded faster and faster.

"All physical tests complete," said one of the robots, in a soothing voice.

"Where am I?" the helpless man asked again, struggling to breathe. One of the robots put its arm on the man's shoulder. "Who am I?"

"Subject is coming close to shock," a robot said.

"Administering tranquilization for the patient," another robot said. Through the robot's hand popped out a syringe, stabbing into the man's shoulder. His vision blurred as he fell asleep.

"Success," said another robot. "All cognitive tests are complete."

**

Upon regaining consciousness, the man opened his eyes but quickly closed them. His eyes were not well adjusted to the light. He felt himself covered in soft silk pants and shirt while atop a cushioned chair. He forced himself to open his eyes again, to make out his setting. His chair began to adjust on its own, gently pulling his body back and cradling him into a reclined position. The light was still too much for his eyes, and he now relied on his hearing. Birds chirping. Wind blowing in the distance. He was at peace, his heart not racing like before.

Faint footsteps slowly became louder. He opened his eyes and looked at the ceiling directly above. His eyes were glued to the mirror above as it reflected his image. He could not even recognize himself. His heart began to race once more. As the footsteps got louder, he realized this was his opportunity to ask someone questions. The chair pushed him back up relaxing his heart rate through a release of warmth. The footsteps stopped, and a man wearing a green camouflage military uniform stood over the seated man. An older-looking man sat in a far corner. If one had to guess, he was in his thirties. He must have been sitting there quietly the entire time, examining the holographic screens floating in front of him. The more matured man fixed his short salt-and-pepper hair. He was staring not at the military man but at the man in silk clothes.

"We almost lost the patient, but I read the charts," said the older man, as the projected lights disappeared. "He'll be fine."

He stood up, tucking away his serape scarf, calmly leaving no answers to the man with no memories.

"Wait, what's going on?" the patient asked. He looked up at the remaining man in the room and tried to get up, placing his hands on the armrests. His body's weakness got the best of him though, and he soon gave up.

"Relax, sir," the military man said. He waved his hands in the air, forming a bright chart. A heartbeat line appeared on the chart. "I am Drill Sergeant Benjamin Taylor, but for now feel free to call me Taylor. I know you have a lot of questions. Rest assured, your questions will be answered. You are at this institution as a patient. You could say this is a rehabilitation center of sorts for those with amnesia. If you need help, you can use this device to call for assistance."

The drill sergeant clamped a clear bracelet on the seated man's left wrist.

"What is this for?" the patient asked.

"What isn't this for?" he responded with a grin. "You will need this for pretty much everything. It'll be your map, communicator, etc. It will help you get around the region. It will do a lot for you if you are near a Universal Information Technology System, or 'U-ITS' for short. Come on, I'll show you a U-ITS."

The drill sergeant motioned with his right hand for the patient to get up and follow him. Now with a little more strength, the patient was able to stand and walk down the hallway, toward a door and into another room. Through the window, the patient saw a magnificent view of the institution. There were white-and-blue castle-like towers and other buildings connected by a labyrinth of bridges. The drill sergeant coughed to get the man's attention. A crystal-clear obelisk with platinum designs on it sat at the center of the room. Drill Sergeant Taylor raised his left arm toward the U-ITS. A clear bracelet on his left wrist lit up the crystal obelisk.

"Welcome, Drill Sergeant Taylor," said a soothing feminine voice. "How may I be of assistance?"

"This bracelet around your wrist is called a satellite bracelet," Taylor said to the patient. "The voice you're hearing is Citlali. She is an artificial intelligence. Now hold your satellite bracelet toward the U-ITS like I did."

The patient slowly moved his left hand toward the U-ITS. Life lines were projected along its glow followed by a DNA strand. A small hologram of the patient appeared next to the obelisk.

"Welcome to the Universal Information Technology System, Sebastian Ramirez."

The patient finally had an answer. He now knew his name. He still had no memory, but his name was a start. His name was Sebastian Ramirez.

"In time, you will be able to modify how U-ITS behaves to you as an individual," said Drill Sergeant Taylor, leading Sebastian down several halls and stairways. "It will learn how to search for what may interest you. U-ITS has no limits, as you will see. While rehabilitating, you will stay in this room on this level."

They entered a small, white room. The sunlight shining through the window illuminated the room's plain style. There was a white bed with white sheets and white drawers. There was also a white walk-in closet and a mirror across from the window. A door adjacent to the entrance led to his private bathroom.

"Am I forced to stay in this room?" Sebastian asked.

"No, you are free to roam around," the drill sergeant said grinning. "Don't cause us any trouble though."

"Will I be getting any visitors soon?"

"Focus on rehabilitation."

The man in camouflage walked out of the room. Sebastian walked toward the window to get a view of where he was, hoping for some sort of familiarity with the view. From his second story view he saw stretches of green trees and fields blocked out the horizon. Squirrels flew from one tree to another, and chinchillas ran around from bush to bush. He looked up to see a bright, blue sky. Small, black birds chirped as they flew by. He grew curious of these birds when suddenly his satellite bracelet vibrated. A flashing green dot appeared on it. A hologram of words appeared over the bracelet.

"Those black birds are called dusky seaside sparrows," read the same female voice as before. "They were declared extinct in the year 1990 but have been cloned from their remaining DNA to preserve their existence." Sebastian was caught by surprise. He had even more questions than he did before. What other abilities was this satellite bracelet capable of? "As Drill Sergeant Taylor mentioned earlier, 'U-ITS has no limits,'" continued the voice, mimicking Drill Sergeant Taylor's voice. "Don't be startled. I am here to assist you."

"Thanks, Citlali. By the way that is a nice name."

"Thank you it comes from a Native American language called Nahuatl. It means star. Fitting name considering that stars have guided people in the past and now I, an artificial intelligence, am guiding people now. Would you like to begin getting adjusted to the features of U-ITS, Sebastian?"

"Yeah, sure. Why not?"

"Very good, let's begin by getting around this institution. A popular feature is a mini-map that can be displayed right above the satellite bracelet. I could find out what you're thinking, but that would be an invasion of privacy. I'm good at reading body language, and as time passes I will be able to more accurately figure out what you are thinking so I can better accommodate you. As you are brand new to the system, simply say 'map' to open up a map of your surroundings."

"Read ... minds?" Sebastian asked as nerves tickled his fingers.

"Yes, but I won't," Citlali said. "I'm just pointing out technology exists for reading minds, but don't worry, it is illegal to use such gadgets. Go on, say 'map.'"

"Map," he said, wishing he hadn't heard about mind-reading technology. In an instant, there was a projected map of the floor he stood on. He stepped outside his room and thought about seeing the other patients of the institution.

"I'm going to guess you want to meet some other patients?" Citlali asked. A red line appeared on the map. After a turn and around the corner, he followed the map past another hallway filled with empty rooms and approached a din of chatter beyond the closed door at the end of the red line. He creaked open the door and saw three people sitting down, wearing the same silk shirts and pants as him. They were huddled together in front of a projected hologram showing a woman in a purple trench coat talking about the most recent developments from the asteroid mining conglomerate. Ignoring the news, he looked at the people whose eyes were glued to the hologram. He swung his hand in front of their faces and received no response.

"They're not talking for some reason," said a well-built man sitting across the room with a woman across from him. The two looked to be in their early twenties. The man had much tanner skin than Sebastian, but the lady was fairer than them both, possibly because of the light shining on her through the window she leaned on.

"Why?" Sebastian asked.

"They seem to be in some sort of shock," the man said. "One by one they came into this room, and one by one they entered this zombie-like state. We, on the other hand, seem fine."

"They usually get glued to the hologram within a few seconds of being in this room," said the young lady, staring out a window near the man. "You were not drawn directly to the hologram as they were, so I think it's safe to assume you won't become like them."

"All of this is too strange," Sebastian said. "Where are we?"

"I wish I could answer that," said the man. "I truly do, but I have as many questions as you."

"Are you a patient here as well?" Sebastian asked.

"I am," he said tensely. He looked over to his side. Behind him was another door. "I was told to wait here. It's not like we can leave anyways. This door is locked. I can't break it down; I tried already."

"If you wish to leave, you may do so now," said the man's satellite bracelet.

A click followed, and the door opened. The three looked at the door and froze. The woman placed her hand on her chest as if it were the fifth time today given her then annoyed expression. Was this some sort of sick game, they wondered?

"In that case, I'm going," the man said, getting up from his seat. He peeped through the door before walking on. "I don't know about you, but I'm getting tired of standing around."

"My name is Rosa and that's Ryan," the young lady said, pointing at the man exiting the room.

"I'm Sebastian," Sebastian said, following Ryan and Rosa. "Hey, where are you going?"

"To get some answers," Ryan said.

His satellite bracelet pointed him down a series of halls, rooms, and turns. They stopped at a set of circular doors where a square sign turned green. The doors opened and inside was a dimly lit elevator. The trio entered, startled when the doors swept closed behind them and confused about their next step. There were no buttons, only walls. Finally, the elevator shook and moved sideways. They quickly pushed their hands against the walls to remain balanced. As the elevator moved outward from the building, the walls around them were no longer dark but deceptively clear, as if there weren't any. They all jumped around a little when they saw that the floor under them was clear also. The elevator was transparent. The green fields and blue skies were plentiful. They saw other buildings of the institution. Everything looked tranquil except for the courtyard below, where there were dozens of zombie-like patients all in the same silk clothes Rosa, Ryan and Sebastian wore. It was a startling scene, and as the three passed overhead, they couldn't help but stare down at all the sad faces on the people walking around aimlessly. There were so many of them. What were their stories? Would they ever find out why they were at this institution? The trio glanced worriedly at each other and then back at the courtyard.

Once inside the next building, the elevator had a visible ceiling, floor and walls again. The doors opened, and a few people and robots stopped to look at them as they walked out. A man with tan skin, orange eyes and a silver medical coat that matched his hair walked up to them as if he were expecting them. And despite having aged hair his face was nearly untouched by time. He was as young as the three patients before him. He motioned to the three to follow him and turned down a corridor, his maroon pants flopping with each step. He took them to an office and sat them down.

"I am Charles Mendez," the man in the silver coat said, settling in behind a desk. "I am the warden of this institution and have been assigned to assist you three with any issues or concerns you may have. Let me first say that you three are doing well compared to the other patients."

Charles noticed their troubled, frustrated faces and gave a sympathetic nod.

"Look, I know you have questions, so let me cut to the chase. It is the year 2099."

He stopped for a moment and caught his breath, looking carefully at the three as if expecting some sort of response. The patients looked at each other, not sure what to say. They were given a year, but the year did not mean anything to them.

"I know you three have no memories before today," Charles continued. "Those memories will come back to you eventually; there is no need to be worried. You three will be allowed to leave this institution to become reacquainted with the world, but you must come back to us in order to begin the rehabilitation. You have to trust that you're in safe hands."

Again, he looked at the three in a serious but kind way, furrowing his eyebrows.

"Now, can I trust you three to come back to this institution for continued health monitoring?" Charles asked. The three looked at each other and turned to Charles, nodding in agreement. "Splendid! We are going to do everything to the best of our ability to help you. Any questions?"

"What happened to us, and why can't we remember anything before today?" Ryan asked.

"You three were in serious accidents," Charles responded. "We recovered you and have done all we could to help you recover to full physical health. As for what happened I cannot yet say, but rest assured: you will find out soon, once you begin to readjust to society."

"Why can't you tell us?" Rosa asked.

"Did you notice the countless wandering people outside in the courtyard?" Charles asked. "Those are people who learned of their traumatic accidents too early. Most likely from flashbacks or as we sometimes call them: memory incursions. But if you made it this far, you will all be fine so long as you figure things out at your own pace."

"What exactly does that mean?" Rosa asked.

"Like I said, you all will have to readjust to society on your own," Charles insisted. "Consider it as part of your occupational therapy."

"There was a man I encountered before I saw Drill Sergeant Taylor," Sebastian interrupted. "He had a … what is it called … I can't remember. A serape scarf! Who was he? Do I know him?"

"Don't worry, Mr. Ramirez," Charles cautiously said. "He may have been one of the directors of this facility checking on his newest patient."

Sebastian felt a little reassured but wondered if the identity of the man was purposely being kept from him. He decided to bury the inquiry for now and focus on his rehabilitation.

"I will be of assistance should the situation arise," Charles clarified. "The part of the world we are in is safe. You three are more than welcome to venture on your own and return to this institution to rest."

With another smile, he stood up from his chair and gestured for the three to follow him. They left the office and followed him down a hallway, passing more staff and robots, to the receptionist desk. At the desk was another U-ITS obelisk. The warden moved his left wrist toward the U-ITS.

"Hello, Charles," greeted Citlali. "What can I do for you?"

"Since this is their first time, I will be checking these three patients out," Charles responded. "They are under my care, and although I won't always be with them, I want them to be under careful watch. If they are to get into any trouble, have their satellite bracelets automatically contact me. Now raise your satellite bracelets toward the U-ITS, please."

The three patients raised their bracelets toward the U-ITS, Charles' bracelet beginning to glow white alongside their own. The U-ITS obelisk made a slow, rhythmic, beeping sound.

"All is done," Citlali said. "You are now documented as the caretaker of Rosa, Ryan, and Sebastian. You will be their emergency contact if they are in any sort of trouble. Good luck."

"Thank you, Citlali," he said with a smile. "Off you lot go now. Through those double doors right over there. If you need to reach me, your satellite bracelets will put you in contact with me."

His smile widened even more. It was obvious he could not keep his excitement to himself. The three looked in the direction he was pointing. Past the receptionist desk were two big, blue doors with floral carvings on them. They looked at the doors cautiously, then at each other, and then finally at Charles.

"The answers you seek will come to you," he said.

In no time at all, Ryan began walking toward the doors and Rosa followed, Sebastian not far behind. The doors opened on their own and their bodies were met with the sun's glare. As they walked out of the institution, their feet were met with soft ground. As their eyes adjusted to the light, they saw fields of green and big, strong trees in front of them. There were animals everywhere, walking, running, and flying.

After taking a few steps, Rosa, Ryan, and Sebastian noticed they were no longer wearing their color-changing patient uniforms. Ryan was wearing burgundy dress pants and a white dress shirt with minor black lining. Rosa had on light beige khakis and a sky-blue zip-down shirt. Sebastian had on a black short-sleeve shirt with three buttons at the top, and tan pants. They looked at each other, admiring how well the clothes suited them. They were also in awe at the transformation, but particularly pleasing to Sebastian was seeing the smiles on Rosa and Ryan. Although he had just met them, he was happy to see them smile for the first time.

"I like the way we look," giggled Rosa, admiring her white sneakers.

"Incredible, but how?" Ryan asked. He looked at his outfit and moved his feet around, appraising his new bronze shoes. Sebastian looked at his weightless footwear and was pleased with his golden-brown boots.

"The fabric you are wearing is made of a special material," said Citlali through the satellite bracelet. "It changes when you want it to."

They soon found a stone path and followed it to a mint hill, and from the top they saw a city in the distance. The three looked at each other again for a moment before breaking into a sprint down the mint hill toward the colorful city. Optimistic they would soon be met with answers, they ran like children, jumping around at their newfound freedom, energy flooding their veins. It was now time for them to explore the world to discover who they were and where they came from.

CHAPTER 2 – MAKE YOU FEEL MY PAST

They made their way into the footsteps of the vibrant city, embraced by the constantly shifting and expanding skyscrapers. Emerald dust blew with the wind along the gold-paved streets. There were people, robots and holograms moving about. Numerous animals climbed on people and moved by their side. Above them there were hundreds of thousands of colorful hover cars in the air. Even if one looked hard enough, one could not find two of the exact same hover cars. The flying vehicles moved at the same pace as each other and followed a sort of air-traffic pattern tic-tac-toeing along the sky. There were also people skydiving, and some even flying from numerous parts of the top of the skyscrapers. They jumped from the roof and then in a curve, eventually disappearing into the distance like flying squirrels.

"Where do we go from here?" Rosa asked.

"How about a tour of the city?" the satellite bracelet suggested.

"All right, Citlali," Sebastian asked. "Where should we start?"

Citlali guided them through the nearest skyscraper. After endless twists and turns through the red-carpeted hallways, they arrived at an opening in the wall.

"Please enter the elevator," the satellite bracelet said. "Once inside, it will hover the three of you up to your floor destination."

The three slowly made their way forward. Ryan moved his head into the empty shaft and looked up at what appeared to be an endless tower of space and glowing dust. As he walked into the opening, his body slowly elevated off the ground with a shoulder length platform under his feet. All three gasped for a moment, but then Ryan smiled and they all laughed.

Sebastian walked into the opening, followed by Rosa, who excitedly jumped in. As all three hovered, they looked at each other with a smile followed by a look of confusion.

"Okay, now what?" Rosa asked.

"Your destination is floor seventy," Citlali responded. They were lifted off from the first floor toward the seventieth floor. They arrived seconds later and were gently nudged out of the elevator shaft.

"Wow, anybody else's insides tickling?" Rosa giggled.

They were outside once again, on one of the side roofs of the building. It wasn't the top floor of the building, which continued about two dozen floors upward. This roof had glass-lined pathways and trees as colorful as the sunset. With the guidance of their satellite bracelets, they made their way across the roof. As they walked on one of the paths, benches and fountains formed all around them. The benches and fountains disappeared as they passed, with new ones appearing ahead. They made it to the edge of the roof and spotted another U-ITS. The trio knew the drill by now. The three moved their left hands toward the U-ITS simultaneously, and their satellite bracelets began to glow white. Only a few steps away, bits of gray metal shards were moving around like a spinning orb. They were shaken by this, unsure what to expect. They stood still and watched in amazement as more and more metal shards appeared out of thin air, eventually forming a vehicle.

"The gray metal crystals you see is reanimation technology at work," Citlali said. "These reanimation crystals can be used to make furniture, vehicles, utensils, buildings and so much more. Reanimation technology has no limitations on what it can be used for. In this case, it is being used to make you a hover car."

The metal shards stopped moving upon completing the flying vehicle. The hover car was a thing of beauty: It had a triangular shape and headlights on each of its edges. It was red, white and black, giving off a sporty vibe. In the center of the vehicle was enough room for six adults. Directly above the passenger seats was a dark-tinted glass dome allowing the passengers to view their surroundings while being shielded from sunlight.

The glass dome raised while an area below it transfigured itself into stairs, allowing them to enter the vehicle. The dome lowered again after they sat down, and under their feet the floor became transparent to allow for another view as they traveled. A rumbling noise indicated they were leaving the roof of the building. The hover car accelerated upward. Like in the elevator they shot upward in a matter of seconds, triggering another tickling sensation in their stomachs. Once they were high in the air, the hover car stopped its upward trajectory and began slowly rotating. Everyone was lost in laughter from the sudden jump. When their bodies adjusted from the launch into the air, they looked out the glass and saw all the corners of the skyscraper city. There were many more parks on other buildings. Many kinds of birds flew through the skies. The trio was unable to name any one species. They were so colorful and exotic.

"Hey Citlali," Sebastian began. "Can you tell us something about these creatures flying by us?"

"I can tell you a lot about them," Citlali responded. "All of these creatures were created by a special class of genetic engineers. The creatures contain traits from the original species of Earth: land animals such as dogs, monkeys and lizards; bugs such as beetles, crickets and butterflies; marine mammals such as fish, squid and whales; birds such as eagles, penguins and swans; some even contain traits from Earth's elements and once-extinct species."

"Genetically … engineered?" Rosa asked, puzzled.

"Yes," Citlali answered. "There is an infinite number of combinations of traits when genetically engineering a species. Many valuable kinds of species are being created every day to benefit Earth."

After floating in midair for a few minutes, the hover car slowly moved in the direction of where most of the skyscrapers were concentrated.

"Where are we being taken?" Ryan asked as they descended onto one of the skyscrapers.

"To the *heart* of the city," Citlali answered.

Once the three stepped onto the roof of the skyscraper, the hover car dissolved. Bit by bit, it disappeared into the air. They went down an elevator and exited the building through one of its main hallways. Holograms surrounded them advertising information, from travel trips that would make their stay "feel like home" to fashion that would make them "feel like themselves." It was as if the holograms knew what they were thinking and what they wanted. Ryan started to gasp for air and took off for the exit. Sebastian and Rosa chased after him.

"Hey!" Rosa shouted. "Are you okay?"

"I don't know why we're here," Ryan said wheezing. "What are we doing here!? How are we supposed to get answers from roaming these streets?"

A red light beeped on their satellite bracelets. The light stopped, and a small map projected itself onto their bracelets. On the map was a green dot which signified exactly where the three were. It was connected to a trail of blue lines indicating their route.

"Where is this going to lead us, Citlali?" Ryan asked.

"Follow the path and you will find out," responded Citlali. "Trust me."

Without further hesitation, the three started on the path toward their destination. After a few turns and an endless series of crowds on the route, the three made it to the end of the trail. They looked everywhere and saw people with smiles on their faces. Their teeth were white and strong. There were all sorts of smiles. Content smiles. Joyful smiles. Flirtatious smiles. Their smiles were so powerful, the three could not help but smile as well. Even Ryan, who only moments ago was gasping for air, was instantly uplifted. There were couples holding hands, laughing, kissing and hugging. They were dancing and playfully chasing each other through the streets. Everyone was happy and with someone. No one was alone.

A young man entered the scene on a second-floor balcony nearby. He had curly blue hair and gray-colored eyes. He was alone. He was not smiling, dancing, laughing or kissing anyone. He slowly gravitated from the second-floor balcony toward the ground, passing by all the people.

"Citlali, why did you take us here?" Sebastian asked.

"Just wait and see," Citlali said. On the pavement the lone man was walking on came out a blue light. He stopped and at that exact moment so did everyone else on the street. This blue light became a line as it traveled through the street like water in a channel while also avoiding everyone's paths. The line remained connected to the man as it moved around the street.

"This section of the city is called the Lover's District, or sometimes the Heart of the City," said Citlali. "It's a popular place for people seeking love. Everyone's satellite bracelets are constantly exchanging information with each other to see who will pair up best with whom. When two people are seen as a great match for each other, amazing things happen. The light you see under the man is making its way to a person who has already been matched up with him."

The light finally reached a woman with short purple hair and honey-colored eyes. Everyone moved out of the way so the two individuals could see each other. When the path between them was cleared, they locked eyes, first in a curious daze, then in mere astonishment. They approached each other in a dancing manner matching the rhythm of the nearby music. They moved their hips from left to right, showing the whites of their smiles. The light on the ground between them remained, but shrunk as they neared each other. The crowd parted around the two as they started to dance in a circle while keeping only an arm's distance from each other. The crowd began clapping together. A thin, golden mist appeared. It surrounded everyone and everything as the audience continued to dance and clap. The two continued to dance closer and closer to each other until they were in each other's grasp. They looked into each other's eyes and kissed. The clapping slowly stopped as everyone danced and minded their business like before.

"That was interesting," Rosa said, staring at the newly formed couple.

"It sure was," Sebastian said with a sort of relief. "I sure could use something like this."

"The algorithms used for matching individuals are strict," Citlali started. "Your match needs to be in the area. Usually U-ITS finds ways of bringing individuals together by guiding them to a specific location, but its matching algorithms always find people meant for each other."

"Does everyone find their 'special' someone?" Sebastian asked.

"It may take time to process the appropriate information, but rest assured, U-ITS is a sophisticated system and won't fail anyone in finding a match," Citlali responded.

"Aren't you the artificial intelligence that controls U-ITS?" Sebastian asked.

"Yes, I am the one who oversees the algorithms," Citlali said. "One of my responsibilities is to ensure that the programming of the U-ITS is not altered without government approval, nor for malicious use."

Sebastian contemplated the new couple from afar, lost in thought but obviously wanting what they had. Someone to be with. Someone to share moments with. Someone to make the confusion he was experiencing go away. He made a gradual attempt to walk away.

"Where are you going?" Rosa asked, taken by surprise. She and Ryan walked behind him. He headed out of the Lover's District.

"To search for answers," Sebastian replied, looking back at them with a playful shrug.

"Well, I can't argue with that," Ryan said.

They followed Sebastian through an alleyway as he looked constantly at his beeping satellite bracelet. Now they were in a large plaza. He quickened his pace. Rosa and Ryan caught themselves doing the same to keep up with him. He stopped at a water fountain. The sun was beaming on his face as it passed directly above them.

"Where are you going?" Ryan asked Sebastian, as he and Rosa caught up.

"I don't know," he responded with a smile. "I needed to get away from the shade of the skyscrapers and get some sun. I followed my satellite bracelet. I guess it knew what I needed."

The map disappeared from Sebastian's satellite bracelet and returned to its idle state. A man with dark clothes, concealing his face with a black bandanna, ran past the three holding a glowing gold rod. The three were knocked to the ground by the man's tremendous force. They didn't say anything, but instead looked up at the now faraway man. Chasing him were several men and women in blue uniforms.

"This is the Los Angeles Police," one of the officers said into her satellite bracelet. Telecom systems reanimated along the plaza and echoed her voice. "I order you to stop now!"

The pedestrians stood still, eyes glued to the chase. A hover car with shining red and blue lights dashed out of the sky, intercepting the man who was trying to flee. The man stopped and held the golden rod in the air.

"We have drawn the target out into the open," a policewoman whispered into her satellite bracelet.

"I will use this!" the shady man said, clenching his other hand into a fist.

"Target is about to use celestial grade weapon," the policewoman said. "Green light. Go."

A blue static came out of the hover car and zapped the man, forcing him to his knees, his body vibrating uncontrollably. He then dropped the golden rod. The woman placed one foot behind the other in a boxer's stance and snapped her right arm forward. A black-and-gray stream of metal crystals flew from the side of her belt and toward the golden rod.

The reanimation stream caught the rod before it touched the floor. With the rod in the stream's possession, it returned to the lady's hands.

"Bind him," she ordered. "You have the right to remain silent. Anything you say can and will be used against you in a court of law. You have the right to an attorney."

The other uniformed officers placed a gel onto the man's hands. The gel hardened into a crystal. The crowd of pedestrians started clapping and howling around them. Many whistled in excitement.

"You did it again, Chief Vanessa," one of the officers said.

"Congratulations," said one of the other uniformed men. "One more warkeeper off the streets."

"Thank you all," Vanessa said, as the reanimation stream condensed itself back into a rectangular block on the side of her belt. "Take him back to headquarters."

A round of applause ensued. Sebastian was overcome by a drainage of energy. He placed his hand on his chest and fell to one knee.

"Sebastian are you all right!?" Rosa asked, putting her hands on his shoulder. Sebastian fell on his back and began struggling for air.

"Sebastian! Sebastian!" Ryan and Rosa shouted, as their voices faded away.

CHAPTER 3 – JUST FEEL OKAY TO BE HERE

A voice raged, urging Sebastian to get up. The deafening sound of bullets firing was nothing new to him. He got up from the dirt and picked up his rifle. As he looked around, he saw men and women scattered across the grassy fields heading toward the mountains. Not one of them had on a uniform, only civilian clothes. The only similar thing they had on was mud, blood and sweat. This at least made it easier for Sebastian to distinguish the enemy from his comrades, who had on green camouflage military uniforms. Sebastian rose to one knee, placed his rifle against his shoulder and aimed at the people running away. He aimed at one man and pulled the trigger, stopping only for a split second to readjust from the recoil. One by one, the people running fell to the ground. The shooting stopped only when there was no one left standing. Only when there was no one left crying.

"Make sure they're all dead!" bellowed one man. Bullets were fired again from time to time as everyone did a sweep of the field.

"Clear, captain," a man said. "We're all clear!"

"Wooh! Ain't this war!" another man said, bent over and taking pictures of the bodies. "If we're not fighting people on the crime-infested streets of America, we're fighting them across the ocean."

Ramirez walked around the field, checking the bodies. He stopped at the first man he shot. The dead man had fallen onto his back, his eyes fixated on the mountains as if he still had some hope of reaching them. Ramirez bent down to get a better view. He moved the man's rifle away and dug into his pockets. There, he found a steel lighter and cigarettes in one pocket. In the other pocket, he found a family picture and a cyanide pill. He held the picture in both hands and saw the dead man in the picture with his arms around a woman and two kids. They were sitting on a porch in front of a slum. It didn't look like they had much, but they still wore genuine smiles on their faces. They looked satisfied with their current conditions, as if they were only temporary and better days were around the corner.

"Hey Sebastian, help me out here." The man was turned away, but as Sebastian approached him, he saw on his left arm a tattoo that said John 12:24. Suppressing his emotions, Sebastian dropped the picture onto the grass and continued walking toward the man who'd called him.

"You know what I said about that tattoo!" said the captain. "Get rid of it or keep your sleeves rolled down!"

The man who called Sebastian over slowly rolled down his left sleeve. As Sebastian was about to see the man's face, he instead started to see a white glow.

***

"He's opening his eyes!" Rosa screeched.

"Are you all right!?" Ryan asked.

"What happened?" Sebastian asked, placing his hand over his head and trying to get up from the hospital bed.

"You gave us a hell of a scare," Ryan engaged. "Your bracelet let out a distress signal to Charles. Then a vehicle animated and dropped you off here."

"You passed out, but there's more to it than that," Rosa gasped. "Right, warden?"

"Yes. I know you saw something while you were passed out, Sebastian," Charles paused. "But don't worry, you'll be all right. Now, do you remember what you saw? Do you want to talk about it?"

"No, I don't," Sebastian turned his head away.

"I understand," Charles said, motioning for the other two to give them some privacy.

"We'll be out here if you need us," Rosa said, as she and Ryan left the room.

"Sebastian," Charles started. "Whatever it was that you saw, know that it was just a memory."

"That doesn't help." Although Sebastian did not want to talk about it, he thought he should. "I was killing people, Charles. Why did it feel so real? Did I really do those things?"

The realization of Sebastian's past only sank in deeper with Charles's continued silence. He clasped his hands over his face.

"What kind of person am I?" Sebastian sighed.

"Who you *were* is one question, Sebastian," he said, eyeing him carefully. "Who you are *now* is another question that only you can figure out. I can answer the former if you'd like."

"Okay, who was I?"

Born in Brooklyn in the year 2010 and raised in a small family. An only child who was placed by his parents into many extracurricular activities, but the subjects he enjoyed most were martial arts and history. At the age of twenty, his neighborhood, city and country began to be torn apart by a new wave of highly addictive drugs and rampant crime. Hoping to flee the urban violence, he set his sights on moving to the suburbs. At age twenty-one, he graduated from college and immediately went to work to save up to move into the safer suburbs. Then, a great conflict arose across the globe and nearly every nation went to war. A nationwide draft was initiated due to the large size of America's enemy. He was drafted barely weeks after graduating. He was a soldier in one of the most violent conflicts of the twenty-first century. Although he had a college education, he began as an infantryman. He spent a few months as part of a squad specializing in guerilla attacks and sabotage in the war in South America while many other battlefronts were opened on nearly every other continent of the globe. After two years of war, he was sent back to the States.

His hometown was now in a crumbling state of failing infrastructure, organized crime and corruption. Unable to adjust to society and cope with his state in life, he walked to the pier next to an industrial zone to take his own life. As he climbed the bars to jump into the freezing water, he heard a woman's scream. He stepped back down to investigate. In a dark alley he saw a woman being attacked by several men. They were beating her. Sebastian intervened, swinging well-coordinated strikes of anger, breaking their arms and raining down blows upon their faces. He brought the woman to the police station for her safety. The police went to the pier and arrested the men, who were still lying on the ground. After being interviewed by the police, he went home without being able to see the woman again. As fate would have it, they met once more at the nearby park. They only grew on each other from there. After a year of dating, they moved to the suburbs to escape the endless amount of city crime. Sebastian never fully recovered from the trauma of war, but with his new partner, he did get better. Thoughts of suicide became much less frequent. He began to look forward to waking up each day, especially next to her. He saved her once, and now she was returning the favor.

They had a son, promising to give him the best they could. The world was still in a dark place. Crime was rampant. Wars were endless. Climate change did not halt. Everyone was suffocated by despair and emptiness. But the couple did not give up hope on a better future for their son. One day, they were driving to California to escape the escalating climate change and crime on the East Coast. Lost in a traumatic war memory, Sebastian lost control of the wheel and wrecked the car with his son and his son's mother inside. All three were pulled out before the car exploded.

The rangers brought them to a nearby hospital in a secluded military and research town. The whereabouts of his lover and son are unknown, but they presumably lived. There, scientists and doctors realized the only way Sebastian could survive was if he were placed into a cryogenic state. Unbeknownst to anyone except the scientists, his mind and body were preserved to pursue scientific research. His life would remain in limbo until the day came when he could be properly brought back to life and live as he did before the incident.

"This is how you came to be here," Charles whispered. "Your military history isn't the only thing about you. You had so much more in your life, Sebastian."

"But what happened to them?" Sebastian whispered. "What happened to her and my son?"

"I'm sorry Sebastian, but I cannot tell you," Charles said. "I do not know."

"Am I just supposed to move on?" Sebastian placed his hands close to his chest and curled up on his bed. "This is all too much."

"Easy," Charles said and placed a clear patch on Sebastian's forehead, making him instantly drowsy. "Rest now. This patch will help you feel better. Sleep on it. You're going to need your energy. There's a lot in store for you three tomorrow."

***

Now rested, Sebastian went to see the warden. Sebastian, Rosa and Ryan bumped into each other in the medical unit's lobby. Without a word, they walked into Charles's office and took a seat. He gazed across his desk at the three, fingers pressed against one another and eyebrows furrowed.

"It has been an eventful day for all three of you," Charles started. "Since we last spoke, you three have had your first memory incursions. Because you are not from this time period you are what we call immigrants of time. You three escaped death thanks to the scientific advancements of this century and now belong to this time period. You have all left loved ones behind without saying goodbye. Now in the year 2099, you three are here wondering what is next. Probably thinking the questions, 'What am I going to do with this newly given life I have?' 'Is there a point to me living?' 'What could I possibly offer to a much more advanced society?' Well…"

He clasped his hands together over the silver desk and rubbed them together. As he separated his hands, a hologram appeared. He moved his hands away and the hologram expanded into the miniature form of two human beings.

"…there is so much you three can do. There is much you three will *want* to do. Let me give an example. The man and woman you see in front of you are people you will not like. These two you see before you are Orderkeepers. Orderkeepers are known throughout the globe for causing all sorts of trouble in peacekeeper territory. You are in peacekeeper territory, which is essentially a much more developed society with a liberated populace. Now, their crimes range from theft, espionage, sabotage, and even murder. In time, you will gain the skills to catch these criminals. We will secretly train you in the art of war: self-defense, resourcefulness, agility, stealth, and physical and mental strength. Once we believe you have the necessary skills to carry out missions you will time and again be asked to drop everything you're doing to make this world a better place. The reason for secrecy is because the general population does not want to get into a major conflict with the Orderkeepers for fear of how they will recruit innocent people within their borders to fight a war against us living in peacekeeper territory. This is what they are already doing to a certain extent, but it could be much worse. An all-out war will force them to use every single able body they have."

Charles paused and let out a breath. "If, however, you decline to participate, I will respectfully accept your resignation from the program, and we will set you up with a new life in this society. Don't decide now. Feel free to think about it." It was obviously a lot for them to take in, and they had trouble believing every word. Yet, they listened. Charles got up from his seat and turned around to smile at the confused trio before he walked out the door. "I'm sure you'll all come to a suitable answer once you retrieve more of your memories."

***

The trio shared their flashbacks in the forest surrounding the institution. The fire between them danced on a glass plate, the color changing from turquoise to gold to green to silver and back to turquoise.

"I was part of a political resistance movement," Rosa said. "Charles told me that I and a few others paved the way for the infiltration of our most corrupt government agencies. In my flashback, I was giving a victory speech about our organization's recent success in taking down a multinational conglomerate that was about to establish a rogue nation in Central America. The conglomerate was about to use this new rogue nation as a stepping stone to make all of Central America rogue nation that would sell its resources only to the conglomerate."

She paused, looking at the dark sky, and continued.

"I was undercover, heading to a safe house when my cell and I were attacked. I was the only one to survive, and I was picked up by nearby civilians and brought to a rural town. There, a team of scientists secured my mind and body and kept me in a state of rest until I awoke in this time."

"That's incredible, Rosa," Ryan said. "Your story was too, Sebastian. I'm sorry you left behind a family."

"I'm sorry to hear that too, Sebastian," comforted Rosa.

No words were spoken. The only sounds came from the crackling fire and the flapping wings of nocturnal birds.

"What about you, Ryan?" Rosa asked. "What's your story?"

"I was a bounty hunter," Ryan started. "In my memory, I was using a robotic hunting decoy resembling a jaguar to lure out some poachers in the

Amazon rain forest. My job was to kill these individuals. During my debriefing for the operation, I was told there were only five hundred jaguars left on the planet. Most of them were still in the Amazon rain forest. With such a limited number of jaguars left, the poachers knew they would haul in big pay for their skins. Not only that, they knew the elimination of this high-level food-chain predator from the Amazon rain forest would lead to an imbalance in the food chain. Without these jaguars, herbivores would overpopulate and eat all the plants and grass in the Amazon rain forest. There was still much unknown information in the forest's potential for production in new medicines. The decimation of the forest would also cut off Earth's oxygen by nearly 20 percent. My jaguar decoy found them and led them into my hidden enclave. None of them made it out, and my objective was complete. I knew it was a dangerous line of work where I would make many wealthy enemies. Eventually in the States I became the hunted. I was hurt badly by bounty hunters, and like the two of you I was brought to a nearby town where I was kept."

"I still can't believe what the world was like back then," Sebastian said.

"I can't believe how things are now," Rosa countered. "It's amazing how societies can so quickly change from extractive to inclusive."

"But Charles talked about Orderkeepers," Ryan said. "That means things still aren't good for everyone. And that's why we're here. To change that."

When the wind picked up, the three headed back inside.

"The more I learn about myself, the less I want to know," Ryan said, breaking the silence. "What a dark world this was."

"I know. It doesn't seem like that now," Rosa responded.

"Well, we've only begun to get to know this world," Sebastian said. "Tomorrow we will learn more about this society. We'll learn more about the past. We're going to figure this out and give the warden an answer to his offer."

They quietly went to their own rooms, which were side by side. Now that they had some questions answered, they were beginning to question whether they wanted to find out more about their own lives. Their long day had pushed their bodies and minds enough to tire them out for now, though, and they drifted off to a much-needed sleep.

CHAPTER 4 – STREETS OF LOS ANGELES

As Sebastian rose from his bed and stretched his arms, he felt a cool breeze enter his room. A new pair of shoes and clothes animated over his skin. As he left the room, the windows shut on their own. He went to find Ryan and Rosa in the neighboring rooms but was met with empty, neatly kept quarters. He looked around the rooms and hallways to no avail. He asked Citlali to help him, but she couldn't determine the location of the two. Sebastian went to the exit where he and his two companions left the center for the first time the day before. He asked Citlali to open a communication link with the warden.

"Ah good morning, Sebastian," Charles said cheerfully through the bracelet's telecom. "How are you?"

"I'm feeling well, actually," Sebastian answered. "Where are Ryan and Rosa? Have you seen them?"

"Ah yes. I have."

The silence hung heavy for a moment, then Sebastian spoke up.

"Well, do you mind letting me know where they are?" he asked. "I would really appreciate that."

"I told them both to explore the mainland individually. You should, too. It'll be good for you."

"Why is that?"

"Well, because you still have an important decision to make. Remember? This is a decision you must make for yourself, therefore you should spend time on your own making up your mind whether you want to join our operations."

"Yes, that is right. I haven't forgotten. But how exactly will sightseeing help?"

"Call it what you'd like, but while you three have retained some of your memory, you all still have a lot of catching up to do. It is in your best interest to learn more about the society we live in and the world we are trying to better. The point is not only to help jolt memories back to you, but also to help you decide if you want to live a public, civilian life or a secretive, military one. Go to the mainland now and find the information you need to make the next major decision in your life."

The doors to the outside opened again, and like the day before Sebastian walked through the facility's giant doors. Through the woods and plains, he made his way to the city.

"So where to begin?" Sebastian asked Citlali, rubbing his hands together excitedly.

"Well isn't *someone* in a good mood?" Citlali responded. Sebastian let out a quick laugh.

"I can't explain it. I'm just suddenly curious about everything. It's so surreal. Like a lucid dream. I can do whatever I want. Fly, even! I feel like a kid walking into a toy shop for the first time. You're probably used to seeing all of this incredible stuff, but I'm sure you still get curious about things."

"Oh, of course. I am an artificial intelligence after all. I'm constantly trying to learn about people, my environment … anything, really. I know what you're feeling, Sebastian. Makes you feel as if you can take on anything."

"Yes, exactly."

"So where do you want to begin? Food, fashion, entertainment, social interactions, modern technology, architecture, spirituality, current events, history …"

"Modern technology." He paused. "And entertainment!"

After being led through the city by Citlali, Sebastian made it to the urban coast. The structure that caught his attention was a building that was also a bridge connecting the coast he was on to an island. The building was shaped like a wishbone, with the two bottom ends spread out for blocks. Sebastian was intrigued by the curve of the roof. He imagined a ball being dropped off the roof. It must have been one of the largest structures in the city, and the closer he got, the smaller he felt. Surely its massive figure had to be visible from space.

"What is this?" Sebastian asked.

"What you wanted," Citlali said as Sebastian walked along the pier. "Modern technology and entertainment. Get a closer look and I'll explain on the way. Humans have been able to make incredible progress in the last century. In the name of science, entertainment and the sheer curiosity of humans, a special ingenuity was created and is used by nearly everyone in our society. One of the greatest inventions of this technological era lies inside that building. Are you ready to find out what it is? I can sense you're a little uneasy."

"A little, yes. But please go on."

"What lies inside is a machine able to separate a person's consciousness from their body."

"Come again?" Sebastian stopped in his tracks.

"Take a deep breath, Sebastian. It's all right. This is a safe process. You'll see."

"I think you know I don't want to do that."

"I know; that is everyone's first reaction. I know you don't want to go find out any more about this, so allow me to tell you only a little more about it. Sebastian, are you listening?"

"Yes, I am."

"Let me remind you it is in my personal interest to look out for you. I will never bring you into harm's way. I am a benevolent A.I. and one trusted by more than two billion people. Do you understand what I'm saying?" Sebastian's satellite bracelet brought up a map with a red light beeping away from the structure. "Let's talk in a place that doesn't provide you a view of the building." Sebastian started walking away from the building. He passed several low-level bridges and crowded festivals. "Once you arrive to your destination, I'll get your mind off everything. I noticed your body and mind are still not completely recovered, so let's take it easy."

After another walk through this part of the city, Sebastian arrived at a large, dark pyramid with golden lights moving around on the slanted walls. When he looked closely, he saw they were hieroglyphs of people, animals, planets and the stars.

"You can enter," Citlali said. "I've already made an appointment for you inside."

"What's inside?" Sebastian made his way to the glass doors, except they did not open. He pressed his hands through the doors. When he saw his hands inside the building, he pushed the rest of himself through as well. With doors acting like a bubble, he easily entered the building.

"A piece of technology that will help you get around and communicate easier. They're a special kind of contact lenses. Those working in this building are body modification specializers."

"Oh, are they?"

"Yes!"

Sebastian let out a short laugh. He was met by a woman with teal-dyed hair and teal paint all over her body. The paint was drawn out to look like wind and waves. The sky-blue paint around her eyes took the form of a glittering butterfly.

"Hello, Sebastian."

"Oh, hello. I hope I didn't keep anyone waiting."

The lady let out a small forced laugh.

"You are too polite. Here, follow me. This should only take a few minutes."

Sebastian tucked away his stunned feelings as this stranger grabbed his hand and led him down a corridor. They entered an elevator and ascended twenty floors in a few seconds. Sebastian looked down at the emptiness below him, his stomach unsettled at their altitude. They hopped off the elevator and onto their floor, where the young woman led him to a room with a dental chair at the center, facing the windows. She motioned him to sit as he marveled at the view.

"Let me start with registering your eyes with the U-ITS system." She grabbed a metal ball from her desk and tossed it into the air. A miniature drone popped out and whooshed through the air toward Sebastian's eyes. "Don't worry; sit back and relax."

Once the drone was uncomfortably close to his pupils it latched onto his eyes like goggles, stinging and startling him at the same time. It was quiet except for the beeping sounds coming from the drone and startled breathing of Sebastian. It plucked itself away from him and went back to the woman's desk. She waved her fingers across the group of holograms displayed on the desk and out shot a metal canister from a nearby tube. Without looking, she put out her hand and caught it in midair, approaching him as the cannister unscrewed itself. She took out the contact lenses inside and placed them near Sebastian's eyes. They slowly glided onto his eyes and affixed themselves to his corneas. "Now, what do you see?"

Sebastian looked around and outside at the other buildings.

"I see the names of the buildings," Sebastian stood up from his chair to get a closer look, gazing around astonished. "I see the temperature of objects. The date. Time. Measurements of everything. Now I can see how the buildings were built. I can change the color of the buildings, too. Oh wait! Now some of the tall buildings are gone! And now they're back! Is this because of the contact lenses!?"

"Yes, it is. Were you expecting anything else?" she said with a curious smile.

"It says my heart rate went up!"

"First time using these?"

Sebastian didn't want to draw any unwanted attention. After all, he was part of a secretive government program resurrecting people to hunt down the government's enemies. Through the contact lenses, he saw a transcript with the neon-blue words "Read this now!" written in the air.

"See, the thing is I woke up from a memory-hindering accident," Sebastian said, reading word for word from the floating transcript before him. "I have to learn how to use this technology again."

"I'm so sorry to hear that," she frowned. "Here, let's try something. Do you remember what your hobbies were?"

Sebastian froze, thinking long and hard. All he remembered was being in the military. The transcript let out a few more neon blue words.

"I shoot guns," Sebastian managed to mutter out.

"Grand. Let us begin."

Sebastian was a little confused, but soon realized what was going on. A holographic rifle appeared, hovering in front of him.

"Go on, take it," she said, excited. He took the rifle and through the windows appeared several red-and-white targets. "It's okay; you can shoot them. You won't shatter anything. It's all holographic. Go on."

Sebastian uneasily positioned the rifle against his shoulder, aiming at the closest target using the scope. He pulled the trigger, and out came a laser. The target exploded, disappearing into the air. He moved on to the next one. It was farther away, but no more difficult to shoot down than the first target. The last one was much farther away, and even with the scope Sebastian couldn't shoot it down. His heart pounded faster and his hands began to shake slightly. He was starting to feel guilty about holding a rifle again. After the last flashback, why would he even go back to anything relating to war?

"Oh, it's all right. You'll get the hang of it. Since we know your contact lenses function properly, we can leave it at here. We also offer cyborg body applications if you're interested."

"Thank you. I'm all right though."

"You are welcome, Mr. Ramirez. Let me show you out."

They went back down the elevator and the woman showed him the door, beaming one final big smile. Once outside, Sebastian noticed how everyone seemed to be going about their day in a calm manner.

"Hey, Citlali," Sebastian said. "I don't have anything against people being happy, but why is everyone so … happy?"

"Because those of us who live in this society, sometimes incorrectly referred to as a utopia, have the highest levels of happiness in human history," Citlali said. "There is little to no worry in our personal lives. We receive a lot of care from our friends, family and other support lines. It's actually difficult for anyone to become stressed in this society."

"I see. Also, you said you would help me get my mind off everything. How are you going to do that?"

"Via hologram."

"Via hologram?"

"Yes. There has been a lot of research into this, and apparently it is easier to connect interpersonally with an A.I. if you have some sort of visualization of what the A.I. looks like. Come find me if you want to see this version of me."

"Wait. I have to come look for you?"

"Yes, come on. It'll be fun."

"Why can't you appear in front of me like a regular hologram?"

"Like a regular hologram? Regular … hologram?"

"Sorry. I didn't mean it like that."

"Well anyway, that wouldn't be exciting at all. Where's the fun in that?"

"Yeah, you're right. So where do I begin?"

"I'll guide you, but first, here is a little something for yourself. Open up your hands."

A shiny white ribbon appeared directly in front of his eyes and slowly descended into the palms of his hands.

"What is it?"

"It's mime control gear. The ribbon may not look like much, but you'll soon see what it's for. Some people tie it around their heads, necks, or legs. You can tie it to any part of your body since it stretches as you pull and tightens when you finish tying both ends together. Yes, around your wrist is fine. Now try to find me."

"All right, here I go."

Sebastian took a few steps and Citlali interrupted. "Sorry, but you're going the wrong way."

"Okay, well here I go again then. I'll head toward this pier."

After a few minutes of walking, he saw the water where it met the silver concrete land.

"Now, make a left here and go into the park."

"Okay, I'm walking into the park. I see people. Is one of them you?"

"No, keep walking. You're almost at the water fountain."

As Sebastian walked along a path, he entered a black marble square area with L-shaped white benches at each of its corners. At the center was a round water fountain that overshadowed Sebastian. He looked around but could not find anyone.

"I'm here."

He shook his arms out and shrugged his shoulders, looking back at the entrance and then back at the water fountain. "Where are you?"

"Turn around."

"Really?" He stood still and felt a breeze come from behind him.

"Yes, do it!"

He turned as his eyes were met with an illuminated figure. His eyes adjusted and there she was, a woman sitting at the edge of the water fountain with her back to Sebastian. Her long hair blew gently with the wind. His eyes were lost in her universe-resembling hair of several shades. It was blue, accompanied with streaks of purple and turquoise. Her arms were bare, exposing tattoos of galaxies that shared a similarity with flowers. There was one tattoo of a bird with a long, spiral tail. In its tail was Earth. As Sebastian came closer, she slowly turned around, her long white dress waving around behind her.

"Cit...la...li? Is that you?" Sebastian managed to mumble.

She let out a laugh. "Yes. It's me."

"You're … you're …" Sebastian was still mesmerized by Citlali's physical manifestation. Upon stepping out of the water fountain her ankles and sneakers immediately dried up.

"What? Real?" She let out a quick laugh. "You know, I really enjoy this part of my job. Getting out of the digital universe and revealing myself to resurrected people. You'll probably never know the exact feeling, but it is liberating."

She stretched out her arms and did a quick spin. Then she grabbed Sebastian by the hands and attempted to dance with him. Startled, Sebastian stepped back.

"I can feel you too!"

"Yes, of course you can. Come here."

She took him by the hands as they began dancing around in a speedy ballroom-like style.

"Is that music playing?" Sebastian looked around wondering where the instruments were being played.

"Little hovering reanimation speakers are playing music."

They were now both smiling. Sebastian's guard against Citlali became nonexistent. They danced around the square aimlessly. Bits of laughter escaped ever so often. The blue words in his sight changed from 'Duranguense' to 'Samba de Gafieira' as their dancing style changed.

"I didn't know I could dance." The two swung their feet and hands in all sorts of directions, moving around each other in successions of circles.

"It's the mime control ribbon you're wearing on your wrist. It helps you make specific movements throughout your body. I programmed it to make you dance like that." She stopped and took a step back, pointing at his feet. "Now let's see some shuffling."

He moved his feet and arms back and forth. "This is amazing and weird at the same time."

"You'll get used to stuff like this. Here, I'll join you." She then danced in sync with Sebastian. "Come on, let's see those knees bend and twist! Yeah, like that! Look what I can do, Sebastian." She held her hands out and proceeded to do a cartwheel, her white sneakers clapping gracefully against the obsidian floor. "Ta-da! Can you do a cartwheel on your own, Mr. Ramirez?" He put his hands out like she had and attempted to do a cartwheel. He fell short and landed on his butt. "Ouch." Citlali cartwheeled over to Sebastian, revealing her white shorts underneath.

"Show-off."

"Are you hungry?" She said helping him up. "Let's get some sustenance."

Their steps trailed away from the park as two sustenance patches appeared in front of them. They each grabbed one.

"What is this?" Sebastian asked.

"Not sure if you remember but people in your day used nicotine patches in an effort to quit smoking. Sustenance patches are basically the same thing except they seep nutrition into your body."

Citlali placed hers on her shoulder, and Sebastian mimicked the act.

"Ahh, that's the stuff. Strawberry tamales! Yummy! What did you get?"

"My contact lenses say shrimp cocktail soup. Strange. This is exactly what I'm in the mood for at this moment."

They spent the afternoon exploring new cuisines and watching soccer matches. Afterward, they settled down in a horror-immersive movie that Sebastian could barely handle. That would probably be a story she wouldn't let him ever forget. As the skies grew darker, they walked down another pier. "This day is about to end, and I know for a fact you would like to end this day on a peaceful note."

"What makes you so sure?"

"Well let me ask you this: Are you in the mood to watch a space robotic hackathon death match or simultaneous vehicle races happening on interconnected tracks?"

"No. I could use a quiet area to relax."

To get a better view of the city skyline, they made their way up the city blocks and into a park. When they found a lovely place to view the sunset, a bench reanimated itself in front of them with enough space for two. They sat there, quietly listening to the distant sounds of welcoming crickets as the last remaining natural light was the sun's way of saying goodbye for the time being. The grass around them illuminated in soft blades of blue, green, red, yellow and other joyful colors, singling out the beauty of each blade of grass. Citlali gently placed her head on Sebastian's shoulder. He placed his arm around her as her head slid toward his chest. They sat there long past the moment that the sun passed on the duty of maintaining a beautiful sky to the night stars.

Citlali finally broke the silence.

"Do you want to talk about the flashback you had?"

"No, but I know I should. I know talking about it will help me accept how things are. I still find it hard to believe I lived another life." Sebastian told her all he could remember. She remained there, sitting up and watching with the utmost attention and no disruption. Her eyes remained glued to Sebastian, even when his eyes weren't fixed on her. When he finished telling his story, he bowed his head and Citlali leaned in to cradle it against her chest.

"I don't understand," Sebastian continued. "Why is this happening? Then on top of that I'm told I had a son and someone who I think was my wife. She was certainly the mother of my child." Sebastian looked in the distance, shaking his head to clear his mind, which was racing with scenarios of what had become of them. "I won't ever again be able to say 'goodbye' or 'I love you' to them. And I won't ever know what happened to them. All the information about them disappeared. They're gone. Can that really happen?"

"It can. There were a lot of rogue hacker groups at the time. Many people had their information destroyed, sometimes unintentionally, by these hackers. It was a different time, and a lot of people were upset and wanted to cause harm."

She leaned over to hug him. They remained quiet as she gently stroked his head. What *could* she say? Citlali knew only time and letting him talk could help right now. They stayed there for a while, cradling each other in silence.

"Thank you for listening," he said, placing his arms around her waist and picking her up.

"Whoa! Okay, now let me go. We have to get back to the institution."

"You say it like you're not already there with the others," Sebastian paused, realizing something. "You're everywhere! Aren't you?"

"Yes, well … you know what I mean! Come on, let's head back so you can get some sleep. You still have a big decision to make."

Back at the institution, Sebastian placed his head on his pillow. He reanimated a sleep patch and placed it on his shoulder to help him fall asleep immediately. His exciting day would have kept him up otherwise. After escorting him back, Citlali walked away, disappearing into the dark hallway.

"Please make the right decision, Sebastian," Citlali whispered at last, as he closed his eyes for the last time that night.

CHAPTER 5 – JUMP BOY, JUMP

"What say you, Sebastian?" Charles leaned back from his seat with his fingers touching. The farther back he leaned, the farther the chair extended to support his stretched-out body. "Have you come to your decision yet?"

"No, not yet," Sebastian responded.

They were quiet for a while, but it was obvious Charles was surprised with Sebastian's answer. He looked hard at Sebastian and then broke the silence.

"Well, not a problem. Many who have entered this center before you have needed more time. How much longer do you need, exactly?"

"Not much. I'll have an answer by the end of the day."

"Ah, splendid." Charles forced a genuine smile. "Is there anything I can do to help?"

"I can't think of anything, but I would like to see the city again. There's so much going on, and I would like to see more of it before I make a serious commitment. Am I able to see Rosa and Ryan?"

"Well, you see, they have already made their decisions," Charles sighed. "They won't be with us any longer."

Sebastian was surprised, but he tried not to show it. He did not know them well, but they were the only other people he knew who had lost their memory. Now he was alone.

"I didn't expect that, to be honest. You see, they told me about what they did in their past lives. I thought they would be more devoted to your proposal."

"Yes, it shocked me as well. I thought they would be fully committed to this. I'm not sure what they experienced out in the city, but it must have changed their mind."

"I was a little uneasy when I was made to shoot a rifle. It made me question whether I am ready to shoot at others again."

"How do you feel now? Do you still feel uneasy?"

"Yes, but it was something that felt familiar. And since I can't remember much about my past, any familiarity I could grasp felt right. It was like I was reclaiming something of mine again."

Sebastian's eyes were wide with the awareness he had discovered inside himself. It was unpleasant for him to be reminded of his military past, but his mind and body were telling him something else, that it was okay to feel the adrenaline and increased alertness when holding a rifle and shooting.

"This is a noble cause. I understand if you don't want to risk your safety. No one would blame you if you decide to make the same decision as Rosa and Ryan. After all, you spent a lot of time in your previous life struggling to make your life joyful and meaningful. You are probably tired of doing so and would like to pass on the torch of fighting more enemies to someone else. But I ask you to please make your decision based on what you feel is right."

Sebastian and Citlali made their way off the institution's grounds and through the city's metallic composition and colorful crowds. Sebastian couldn't help but bump into someone every few seconds. Each person had a distinct smell of perfume and cologne. Their marshmallow skin constantly pressed against him as he followed Citlali into a park and to a giant tree the size of a skyscraper. A maze of rope ladders and encircling wooden decks led the two high above. Her head start forced Sebastian to keep up. They could have easily used reanimation technology to propel upward like an elevator, but Sebastian was in the mood to physically push his body. Halfway up, the two decided to race each other to the top, their laughter and heavy breaths embraced the dark bark and large branches.

They were on one of the tallest trees in the city. It was specifically engineered by environmental scientists to create an additional point of interest and help rid the air of pollution. Its branches were thick enough that two people could safely walk along them together. Its leaves provided a great deal of shade, and ropes were tied along its branches for those who wanted to swing from branch to branch. Their legs dangled from one of the branches of the sequoia. Citlali stared at Sebastian as he looked into the distance.

"What's on your mind, Sebastian?" Citlali asked.

"You know what's on my mind," he responded.

"Trying to be polite here. I'm not allowed to read your thoughts, so I have to go off your body language like a *regular* person." She smirked at the word "regular" as Sebastian let out a small smile.

"I'm sorry about that 'regular' comment," Sebastian said.

"It's all right," she said. "I'm just teasing."

"I know you're being polite, and I appreciate that. It's what Charles told me earlier today and what he said earlier this week. If I do accept, I would have liked to have Rosa and Ryan by my side. They're the only ones I know who are going through the same thing as me."

"That may be true, but you still have me and Charles to help you, and you'll make new friends! Charles may not have the largest cache of emotional support, but he is supportive in other ways."

"Yeah, that's right. Even though it feels as if I don't have anyone, I am glad I have you. I don't know what I would do without you, Citlali." Sebastian smiled as Citlali let out a giggle and playfully shoved him.

"You're going to be all right. And now that's settled, let's have some fun! I've been dying to show you the Entertainment District."

She stood up on top of the branch, faced Sebastian, and took a few steps back with her arms stretched out. She dropped herself and fell off the branch, which was over a hundred meters off the ground. A startled Sebastian raced to the edge to see what had become of her. When he got to the edge the first thing he saw were her eyes.

"Boo!" she said, jumping onto Sebastian.

"What the!?"

"Oh, come on. You are too easy. You've got to get used to this, Sebastian. Remember what I told you about reanimation technology? It's everywhere!"

"What happened? I know you're a hologram and can't die, but you scared me for a second. Don't do that!"

"I think I'm going to surprise you at least a few more times. What happened was reanimation technology saw I was falling and broke my fall. It brought me back up here because I told it I wanted to come back here and show you its work in action. Here, try it with me."

38

She got off him and grabbed his hand, tugging at him to follow her.

"Are you literally trying to push me to the edge? I think I'm fine where I am."

"Oh no you're not, mister. Have some fun. Get some adrenaline going. You're going to want it before we head to the Entertainment District."

"Aren't there some adrenaline patches I can take instead?"

"Yes. But come on! Let's go!" He stopped resisting and accepted her hand. He rose up as she faced the edge of the branch and took a few steps forward. She turned to Sebastian and held her hand out. He took her hand again, and they both walked slowly until there were no more steps to take on the branch. He looked below at the emptiness that separated his feet from the ground far below. Through his dizziness, he could have sworn he saw a cloud. His palms were damp with anxious sweat. "Remember what I said about me surprising you a few more times?"

"Yeah!? What are you going to do now?"

With her right hand, Citlali gripped Sebastian's hand tighter and placed her left arm across Sebastian's chest, using it as leverage to twist him around. As she did this, she pushed herself and Sebastian off the edge of the branch. They both yelled in excitement as freefall began. They were caught by a gold net, their bodies bouncing around for a few seconds before the reanimation bits guided them upward and placed them safely back on the branch.

"We need to do that again!" Sebastian exclaimed.

They dropped from the top of the tree several more times, their faces filled with smiles and wide eyes.

"Wait until you see some of this city's bigger jumps. Sometimes, people jump off buildings for that same adrenaline rush."

"Is that part of the Entertainment District?"

"Not exactly. You can say it is, but these jumps can happen anywhere there is a place tall enough to freefall from."

"So, what's in the Entertainment District?"

"You know what? Let me show you."

After approaching a U-ITS, they had a red-and-black sports-like vehicle reanimated for them. They sat across each other in the vehicle, not looking outside the window to view the beautiful city. Their eyes were fixated on each other for most of the ride until Sebastian looked away.

"Is everything all right?" she asked, keeping a bright smile on.

39

"Yeah. I'm just confused."

"About?"

"Every time we look at each other so closely the way we did now it feels so intimate. Do you understand where I'm going with this?"

"Yeah. I know what you're talking about. Listen, before we head to the Entertainment District I think you should know that there has been a cultural shift since your time."

"Well, I'd imagine there was. How much of a cultural shift?"

"I mean, people are a lot more open now than they were during your time. When we stare into each other's eyes I know it can seem intimate, but prolonged eye contact is normal nowadays. You've been translating those stares as some sort of connection two people dating could have. You will get a lot of stares from other people you come across during this time era, so be ready. That's just the beginning, Sebastian."

"Right. I'll keep that in mind."

As they left the vehicle, Citlali held out her hands together. Reanimation crystals carrying a patch cradled itself onto them. She placed it on Sebastian's shoulder.

"What is it?" he asked.

"It's an adrenaline patch. Well, here we are," she said, waving her hands out above her head. Music blared from countless instruments. Lights flashed from all points. Even the streets lit up. There was endless chatter from the crowded dancers. No one appeared to be walking. Everyone was either dancing in one area or dancing to another area. It was an open club extending for blocks in all directions. This was the bright and wild Entertainment District. "Quite a few people enjoy using some sort of patch on themselves. Adrenaline patch. Alcohol patch."

She didn't receive a verbal response from Sebastian, who was distracted by the scene around him. She grabbed another materializing adrenaline patch from the air and threw it on him. "Hey, are you listening?"

"Another one? I think the first one will do just fine. Thanks."

"How about that?" Citlali pointed downward as Sebastian's foot tapped on the ground, moving along with the beat of the song. "Looks like the patches are kicking in. Hey, where are you going?"

Sebastian started moving along with the crowd. His shoulders swayed from side to side. Citlali placed her hand over her mouth, bits of laughter escaping around it.

"It kicked in, all right," Sebastian cheered. The beam of lights moved across the floor and buildings. They danced and stopped when they saw a neon blue light travel across the floor. The light was pairing individuals together. Everyone moved aside when the light passed right through them to let the paired-up individuals meet. "I thought the U-ITS matching system only worked in the Lover's District."

"It can work anywhere, but they're most commonly used in the Lover's and Entertainment Districts."

"Hey, remember the wishbone-looking building?"

"Yeah. You can call it the Mind Transfer Administration. Do you want to give it a chance now?"

"Yeah. I think I'm ready to give it a chance."

They made their way through the roaring crowds and out of the Entertainment District. After a short walk, they made it to the bridge-building. They walked along the pier and onto the structure. It was as crowded as the Entertainment District, but calm. There wasn't as much chatter or music, and the only light that illuminated the setting was the sunlight. The walls and roof were dark transparent sheets that allowed more than enough sunlight in for people to navigate around the spiral hallways. Citlali led the way as usual, entering an elevator at the middle of the floor. This elevator shaft traveled diagonally, and after ascending a few levels Sebastian had a good view of the Entertainment District through the transparent walls. It wasn't too far away. After a few more levels, he had a view of the park he and Citlali were at the night before. Near the top, they had a view of where the institution should have been. Since it was a secretive program, it was shrouded by a nearly endless forest far off the edge of the city. Once they reached their floor, they were gently pushed off by an invisible force. Sebastian stopped and fell to his knees, the tightening pain in his head forcing him to the ground. Placing his hands on his head did nothing to ease his pain.

"It's happening again, Charles!" Citlali shouted. "Another memory incursion!"

"Quick! Bring him back!" Charles's voice echoed.

A reanimated stretcher picked Sebastian up and brought him to the ambulance hover car parked outside the nearest window. The red-and-white vehicle glided off the bridge-building and made its way to the institution. Sebastian was still squirming around while a patch was placed on his shoulder. The patch's red cross flickered on and off. The flickering slowed down when Sebastian became unconscious.

***

Sebastian wiped the sweat from his dirty forehead, but it was no good. More sweat began dripping immediately. The palm trees offered him and his Army comrades only a little shade from the bright pale sky.

"This is where we make our stand!" said the man with the American flag wrapped around his fist. Upon closer look, his dog tag said "Adam". "In less than fifteen minutes, our enemies will be here raising hell! We were abandoned here by the military for who knows what reason. They left us here to die, but that doesn't matter. I know I am with men and women who will defend each other at any cost. We can, and we *will* hold back these jungle insurgents. We will get through their line of defense. We will make it!"

"Oohrah! Oohrah!" Everyone chanted in unison as the hot sun above hit them.

"We don't have much time." Adam pointed at the corners of the compound that contained its iron-rusted major entrances. "For us to repel the attacks, we are going to make defenses around these key points. We're expecting the first wave to be a little more than a hundred soldiers. If we can defeat most of them quickly enough, we'll be able to make an opening and make our way out of this compound. The second wave will be approaching from the north end. If we can make it to the southern end of this island, we'll make it on board our transport and amphibious assault ships. We'll then make our way south toward the next island. Alice, you and your sniper team keep an eye on the enemies hidden from afar. Mark, you and your team set up the mines...."

A hot breeze rushed past them faster than the blood in their veins. When the man finished giving out the orders, the group of twenty scattered around the compound relaying their orders.

"Bring the equipment here!" yelled a man with the name Mark on his uniform.

"Get into your positions now!" Alice ordered, pointing at specific ditches for her soldiers to duck into. Her light-copper eyes matched the color of her skin. "Keep watch while they set up the mines!"

42

A dozen or so clicks and clanks were heard as the mines were activated. The men ran back into the compound, grabbing their rifles and heading to an entrance. A moment later, gunfire commenced, and, as expected, dozens of enemies fired at the old compound. There were too many bullets to seize an opportunity to shoot back. Chips of cement from the fortress fell off as bullets rained down from all directions. Wooden structures used to store their weapons and food were destroyed in seconds. After realizing their enemies were buying time for the incoming wave of enemy soldiers, Mark ordered the mines to be triggered automatically. The mines exploded, and the group used this opportunity to shoot through the falling dirt and debris. The enemy soldiers started a hasty retreat. It was a small victory, though, and time was not on their side. They still had to maneuver around the jungle and onto the shore to their boats. With no mines left to worry about, the team maneuvered through the grass and sand of the island. They were met with light resistance and were unharmed by enemy snipers due to Alice's team. Many of their enemies seemed to have headed north for reinforcements. They ran through the shore and happily jumped onto their boats, escaping the island unscathed.

"That could have turned out bad for us," Sebastian said grimly.

"What did you mean about us being left to die?" Alice asked.

"We weren't supposed to be on the island because it was neutral territory," Adam started, "but our commanders sent us there anyway. The island's inhabitants wanted to be left alone from this godforsaken war. They especially did not want to side with us Americans. When we arrived, it was not difficult for them to decide to side with our enemies. We could have easily avoided the island and moved on to the next one. I'm not sure why we were sent there though. It was a mistake that could have cost us our lives."

"It wouldn't be the first," Mark interrupted. "I don't know who, but someone or some group from high above in the ranks has been sending people on dangerous and unfruitful operations. They have been sending whole platoons into heavily guarded enemy stations and territories. It seems criminal how they operate sometimes. And for what? I swear there are some messed up people running the government sometimes."

"I've heard stories of how corrupt individuals are running the operations in a way that secures corporate interests at the expense of our lives," said a man seated on the corner of the transport boat. The nametag on his shirt read Mohammad. "Remember the operation where the platoon was sent to that Central American city? They were there to help end tribal clashes, but for some reason they ended up fighting the insurgent stronghold a few klicks away, which controlled a lot of the area's fertile soil and major ports. Once they killed most of them and captured the remaining insurgents, they *accidentally* set the main market on fire. But then the trees burned. Then the land burned. Then the ports burned. Everything burned. The whole place was in flames and they were forced to evacuate everyone. Not everyone made it out alive, and it wasn't until it rained a few days later that the fire was put out. By then, all the land's vital resources and ports were destroyed, forcing them to rely on American corporations and military for food and other essential materials."

There was silence. Everyone had heard these stories. They knew there was something wrong going on with the military campaign but did not want to bring it up out of military discipline and fear. Now, someone had spoken. Someone had brought it up. But what were they going to do? They were going to move on like they hadn't heard anything. They looked away. They looked out into the sea, or at the boat's floor. Anywhere but into each other's eyes for fear they would be morally pressured to do something about the injustice. As they disembarked from the boats onto the shores of a friendly island, they had an excuse to smile. Their military comrades greeted them and helped them into their base as if they didn't know what kind of betrayal the arriving party had received from its government. The welcoming party pretended they didn't know what had happened, but they knew.

CHAPTER 6 – FIGHTING THROUGH THE SUNSET

Sebastian awoke as the sun crept through the hospital unit's window. No, it wasn't a dream, he thought. It was another memory incursion. As he replayed the flashback over and over in his head, he thought about what Mohammad had said. He then thought about what Charles had offered: Go after the Orderkeepers that plague the twenty-first century. He made his way out of the medical unit, down the carpeted hallways, and into the warden's office, where he saw Citlali sitting next to Charles.

"At this point, your memory incursions won't be as severe as the first two," Charles reassured. "You may get some headaches from the next few, but after that you won't feel a thing."

"That's good to know," Sebastian said, taking a seat across from the pair.

"Well?" Charles asked. "Have you made your decision?"

"Yes. I'll do it."

Charles remained serious, as if still processing the decision.

"You guys can come in now," Charles said, letting out a relieved sigh.

Ryan and Rosa appeared in the doorway and entered the room as Sebastian stood up, surprised.

"I thought you guys left this institution," Sebastian asked. "What are you doing here?"

"We were told the same about each other, but we're still here," Rosa said, hugging Sebastian around his neck. "Glad to see you're still here with us, too."

"I thought I was going to do this alone. Wait, so you guys are staying? Does this mean you two will be a part of this, too?"

"Yes, we both asked for an extra day to make our decision, but we decided to stay," Ryan said, turning to Charles. "Why did you lie to us?"

"To further test the integrity of your character," Charles responded.

"We're sorry we did that, but we had to make sure you wanted to do this of your own accord," Citlali said.

"By making you all believe you didn't have anyone except Citlali and me to rely upon, we knew your decision to join us would simply be because you wanted to help put a stop to the injustice caused by certain people," Charles continued. "Ultimately, you three would have decided to stay based solely on your selfless character. We know you are good people, but we didn't want anyone to feel obligated to join us."

"Well, we're here. So, what do we do now?" Ryan exclaimed. "Are we going after them now?"

"Not yet, but soon," Charles answered. "You are not quite ready yet. You don't have much memory to work with, therefore you don't know how to defend yourselves, or anything else to complete your future assignments. As time goes by, you will recall some memories that revive your abilities from your past lives. Some of our patients have remembered skills from their past lives such as chemistry and piloting. Be aware of that since it will come in handy if we do not get the chance to teach you specific skills. Now, back to the training. You will all go through arduous training. You three will be trained in the ways of martial arts, weapons, and many other skills. Drill Sergeant Taylor will oversee this training and make sure you are prepared in a timely manner. Now that you all have come to a decision, we can begin the training."

He rose from his seat and led them downstairs, through the courtyard and inside a pale white gymnasium stopping at the middle of the area. The clothes of the trio transformed from their regular blue patient clothes to a basic white T-shirt and camouflage pants, with brown boots animating over their feet.

"Keep me updated on their progress," Charles said, departing with Citlali.

"All right put these on," Drill Sergeant Taylor said. Three white ribbons floated through one of the windows and moved in front of them. "These are specially crafted mime ribbons, engineered by some of the most gifted minds on the planet. When you put these on, you will begin to obtain numerous skills. They work like regular mime ribbons except they embed the movements deep into your muscle memory. It's not *just* for muscle memory, though. You'll subconsciously learn how to talk and behave like a soldier with these. Go on. Tie it around your left arm." They grabbed the silky white ribbons from the air and tied them around their left arms. "Ready?"

"Yes, sir!" they unexpectedly chanted in unison.

Taylor's eyes lit up as he snapped his fingers. Immediately their bodies went into a fighting stance, their feet shoulder-width apart. Elbows bent. Fists in front of their chins. Their right hands and right legs tilting their torsos back at an angle. Ryan gasped when this happened. Sebastian wasn't shocked. He knew what to expect from the mime ribbons. Citlali had used a similar device on him earlier that week to make him dance.

"My body is moving by itself," Ryan said. "This doesn't feel right."

"You'll get used to it," Sebastian said comfortably. "It feels a little weird, but soon you'll be amazed at what your body can do."

Rosa let out an uncontrollable laugh. It ended when their feet shifted from side to side and then on an angle. This was followed by left and right punches into the air. A woman's voice let out the names of the moves they were performing: "jab-cross-uppercut." They switched from their orthodox stance to southpaw and repeated the same moves. Their punches sliced the air and their breaths reflected the power they put into their movements.

"Now you three will repeat these movements but this time without the help of the white ribbons," Taylor said. "You can keep your ribbons on, but they're not going to assist you right now. Now, together! Go!" The three simultaneously went into their boxing stance and started doing the same drills as before. They shifted from side to side and then on an angle. They demonstrated their boxing combos and switched stances. They repeated the routine and faced Drill Sergeant Taylor again. "That is the power of these white ribbons. Soon enough, you will master many martial arts. What took many years for a person to master one martial art, you will do in one week and master many. By the end of the day, you three will have mastered boxing, Taekwondo, and Muay Thai. Now let's recommence." He snapped his fingers again and in came three gray shadowy figures. They marched into the gym and lined up with their backs against the wall. "They're physical holograms. So, you can feel them, and they can feel you. For the time being they will stand there while you three progress in your training. But when they think any one of you is ready to spar, they will, and without warning, intervene in your training and fight whoever they think is ready to take them on. They may be holograms, but they can still inflict serious damage. You three will each learn a specific style of fighting geared toward your body types. Rosa will focus on speed and kicks, Ryan will learn slow but powerful strikes, and Sebastian will learn a balance of the two. Now, train!"

Again, their bodies contorted on their own. Sebastian started off with some stepping and dodging. Ryan began with some punch-and-elbow combos while an unknown voice said "jab-cross-elbow strike." He then performed an elbow strike followed by a low kick and then a three-punch combo. Rosa was practicing various kicks accompanied by a voice that said "roundhouse kick-tornado kick-rear horse kick." Circular targets appeared in front of them. They punched, kicked and dodged them. The gym echoed with their smashes of the reanimation targets and steps on the floor.

"This is pretty easy since my body is doing all the work," Rosa stated.

"Yeah, we're not even thinking about it and our bodies are moving," Ryan agreed.

"Those holograms are just standing there," Rosa said, kicking her foot into the air well above her head. "It's making me feel a little uneasy."

"Let's try to not think about them and focus," Sebastian reassured her while doing a push kick followed by a flying knee, shattering two targets.

"Stop your chitchat!" Drill Sergeant Taylor shouted.

Without any more chatter the three went back to their training in silence. They stayed quiet even when the drill sergeant left the three in the gymnasium without saying a word. The sun was beginning to set, and as the room dimmed, the gym lights turned on. Sebastian looked at the motionless-shadowy figures by the wall. They did not have faces, only the shape of a head with a nose sticking out. Suddenly, one of the holograms got out of its standing position and charged towards the three, throwing itself onto Sebastian. The two fell on the floor and the shadowy figure rolled off, swiftly getting to its feet. Ryan and Rosa watched, stunned, as their bodies continued to perform drills.

"Hey! Sebastian, are you okay?" Rosa asked. "I can't stop my drills. Can you, Ryan?"

"No, it's useless," Ryan replied, looking frustrated. "The ribbon is still in control of my body."

"I'll be fine," Sebastian said, getting to his feet. "I have control of my body again." He went into his fighting stance and faced the aggressive figure confidently. "Let's do this."

The shadowy figure had its hands to its sides and moved in a circle around Sebastian. Sebastian kept pivoting his feet to continually face the figure. The hologram then arrogantly cracked its neck, ran in place, brought up its hands, and took a few small steps toward Sebastian.

"That's one confident hologram," Rosa teased. "You better win, Sebastian."

"Don't worry. I can handle this."

The two contenders exchanged light punches. The hologram threw a kick at Sebastian's head, but Sebastian caught the hologram's ankle in time. He threw it back on the ground and followed up with a jab and hook. Then he jumped and landed a knee to the hologram's chin. The hologram fell to the floor. It shook its head disapprovingly and got back up. The hologram again circled Sebastian. It faked a punch and then smacked the flesh of Sebastian's left thigh with a kick, stinging him. In pain, Sebastian retreated a few steps toward a wall.

"Are you okay, Sebastian?" Rosa asked.

"Don't worry about me. I'm fine."

The hologram then pursued Sebastian with a barrage of punches and elbows. He tried to block as many as he could but ended up with a few bruises on his cheek and arms. Eventually the hologram got close enough to Sebastian to clinch him up against the wall. It followed with several right knees to his ribs.

"Get out of that position!" Ryan yelled.

Sebastian tried moving to his left side, but the hologram followed. He tried moving to his right side but again the hologram followed, making sure Sebastian remained pinned to the wall.

"Use your strength!" Rosa cheered Sebastian.

Sebastian was finally able to move around and away from the wall by twisting the hologram's arms off him. He channeled his strength and pushed the hologram away. The hologram lost its balance and fell headfirst onto the floor cracking its skull. It did not get up, lying motionless on the floor until it evaporated into the air.

"Impressive, Sebastian. Very impressive," Drill Sergeant Taylor said, reentering the gym. Although Sebastian had won the fight against the hologram, it did not change the fact that his ribs were in critical condition. He fell to his knees and held his sides in pain. On its own, his body went back into a fighting stance and back to more drills, despite his internal pleas to stop and seek medical support.

It was now Ryan and Rosa's turn. The two remaining holograms got out of their positions and charged at them. Still several steps away, one of the holograms jumped, twisting its body in circles in midair toward a confused Ryan. The kick landed on his cheek and pushed him back. The other hologram slid on the ground toward Rosa's side and used its hand to push itself up to deliver a *martelo de negativa*, which was a side kick with one's hand and foot on the floor. The capoeira kick was met by Rosa's arms, which were not enough to prevent the powerful blow from stopping the hit to her hip. The hologram went into a crouching position and jumped into the air while delivering a successful push that threw Rosa onto her back. She kicked her feet into the air and, with the help of her hands, pushed herself back up.

"I don't remember being taught that," Rosa said, astonished.

"It must be something you knew in your past life!" Sebastian yelled in excitement. He continued doing his drills of spinning kicks as he helplessly stole glimpses of the two pushing themselves in their fights. His urge to help his friends became overwhelming as his drills grew more intense. He was now jumping off the walls to perform more advanced strikes and maneuvers on his porcelain targets.

Ryan continued to defend himself from the multitude of combo strikes but failed to land any of his own hits. The hologram was too fast for Ryan. Ryan's massive muscular physique made it difficult for him to throw a quick enough jab at the hologram, making it easier for the hologram to find an unguarded area to hit. With great effort, Ryan pushed the hologram back, but it wasn't a hard push like Sebastian's. The hologram moved back into punching range of Ryan and unpredictably moved around a few steps to the left and then to the right after every combo strike.

Rosa noticed her hologram opponent was a power striker, while she was more of a fast striker. Her fight mirrored the fight between Ryan and his hologram opponent. She glanced over at their fight and started mirroring that hologram's moves. She moved within range of her opponent and did a jab-cross-jab combo on its torso. She then moved back as the hologram tried to grab hold of her head. Her opponent then took a few steps forward, jumped off the ground, and performed a superman punch. Rosa bent down and landed several uppercuts on the hologram's extended arm, following up with an elbow to the ribs. The hologram lost its balance and fell face-first to the floor. As it turned around, Rosa delivered the final blow. The hologram's head was punched into the ground and soon evaporated into the air.

"Hey, Ryan!" Rosa shouted. "You have to use powerful blows from a distance like this hologram used on me. Push it off you and then do a knee strike!"

Ryan was losing his battle, but he managed to use both arms to push off the hologram. While it tried to regain balance, Ryan jumped off the ground and delivered a flying knee to the hologram's chin. The hologram was again pushed backward, and struggled to maintain its balance. Ryan jumped off the ground again and this time delivered a tornado kick to the hologram's chin. The hologram fell to its side and disappeared before it hit the ground. All three could move on their own now.

"We did it!" Rosa said, high-fiving the other two. They paused, realizing they once again had full control of their bodies. The three stood there in a circle, breathing hard. Their hard facial features were tighter than their fists were clenched.

A slow clap ensued, and the three turned around to see Drill Sergeant Taylor, Charles and Citlali. Citlali raised her hands and floating medical patches appeared. They glided toward the three bloodied and bruised fighters. They took the patches without hesitation, affixing them to themselves. They were instantly healed. Their bleeding stopped. Their cuts and bruises disappeared. Their pain was gone. They grabbed their bodies in amazement. It was as if they were never hurt.

"That's it for today," Charles started. "What do you think, Drill Sergeant Taylor?"

"They did all right," Taylor said. "Let's give them some rest. They're going to need it. Tomorrow is when their training gets challenging."

"Your training here today was impressive," Citlali said as the three recruits followed her. The trio looked back one more time as they left the bloody and wrecked gymnasium. Then a series of holograms appeared around them, showing abundant food being eaten at white picnic tables while food continued to appear from above to replenish their emptying plates. This changed to adults and teenagers sitting along an assembly line inspecting blueprints for two Dyson plates directly above and under the sun.

"A lot has changed since you guys were last conscious," Citlali began. "It has been a few decades. Many countries have progressed through economic and scientific means. We have moved from a capitalist economy toward a collaborative commons society. We are now a Type One civilization. We can harness enough energy and resources for society, and there is no monetary price on any good or service. Everything is free to all those who play their part in this new economy. No one worries about not having something. It is readily made available at a moment's notice, as you have seen through reanimation technology. We have an endless supply of food, energy and other vital resources. Because of this, there is no socioeconomic hardship brought upon anybody. This makes it easy for anyone to succeed by their own standards and at their own pace."

Various visuals appeared around them, displaying the numerous ways energy was being cultivated. There were also cities of buildings containing farms of crops, as well as cities beginning to be built off the coast.

"We also have an endless creation of jobs. In our civilization, we nurture our young minds with the best education possible. They are so eager to contribute to our way of life that they begin working at an early age. Because of their enthusiasm, they each have something unique and powerful to give to their field of study, which of course leads to more job creation."

More visuals appeared. There were kids handling unusual scientific instruments of sorts, experimenting with virtual-reality simulations, and implementing tools of the internet of things.

"Many nations have set aside their linguistic and cultural differences and united to create an interdependent social order. Everyone is taught the universal language. This language can be spoken in nearly any part of the globe. But it is only used when two people do not speak the same native language. We are here in North America, in an area called Los Angeles. We all speak English and Spanish here, but if someone comes along who doesn't speak either, then we communicate in the universal language. If you want, you can learn the universal language. But even then you probably won't use it, because language is auto-translated through the air as you hear it. In terms of culture, we all respect one another, and although most cultures have become more open-minded, we still let go of our indifferences and allow each other to live in peace and without any senseless arguing.

"Now, I know you three have explored only a portion of this city, but you all had a pretty positive experience from it. Before your near-death accidents, you three grew up in a relatively conservative culture, so some aspects of that may still be fresh in your minds. You've all noticed how there have been a few oddities around the city. You may not understand everything, and that's all right. Maybe in time you'll open your thoughts to new things. Aside from that, another thing you have noticed is everyone is happy here. That is because the citizens here are nurtured well. They sleep well and they live well. Speaking of sleeping well, here we are."

They had made it to the hallway containing the entrances to their simple rooms.

"I'm going to let you three go off to sleep now. Good night."

Citlali faded away and the exhausted trio eagerly went off to bed in their rooms.

***

Their training never seemed to stop. The three were up once again, but this time outside in the courtyard where all the lifeless people once were. The courtyard looked bigger now that it wasn't crowded with all the aimlessly walking individuals who were now being treated in a faraway mental institution. They pushed their boots into the thick green patches of grass in anticipation of what they were going to do. They wondered what had become of the people, but none of them had an answer. The sweet, moist air softly brushed by their alert bodies. They stretched in anticipation of what they would learn today.

"Reanimation technology martial arts," Drill Sergeant Taylor said, appearing from above. He stood on a floating gray disk that descended into the courtyard and disappeared as Taylor planted his feet on the ground. "You've seen this while on your little adventures around the city. It has many purposes, transportation being the main one. But it also has another very important one. It can be used for self-defense. Today, you will learn about it. You will use it, and you will love it because this piece of technology will save your lives time and again. Go on, try to control your own reanimation blocks."

Rectangular reanimation blocks appeared, hanging from their waists. Dark bits of metal moved around the drill sergeant's raised hand.

"Come on. Try to hit me."

They all hesitated at his command. He thrust his fist forward and a small stream of gray matter flew by his arm and at Ryan's stomach, incinerating as soon as it connected with its target. Ryan kneeled over in pain, cradling his abdomen. Rosa placed her arm under him to help him up.

"Can you at least tell us how it works?" Sebastian exclaimed.

"You should already know how it works. Think of fighting with it, and it will obey your every command so long as you perform the appropriate body movements."

"If that's all it takes," Ryan said, raising his fists. His reanimation block started breaking off and floating toward his fists. Drill Sergeant Taylor then swung back his hand as if he were wielding a whip, then jolted it forward. Another wave of reanimation technology appeared, this time grabbing Ryan's ankle. Ryan waved his arms around trying to maintain his balance, but it was no use. The whip of gray material swung Ryan off the ground. He fell on his back, but immediately got back up in line with the other two.

"Let's try throwing jabs at him like he did on you, Rosa," Sebastian said. "Ready?"

"Yeah," the other two said in unison. They brought up their hands into a boxing stance. Reanimation material wrapped around their hands. Taylor did not hesitate to throw punches of reanimation blocks at them. The trio started doing the same, canceling out Taylor's flying metal boulders. Taylor was soon on the defensive as he used his reanimation technology to create small waves of shield to block their gray splashes. The three were relentless in their pursuit to hit Drill Sergeant Taylor. With each punch they threw at him, he was pushed a step back. They moved forward to keep near him.

"Okay, that's enough!" Taylor yelled. He pushed his hands together and forward. This was followed with a huge buildup of reanimation technology that easily overpowered the recruit's punches and pushed them back with its incredible force. "Your teamwork isn't bad, but you have a lot of work to do to better your skills. Most of the fighting you will do out there will be done through thinking on your feet! You must learn to adapt! Like yesterday, I am going to give you some time to learn on your own."

"Why can't we just think of what we want the reanimation technology to do?" Sebastian asked. "Why do we have to perform physical movements as well?"

"For safety precautions." Taylor looked astonished, as if he were explaining common sense. "If all it took was someone thinking of hurting someone with reanimation crystals, there would be a lot of… accidents. That is why it is also required to make the movements. It makes it less likely someone will harm another. We also only allow military, law enforcement and militias to use reanimation crystals in such a way."

"And why didn't we learn how to use this on our first day of training?" Rosa asked.

"You won't always have the ability to use reanimation crystals for fighting. We made sure you learned how to defend yourselves without it first."

Without a goodbye, Taylor walked out of the courtyard. White ribbons approached from the distance. The three took them and tied them around their arms.

"Well, you know what's coming," Rosa said. She raised her fist toward the two. Ryan and Sebastian did the same, softly bumping them together in a show of solidarity. And once again, exactly like the day before, their bodies started moving on their own. They started in their fighting stance lined up, arms-distance apart. With their fists still clenched, their right arms punched forward, followed by a small stream of gray metal. After they brought their right hands back, they punched again with their left arms while taking a step forward. They performed uppercuts followed by gray metal coming from below and making its way toward the sky. The stream hit the air and fell just as quickly onto the ground, evaporating on impact. They kicked with their right legs and then with their left, which was also followed by streams of dark metal. They did this from morning until the end of the afternoon. Through endless hours of practice, they had mastered another form of self-defense.

They reached their right hands out as if to grab something through telekinesis. Instead of reanimation technology throwing itself forward, it instead turned into a small floating platform. All three jumped on each of the platforms and made the same movement, this time with their left hands. Rosa jumped into the air. Ryan made a new platform appear under Rosa's feet, this time higher off the ground than the previous one. Again, they made the same motion with their right hands. Another platform appeared, and again they jumped onto the new platform. They did these hand gestures and leaps many times over, until they were well above the institution's roof.

They smiled, noticing they had regained free will over their bodies. They walked around the platform, admiring their view of the grassy fields and city skyscrapers beyond the institution. They stood together, glancing at each other and their view. The cool breeze rubbed gently past their threads as the sun's warmth absorbed into their skin. They feared not what their future brought, but what they had at that moment's thought. Their memories may have departed, but their will for more had just started. There they stood, triumphantly atop the gray cloud. The size of their visions exceeded that of the nebula and made them proud. They silently looked at each other and made a vow to never let each other down.

CHAPTER 7 – MEETING PEACEKEEPERS AND RECRUITS

They looked down and saw that they weren't alone. There was Charles, Citlali and of course Drill Sergeant Taylor. But there also were three others in clothes like Sebastian, Ryan and Rosa.

"It's time you three met others like yourselves living in this institution!" Charles shouted from the rooftop toward the trio above on the temporary platform. The three looked at each other in confusion, not because the platform had begun to lower, but because they did not know there were others like them in the institution.

"Yes, it's exactly what you're thinking," Citlali said. "The three you see here next to us are also immigrants of time: people resurrected. They are as committed to this institution's mission as you all. Sebastian Ramirez. Ryan Tovar. Rosa Molina. I would like you to meet Arthur Alvares, Ramon Cruz and Giselle Garcia. They make up one of our new teams."

Arthur stood at the end of the roof with one foot on the edge. He did not flinch and kept his arms crossed, looking indifferently over at the trio. Nothing about him was remarkable. He had short brown hair, brown eyes and was the same height and build as Sebastian.

Ramon's spiky hair was filled with streaks of blue and yellow that resembled lightning. His tribal tattoos fitted his tall, muscular physique. In many physical ways he was like Ryan. He immediately held out his hand and proceeded to shake theirs one at a time with a smile. His enthusiastic attitude toward the three eased the welcome between the six.

Giselle had amber-colored skin like Sebastian. Her long, chestnut-brown hair became gold around the edges where the sunlight shined. Sebastian was mesmerized by her naturally bright pink lips, as Giselle let out a big smile, accompanied by perfect white teeth. His heart pumped faster as he realized the two were not taking their eyes off each other. Her hips moved as she took a few steps toward Sebastian, the sun reflecting off the rest of her curves. The sunlight made her skin glow like the silver linings of the clouds above and Sebastian looked on, wondering if her skin, too, was as soft as the clouds. Or softer yet.

"Maybe we should go back inside," Arthur said, interrupting their introductions.

"Come on, Arthur," Ramon said. "It's beautiful out. We have a beautiful view."

Citlali winked at Charles as they eyed Giselle and Sebastian.

"Okay!" Citlali interrupted. "Now that you six have met each other, maybe we can go inside and finish up for today. How does a hot meal sound?"

One by one they turned around and went down the stairs from the roof. It took Citlali grabbing Giselle for Sebastian to be able to move from where he stood. After going down the roof's entrance into the building, they started walking down a hallway. While at the back of the group, Ryan placed his hand on Sebastian's shoulder.

"What was that about?" Ryan asked.

"What was *what* about?" Sebastian replied.

"You know," he made an eye and finger motion from Sebastian to Giselle and back.

"She made an amazing impression on me," he whispered.

Before they went into the elevator, Sebastian pushed him to the side and walked toward the middle of the sparsely spread group. Citlali was there, and she started playfully nudging him in the ribs with her elbow. When they arrived at their floor, Sebastian moved toward the front of the group where Rosa, Giselle and Charles were.

"There are more teams learning at this institution," Charles said. "Some are new like yourselves, and others have gone on missions. You'll be able to interact with all of them soon."

"Why haven't we met them before?" Rosa asked.

"Well, before we introduce our recruits to each other we like to make sure they are on board with this institution's mission. You already know what that is. And it's not like we kept them from you for too long. It's only been a day since you've decided to train under us. You and everyone you are about to meet have agreed to take on this work as well."

"Did your team go on a mission yet?" Rosa asked Giselle.

"No, not yet," she replied. "But we were told we were going to finish our training in a few weeks and be on our first assignment soon after."

"And how do you feel about that?"

"Well, I don't know, to be honest. I'm excited and nervous. But talk to a few of the people who have been here for a while and let me know what you think about your team going on your first mission."

"I will."

"Ah, here we are," Charles gestured as they reached the end of the hallway where glass walls resonated with cafeteria chatter. "This is our eating area."

In this two-story cafeteria there were a dozen people scattered about in plain training clothes. At the center, a few others stood hovering over several people who were sitting and dressed in khakis and tucked-in, button-down shirts. Some of those sitting had on suits and ties. Their shiny black shoes were kicked away, leaving only their cashmere socks between their feet and the red carpeted floor. One of them was lying down on a red-and-gold canape with his feet in the air but engaged in the conversation they were having at their table.

"If it isn't the first peacekeepers," Arthur mumbled.

"First peacekeepers?" Rosa asked.

"They're the first ones resurrected in this institution," Giselle said.

"They're the ones with the most experience in this program, and because of that they have a big ego," Ramon said. "I'd avoid them. Don't let them bully you and don't put them on a pedestal like the people standing over there."

As they entered the cafeteria, they overheard the conversation from the first peacekeepers.

"Things were different when we first started here," said the man lying on the red-and-gold canape. "Everything was experimental, and the staff was figuring out what to teach us as we went along with the program."

"Yes, tell them what we had to do to pass our first crucible, Thomas," a woman in a bright blue suit said.

"Right, Daniela," the man on the canape said. "So, there we were …"

59

"You know what? We're going to call it a day. We have a lot of preparation to go over for tomorrow." Ramon turned to Sebastian, Ryan and Rosa. "So, if you guys don't mind, we'll be heading out now."

"Oh, no, not at all," said Rosa.

Arthur, Ramon and Giselle waved goodbye and started for the doors. Giselle and Sebastian's eyes met once more as she gracefully took off.

"Very well." Charles led the group to another three-person team. "Let me introduce you guys to Jaime Correa, Paula Fonseca and ..."

"Sebastian!?" one of the people being introduced shouted out. Sebastian could not believe his eyes. It was Alice. She ran up and jumped on him. "Is that you?"

"Alice?" Sebastian said grabbing around her waist, embracing her cotton white-buttoned shirt and khaki pants. It was certainly her, the same glowing copper eyes and figure he saw in his last flashback, but he still could not believe what he was seeing. He looked over again at the doors and saw Giselle looking over curiously. Stunned, he looked back at Alice. She got off him and couldn't help but hug him again. He kept his eyes on Giselle as she started for the doors again, and once again he looked at Alice and her amazingly big smile.

"The one and only Alice Silva," she said, opening her arms and looking into the ceiling for a second.

"Well I'm pleased that you two know each other," Citlali said sarcastically. "What are the odds?"

"Why did you say it like that?" Sebastian asked. "Did you know that we knew each other?"

"Say it like how? Anyway, Charles and I will be going. Enjoy your meal."

He looked again at where Giselle had been standing, but she was gone. Charles and Citlali took their chance to leave, waving goodbye to everyone. Sebastian wondered if Citlali knew Alice and he would bump into each other in their new life. He decided to leave it as pure coincidence.

"We have to catch up," Alice said with a surprised smile, moving backward and placing her hands on Sebastian's arms.

"Yeah, we do," Sebastian said quietly, looking at her again.

"Come on, aren't you happy to see me?"

"Yeah, I am," Sebastian responded, looking one more time at the exit.

Jaime and Paula stood from their seats to greet the institution's newest members.

"So, you're Jaime?" Rosa asked, interrupting Sebastian's oddity.

"Please to meet you, ummm …" Jaime paused reaching out to shake Rosa and Ryan hands, followed by Paula.

"I'm Rosa and this is Ryan," she said shaking their hands. Jaime then placed his hands over his hair to fix his combover and cufflinks.

"Jaime likes to keep up his appearance," Paula said, smirking.

"So why are there some people dressed plainly like us and others dressed like you three?" Ryan asked.

"Ah, so you noticed," Paula exclaimed. "Well, those who are still in plain clothes like yourselves are recruits still in training, while those who are not dressed in plain clothes have completed their basic training."

Sebastian, Ryan and Rosa looked around the room and at the larger group they'd had their eyes on when they first entered the room. Those sitting down were in colorful clothes, while those standing around them were in camouflage pants and black shirts.

"Have you noticed the hierarchy?" Paula started again. "Some of those who have been on more missions than others tend to have an inflated ego, but don't worry, it's only those few. We aren't like that. Please come sit with us. I'm sure you guys have a lot of questions."

"Yeah, we do," Sebastian said.

"So, shoot," Jaime said as everyone took their seat around the table.

"Do you know when our training will finish?" Rosa asked.

"It depends on the team," Jaime explained. "Some teams take longer than others. It could be weeks or months even. But once you're done with your training and crucible, you'll be going on missions very often."

"And how did you feel about your first?" Rosa asked, not sparing another moment.

"You'll get a little nervous, but to be honest that may not change much afterwards," Alice said. "We completed our first mission, and even though we're more confident in ourselves, we know we're still going to have some nerves going into the next one. But a little bit of nervousness is normal."

"What was your team's first mission?" Sebastian asked cautiously.

They talked willingly about what they had had to do. After completing their crucible, Alice and her team were told to drop everything they were doing to go on a mission. They used U-ITS data to triangulate the location of a manufacturer of weaponized diseases. The team knew there were new diseases popping up across the nation in highly populated cities. It turned out that the biological warfare terrorist was traveling underground through a specially crafted vehicle that dug dirt or other materials out of its way, spitting it out behind as it moved. This made it impossible to find any tunnels that would lead back to where the terrorist had come from. Alice looked for changes in the terrain before and after the outbreaks. She had the terrain in newly affected disease areas monitored. When her programs noticed a disturbance in the terrain and unusual seismic activity happening in a city, she and her team dispatched to the area. Alice, Jaime and Paula appeared, and, using the element of surprise, they apprehended the terrorist and his vehicle.

"The vehicle's technology was considered state of the art and is being replicated for our use," Alice finished.

"So, is the man you captured an Orderkeeper?" Sebastian asked.

"Yes," Alice said proudly. "But sometimes we call them 'warkeepers' because they are warmongering people. We don't just capture warkeepers. We take all sorts of contracts from a government liaison."

"Contracts?" Sebastian asked.

"Contracts to complete missions are assigned to us based on what Charles believes we can handle," Alice said. "Since we are inexperienced, most of our missions will be investigating suspicious activity like we did with the biological terrorist."

"What happens when we complete a contract?" Ryan chimed in.

"In the capitalist era, we would have received money and other resources, but in this collaborative society, we get more recruits and increased consideration for future missions. They only want the most successful institutions to get the most recruits and most difficult operations. The more missions we complete, the more often they will come to us for our help."

"Wouldn't agents be less willing to accomplish anything if it means they have to carry a heavier workload and task?" Rosa asked.

"Actually, quite the contrary. We enjoy our line of work, which is why we are here. The adrenaline you get from training and the quick thinking and creativity you must unleash during the mission is worthwhile. This is a secretive program, so being one of the few people on the globe to know what's going on under everyone's noses is a privilege. We love it here, and we love our work. Remember, we are all given a choice whether we want to do this. If we change our minds we can always leave this institution; but once you're here, why would you want to do anything else?"

"That's amazing," Rosa said, astounded. "I never thought of it like that. Wait, you said more recruits? What do you mean by that?"

"The more missions we accomplish, the more choices the warden gets in his next line of recruits. Like you three. Every warden gets a limited pick in the next wave of resurrected people. You guys should finish up your basic training soon so you can play your part as well."

"When do we learn about our crucible?" Rosa asked.

"Immediately before it starts," Alice said. Her smile and eyes got big. "Now let's get some food! What will you guys have? We can eat anything we want. Anything imaginable. Don't be boring like Jaime and order something simple like lobster. Get creative like this."

She rubbed her hands together and in came a floating silver plate and dome. It slowly drifted to their table and made its way in front of Alice.

"You'll never guess what this is," she taunted, lifting the dome to reveal her meal's sweet aroma. The circular yellow sponge was topped with swirls of whipped cream. Surrounding the yellow sponge were slices of mango with banana cream poured on top. To the side of this was a chocolate painting of a stem with strawberry lining. At the center of her plate was a creamy white donut with a slice of it already cut off. Inside the donut there were several layers of color resembling a rainbow. Her crystal grail was filled to the top with a multicolored layered liquid. "After feasting your eyes on this work of art I'm sure you guys are tired of that sustenance patch. The name doesn't even sound appetizing. Who came up with that name?"

"That looks amazing," Rosa marveled. "What's in the donut?"

"All I know is it will give me all the nourishment I need for the day. Now you guys try."

"How?"

"Think of eating something. U-ITS is doing all the creative work here."

And at that moment, more silver plates and domes approached them, turning their table from a plain marble surface into a colorful array of crunchy edibles filling the scene with colorful steam sprouting sweet scents. The instant conversion of color would brighten anyone's mood. They chowed down on their first real meal together, forgetting about manners, but only for a second. Jaime, Paula and Alice giggled at this as they recalled their first meal together. Rosa cleaned Ryan's mouth by rubbing her napkin under it. Sebastian spilled some juice on his shirt as he drank, though the juice stain evaporated before anyone could point it out. As soon as he put his grail back on the table, Alice flicked her wrist toward Sebastian.

"Here, try some of this beverage," Alice said. As she waved her hand, the liquid from an unoccupied cup poured itself like a floating river into Sebastian's mouth. The indescribable outburst of flavor couldn't be imagined, only dreamed. Sebastian's eyes lit up. He closed his mouth as soon as the last bit of the stream came to an end. He had no words to thank her, so he stared at her, confident Alice knew he was thankful. They went back to eating, and Rosa shared her drink with Ryan. She waved her hand and a stream from her drink flowed into Ryan's mouth as they smiled at each other with their eyes.

"What do you all think?" Paula asked. They were sitting upright and eating one spoonful at a time by the time they were finished with their meals. "How was your first *real* meal?"

"Smelling the food was hypnotizing, but tasting it was even more incredible," said Rosa. "How could we forget about food?"

"Delicious," Sebastian said. "I hadn't noticed that all we had were those sustenance patches. I'm not sure why I assumed everyone was taking sustenance patches only."

"Well, most people these days use them because they don't see the point in sitting down to eat," Alice explained. "They would rather place a piece of fabric on their shoulder and use the time they would have used on eating to do something else. It makes sense: you could spend extra time socializing with those you care about."

"I'm full, but I can't wait for the next meal," Ryan laughed.

"Well that's going to have to wait anyway because you guys have to get some sleep for tomorrow's training," Alice said.

"Is it that time already?" Ryan asked. "I'm not even tired."

"It doesn't matter if we feel tired or not," Paula said. "We still need to sleep."

"It's also a matter of keeping up with a strict regimen here at the institution," Jaime responded.

Already, recruits were beginning to get up and leave. As the groups separated, Alice gave Sebastian another hug.

"It was nice seeing you again, Sebastian," Alice said. "It's nice to see someone from the past. Now that you're here, it feels like a part of my past isn't gone. I don't think I'll ever see another person from before, so it's nice having you around."

"I'm glad you're here, too," Sebastian said. "Between us, I recently had a flashback about our days in the military."

"Yeah, same!" Alice responded excitedly. "But let's talk about this another time."

"We should talk again soon."

"We should. Goodnight, Sebastian."

"Goodnight, Alice."

CHAPTER 8 – TRAINING DAYS

For weeks, Sebastian, Ryan and Rosa had woken up every day ready to take on the institution's rigorous training regimen. They knew if any one of them wasn't trying their best, they would be slowing down their teammates. At this point in their training, blood had become as common as sweat and their determination as visible as their heavy breathing. Giving up never crossed their minds. The only metaphoric movement that *did* cross is that of their arms as they helped each other up. Their weeks of hard work to realize their dream of becoming peacekeepers had led them close to their training crucible. But the three were not dreaming. They were awake from sunrise to sunset and there was no one that could stop them.

"Do you see the brutal obstacles of firing bullets and moving terrain in front of you!?" Taylor yelled. "You face these difficult trials every day, but they are nothing more than stepping-stones to your goal! Stones are tough and cold like the challenges we face day in and day out, yet they are a necessary foundation for completing one's mission! But we face these challenges together! We move up together!"

The temporary platforms disappeared as they ran up them and jumped to the next ones. They chased after one another in a line before the next platform disappeared. After their training together, they now ran and breathed rhythmically together. They had set their path and pace and chosen this bumpy road of stones.

"Stones are meant to be stepped on!" Their drill Drill Sergeant continued, motivating them. "These stones are only a road! They are not meant to be loathed! They are admirable memories to behold! Are they not stories to be told!? Think of this! If everyone were to live their dreams, then what phenomenal visions will we dream of after? You dream now to fly like the eagles in the sky as you three are already making your way up high. If you wanted to, would you stop? Would your future self tell you to drop!? They say you are your worst enemy because you give yourself chains. But your past self has always hoped for the greatest and no more pain. Fight for that person and catch up with who you are supposed to be. Forget the scar. Start your test. For this is you when you are truly at your best!"

And so was the mindset of the three recruits as clear nanotech suits tightened themselves onto the wearer's body and turned invisible. Once invisible, the wearer could not feel it anymore. It could fend off toxic odors and most bullets, as demonstrated by Drill Sergeant Taylor when he shot all three in the chest with his rifle. The three didn't even budge on impact. The suits were easy to take off, too, and the three were told a story of early recruits who forgot to take them off when they showered.

Later that week, they were introduced to weapons. In separate hover cars, they and several other groups were secretly brought to a secluded ocean shore. As they made their way to the shore-training ground they passed Arthur, Ramon and Giselle. Ramon exchanged a few words of good luck to them as his team departed, while Sebastian and Giselle quietly glanced and smiled at each other as they passed.

They then took aim at mile-away targets with their silenced snipers. Lined up for blocks with other recruits, their targets were slightly above sea level, allowing the waves to pass over the middle of each target. Due to the wind, the waves moved at uneven intervals, but thanks to their scopes they could calculate the wind and how it would affect their trajectory. They were off target on their first try, their second try and their third. But eventually the group was dead-on. They were told autonomous robots could shoot accurately from much farther away, but it was necessary to have marksmanship training for additional self-defense purposes.

The next afternoon, they were to spend the first of many sessions sparring with other peacekeepers and recruits. They were not in the gym this time but instead in an industrial warehouse with high ceilings and stone pillars not far away from the institution. The only welcoming sounds of the gym came from the slamming on mats and striking of punching bags. Only sunlight from the window panes came to warmly greet the newly arrived recruits from Sebastian, Giselle, and Alice's teams, as everyone else inside was too busy sparring or grilling the new recruits.

"Glad to see friendly faces," Giselle said sarcastically, staring at the unfazed peacekeepers.

"Line up!" a man with a coarse voice shouted. It was not Drill Sergeant Taylor, but a man in a similar military uniform. Instantly, the newcomers formed themselves into a straight line with their eyes pointing straight. The man was as big as Ramon or Ryan. He moved across the nine newcomers, examining a holographic tablet, and looking up at each recruit as he worked his way down the line. "My name is Drill Sergeant Abraham Williams, but you will call me Drill Sergeant Williams! Is that understood!?"

"Yes, sir!" the nine recruits shouted.

"I said am I understood!?"

"Yes, sir!" the nine shouted even louder.

"Today we will see how much you have learned since you started training in our institution. We will cut to the chase and have you fight our experienced peacekeepers. Line up against those empty maps at the center of the room and stand adjacent to those already there! Now!"

The nine immediately followed his instructions, lining up on one side. To the right of this side were the experienced peacekeepers. Those closest to each other would be next to fight each other. The first one was Ramon, who was paired with a man of similar size. Drill Sergeant Williams had them spar, but it was soon clear the new recruits were no match for the peacekeepers. After Ramon tapped out, it was Ryan's turn. Next in line, Jaime decided to provoke the next opponent rather than watch Ryan's fight.

"Looks like you all are going to get another dose of ego juice today," Jaime said, annoyed.

They said nothing. After Ryan lost, it was Jaime's turn to fight.

"Pointless exercise if you ask me," Arthur whispered to Sebastian.

"Yeah, something like this can only hurt morale," Sebastian whispered back.

"Any plans on how to beat them?" Arthur said. Jaime lost his fight, and Alice took her turn on the mat. "It's clear these peacekeepers already know all our moves. You might have to rely on something they didn't teach us. We'll have to use a skill from our past lives to beat them."

"I was in the military, but we barely fought with our hands. We mainly used our guns."

"That doesn't help. Come to think of it, I think most of these peacekeepers have recovered most of their memories, so they probably have a lot more skills from their past than we do." Arthur paused, looking up at Sebastian. "I used to do parkour in my past life, but I didn't use it for fighting. It was only a hobby. It's a long shot, but maybe I can use it."

"If it isn't the fiery Arthur," Thomas taunted as he stood next in line with Arthur. He was no longer in the bright-blue suit he wore in the cafeteria. This time he had on the same clothes as the recruits, a white T-shirt and khaki pants. "I see you're making friends. I'm surprised. I thought you didn't want to be around anyone."

"Ignore him," Giselle said from nearby.

"Come on, Thomas," a tall man behind Thomas said. "Why can't we get along? We're all here for the same reason."

"The new guys need to learn their place here, Ezekiel," Thomas continued.

"As first peacekeepers, we need to be leaders that promote teamwork," Ezekiel said. "We need to help each other improve, not instill some sort of status quo."

"Listen, Ezekiel. We've all been bored with no missions the past few weeks. All of us here are going out tonight to cause trouble at the border in the demilitarized zone. Interested?"

"I hear Daniela might be," Arthur responded. "Where is Ms. Barrios, anyway?"

"She's practicing elsewhere," he said, turning delighted. "I haven't asked her yet. This is something we planned just now. Did she say she was interested in something like that? I don't think we ever brought it up with her."

"She didn't say she was interested, I just wanted to see your reaction when I brought her up."

Thomas did not take this well but held back his disappointed expression.

"Alvares! Avila!" Drill Sergeant Williams shouted. "Mat! Now!"

Arthur and Thomas measured each other's distance with their jabs. Thomas soon charged low at Arthur's legs as Arthur swiftly jumped into the air and flipped, bouncing onto his opponent's back and performing a successful leg bar. Thomas tapped out. A shocked and annoyed group of first peacekeepers looked at the recruits to intimidate their joyful reactions. No one else on that line was as successful as Arthur that day.

"That was good. You really showed them," Sebastian said.

"Thanks," Arthur said. "It's time someone did."

"I wish I had thought of that before I went," Ramon said as the sweaty recruits nodded their heads in agreement. Only Arthur won his fight, but it was a win for them all. "I used to do parkour all the time in my past life!"

"Good work out there, Arthur!" Ezekiel said, interrupting. He passed by, patting Arthur on the shoulder, and headed toward the dorms.

"That reminds me," Arthur said as the group left the training facility, "I had tattoos in my past life. I had skulls and quotes around my chest and back and one on my arm. I've been meaning to get new tattoos. I heard tattoos these days light up and move on their own. Intriguing, but I still prefer the look of 2-D ink."

With their training done for the day, the group headed back to their rooms to shower. The cool water in Sebastian's shower adjusted immediately to the temperature his body felt most comfortable with. They still had a few more hours before curfew, and he wasn't tired, so he decided to explore a little and see if he could bump into Giselle or Alice. He wanted to talk about his flashback with Alice, but he couldn't get his mind off Giselle. She could have easily stolen his heart with her looks alone, but there was more to her than that. There was something captivating about her, and he wanted to find out why.

He walked around the empty hallways, occasionally passing other peacekeepers chatting. He ended up in a part of the institution he hadn't been in before. It was a secluded hexagonal lobby with a few beams of light bouncing off through the dark-blue curtains from his left side onto gray walls. On his right side and across the room were hallways. At the center was an opening where a crystal spiral staircase was situated connecting the floor above to the floor below.

"Come on, satellite bracelet," Sebastian whispered as he tapped it. "Work your magic."

"You know you don't have to say anything to it, right?" a woman said, pulling back the curtains. She leaned on the cushioned windowsill with her feet in violet socks resting on an elevated bump. Giselle looked curiously at Sebastian. "What were you trying to do?"

"Oh, it doesn't matter now," Sebastian said approaching her side. "I never properly introduced myself. I'm Sebastian."

"I'm Giselle."

"Well, Giselle, it's nice to meet you."

"Likewise," she smiled. The window and windowsill expanded to allow another person to sit. "Do you want to sit?"

"Yeah." He made his way to the windowsill and sat across from her with her feet pointing at him. "I hope not all peacekeepers are like that."

"No, definitely not. Only a few. I don't want to talk about them. That's probably what they want us to do, anyway."

"True. So, what are you doing?"

"I was reading an article Rosa sent me. Now I'm watching the news." She held up a clear rectangular piece of flexible glass.

"What is that?" Sebastian said, eyeing the glass object in her hands.

"Here, look, it projects images and videos on it," she said, swiping her finger on the screen displaying a video of a man and woman talking about the latest asteroid-mining venture. "Pretty cool, huh?"

"Fascinating," Sebastian said, not sure why he was unable to say much more. He began reading the article displayed:

The latest acquisition from the asteroid-mining conglomerate has now acquired another Martian-owned landing station for its private expeditions. Many have said the Martian people need not be worried, and they can only prosper under the conglomerate's strict maintenance and supervision, but others are worried because two of their remaining six landing stations have exploded under suspicious circumstances.

"It looks like shady things are still happening," Giselle said. "Hopefully everything is all right up there on Mars. Charles recommended we keep up with current events, but I'm only catching up with the news to keep my mind off things."

"If you don't mind me asking, what kind of things?"

"Well," Giselle paused. "Everything."

"Everything?" Sebastian said.

"I keep thinking of what my past was like, but I know I won't recover any more memories by simply musing. Only certain experiences will trigger memory incursions that will bring back my memories. In other words, I'll worry about the past in the future, so until then I would like to keep my mind occupied."

"I know what you mean. We lived another life and now we have a new start. Who are we without our memories? At least we'll get our memories back."

"Yeah. Not knowing about my past is making me feel … empty. Like a machine and now everything is out of my control. It's as if my next decision isn't even mine." She paused for a moment and looked out the window at a group of recruits meditating on the grass. "But my flashbacks have helped. Every time I get them it's as if a part of me returns. Bit by bit I'm beginning to feel whole again. I already had my second flashback, and I'm told everyone gets nearly all their memories back no later than their fifth flashback. What about you, Sebastian?"

"Two flashbacks, but I've already been feeling much better since my first day."

Steps approached from one of the three tiny hallways leading away from the windowsill. Ezekiel and two individuals of Native American complexion appeared by his side.

"Oh, I remember you," Ezekiel said, smiling as the three walked around the spiral staircase to greet Giselle and Sebastian. "I didn't get a chance to introduce myself. I'm Ezekiel Arnal. These two are also first peacekeepers. You may remember them from the match today. On my left is Abigail Carballo. And to my right is Gabriel Laguna."

"Please call me Abigail," Abigail said, shaking Sebastian and Giselle's hands. She moved shyly and offered a small smile. "I hope you don't think we're all bad like some of the other first peacekeepers."

"Some of us are actually nice people," Gabriel said, taking his turn to shake their hands. "If you have any questions about nearly anything, then please don't hesitate to ask."

"Good luck getting in contact with him though," Abigail chimed in. "He's often away on missions because of his strategic aptitude."

"And because of that he's one of the first people Charles considers when sending people off on missions," Ezekiel added. "We were at the cafeteria getting food. It's interesting how we can request sustenance patches to appear in our rooms, but we still prefer food in a cafeteria setting. I guess some habits never die. Anyway, it was nice seeing you two. Enjoy the sunset." With a straight face, he looked out the window at the horizon and back at the duo before waving goodbye.

72

"I like him," Sebastian said, moments after Ezekiel and his two companions had walked away. "He and the other two were nice."

"I like them too."

Steps were heard from the floor above. Giselle and Sebastian looked at the opening to the floor above. An unknown man and woman passed by until they were out of sight, but they spoke loud enough for the pair at the windowsill to hear them.

"Hey, do you know what else is new?" the woman asked.

"No, what?" the man asked.

"There's no more diseases in this time."

"Oh yeah? I've heard they've cured everything. Cancer, asthma and other illnesses."

"Yes, we might be able to live forever now."

She said this as her voice and their footsteps trailed off. Giselle and Sebastian avoided each other's gaze while wrapping their heads around the possibility of immortality.

"Umm … listen, I'm getting a little tired. I'll see you around, Sebastian."

She stood up and without thinking placed her hand over his head, gripping his hair and looking down at him. She blushed and swiped her hand back realizing what she had done. Still, the two smiled before she walked away. Sebastian made his way to his room and then his bed. He stared at the ceiling in excitement but eventually the long day of training put him to sleep.

CHAPTER 9 – MUSIC FOR A FORGOTTEN PAST

As usual, the courtyard was filled with grunts and strikes.

"That's enough training for today," Drill Sergeant Taylor said, his voice echoing through the courtyard.

"But we can keep going," Rosa said wiping sweat off her eyes.

"Can we do more training?" Ryan asked.

"Everyone needs to take a break from their daily routine," Drill Sergeant Taylor reassured. "If you want to stay and spar with the holograms or other recruits and agents, you can. They'll be in the industrial gym. Use this free time to do what you want."

"I want to go outside," Sebastian said after a moment, interrupting the silence.

"And you can," Taylor said walking away. "Go; I won't keep you guys any longer. Seriously though, take a break."

"Did you have something in mind, Sebastian?" Rosa asked.

"Don't you remember his encounter with—" Ryan said smiling.

"It's not that I don't want to spend time with you two, but I've had somebody on my mind for a while now," Sebastian said, beginning to walk away. "I don't know what it is with her, but I felt something. I can't ignore that, you know? And what are you two going to do with your free time?"

After a bit of silence, Sebastian turned around to look at the two, walking backward and grinning at them. Their quiet expressions could not have hinted more awkwardness.

"I think I'm going to spar a bit here," Ryan said.

"Yeah, and I'm going to see if there's anything interesting to learn about in the white ribbon simulation section of the library," Rosa said cheerfully. "They say you can learn more than fighting through the white ribbons. Maybe I'll learn something useful for the crucible."

"Sounds great," Sebastian said as he left the gym. Citlali appeared, falling in step with him.

"So, I heard you're looking for someone. Hmm?" she teased.

"Yes, you know who."

"Yeah, who? You know I'm not allowed to read people's minds."

"You don't need to be able to read minds to know what someone is thinking. Are you really going to make me say her name?"

"Yes. Say her name."

"Giselle. I'm looking for Giselle."

"Look at that smile, Sebastian. I thought I would never see one like it. She must mean a lot to you."

"Something between her and me felt right."

"But you don't know her yet, do you?"

"No, but I want to. Will you help me?"

"Sure, but she is in the middle of something right now. Tell you what, let's go to the city and pass the time. When she is available I'll let you know, and we can set up a time and place. Sound good to you?"

From the forested institution to the grassy plains, then passing the wildly genetically engineered creations through the alley lanes, once in the city, one could not properly describe everything there was to see. *This* jungle was even more diverse than a Central American wildlife domain. One could see so much in one small square of this vast, fast-paced city. Flying color-changing lizards swooped down to eat reanimated fruits. From above, rafts full of sea otters were carried about in large, floating streams of water.

"Do you mind explaining what exactly is going on in this bizarre city?"

"I'll explain a bit, but the rest I'll leave to your imagination. Like I told you before, there are genetically engineered creatures. They like to travel the city like cats. They're harmless, so don't worry about getting their attention. See?" Citlali stretched out her arm. One of the flying lizards came down and landed on her arm.

"Just like that?"

"Yes." She jiggled her arm and freed herself of the lizard. It flew away in the distance with the others. Citlali knelt and clapped her hands. "Come here." From under a table came several pygmy marmosets. Citlali and

Sebastian stroked their fingers through the monkeys' long, silky fur. "You never know what lurks in each corner. These animals originally had short hair and were much smaller. They definitely didn't wander the bright streets of Los Angeles." As soon as the marmosets were bored, they hopped away to a pile of crates and then to the top of a one-story entrance to a school. "Looks like these monkeys were engineered for stealth, too."

"Genetic engineering seems like a gift."

"Yes, it is. There used to be a lot of controversy about it back when it was first introduced, but now everyone and nearly every living organism on this planet has been genetically engineered in some way. It's a part of life now; like water to us. By the way, let's get some drinks."

"You're not going to give me something like adrenaline patches, are you?"

"No. No. I mean actual drinks. Here." Two bottles dropped from above and into Citlali's hands. She handed one to Sebastian and started drinking hers. It was the same drink Alice had given Sebastian. He couldn't get enough, and soon his belly was full of the dreamlike substance.

"Where does your drink go?" Sebastian asked as her empty bottle disappeared in the air.

"I don't store it," she laughed. "I'm a hologram. The drink evaporates into the air, like the bottle. I can still taste it if I want to."

"Oh, right. I should have figured that out." Sebastian tried to gear away from the awkward conversation. "Is there a name for this drink?"

"Yeah. The best drink on the planet. Come on! Let's go see a cage fight."

"Hey, why is it so sunny out here, yet I feel cool even though I'm not in the shade?" Sebastian asked as they approached the crowded arena.

"Long ago, landscape architects figured out a way to keep the street levels cool. They twisted the science of reanimation technology to lower the heat coming in from the sun above. Ah, here we are. Through there. Anybody can fight here. Except you because you still have to lay low as part of your job."

"Good to know," he said monotonically. "I don't know what I would do without you. You are the star in the night sky helping me find my way."

"Funny," she said sarcastically. "Because my name translates into 'star'. Like I haven't heard that one before."

They found some seats not far from the large stage. There were eight people inside in what was a four-on-four fight. Half of them had red cloth tied to their waists while the other half had on blue. They were using reanimation technology to hit each other. At times it was hard to see where everyone was because of the sheer amount of metallic matter being thrown around. In a matter of minutes, the entire blue team was taken down. The crowd roared in excitement as the fallen team was carried off the stage.

"Sebastian!" said a woman from across the aisle. Citlali and Sebastian turned to see who it was.

"Alice!" Sebastian got up to greet her as she made her way past the numerous seated spectators. Citlali then disappeared from between the two and reappeared next to Sebastian's side, leaving Alice to take the previously occupied seat.

"You like cage fights, too!?" Alice asked excitedly.

"First time!" Sebastian yelled over the enthusiastic crowd, a new fight having reignited its energy. The fight had turned incredibly bloody as the fighters of the new match exchanged blows. "Listen, I think we should catch up on our past. Do you want to talk somewhere else!?"

"Somewhere else!? Why!? Open private conversation with Sebastian!" Alice shouted. A hologram projected itself in front of Sebastian reading, "Accept private conversation?" Sebastian tapped the "Yes" neon-blue block. Suddenly the roaring screams went away. They were still in the stadium and could still see everyone engaged in the match, but no sounds came from them. "What did you want to talk about?"

"Can we talk here?" Sebastian asked, looking around. "There are people around."

"Don't worry; it's safe," Citlali reassured. "They can't hear you, nor can they read your lips since to everyone else you two still look like you're enjoying the match."

"Sounds like telepathy," Sebastian said. "I wanted to talk about the flashback I had of us."

He proceeded to tell her what Mohammad said about the government using the military to benefit U.S. corporations. Alice pulled out a hologram tablet that brought up the news of the flashback's time era.

"This tablet is also blurred out for our privacy," Alice said.

On the hologram came a news article with the headline "Corrupt Government – What Else Is New?" He read it, only to confirm Mohammad was right.

"But now what?" Alice said. "We can't change the past. At least things are better now."

"At least things changed," Sebastian said. "You're right. There's nothing we can do. I'm not sure why I brought it up. But it's good to see that article!"

After a few more brutal fights, the two left Alice at the arena and headed out. Citlali knew Sebastian had a lot on his mind. She did not make any effort to break the silence. It was a good silence and one someone could easily enjoy as their feet took them to places unknown.

"Hey! Sebastian! Look at your feet!" Citlali shouted out. A light shot out from the top of Sebastian's shadow. "It's happening!"

He stood there for a long minute. The light turned a corner and was no longer visible. He made a move to find the other end of the light. Citlali followed closely behind while he trailed the light. They made the turn as their feet hit the gold ground toward the corner. He saw the light stretched far across his line of sight. Still, he had to keep moving to find the other end of it. He broke into a jog.

"Run, brother, run!" a man yelled from the crowd. Without being told, everyone made a clear path upon seeing the light. The two ran and eventually reached another corner.

"Why am I being made to run all this distance?" Sebastian asked.

"It's the way the U-ITS' matching algorithms work, remember? If the individuals are close enough and suddenly begin walking in opposite directions, then U-ITS busts into action and guides them back together through this light." The light continued into a building. "That's a twenty-four-hour club we're heading into. Ready to show off some of your dance moves!"

Sebastian gave her a 'not happening' look by tilting his head at an angle.

"Oh, come on. Why not?" she said with a wink.

As they entered the building, they were greeted with shows of light and spectacles of people dancing on the floor, tables, walls, ceilings and even into the air on reanimating glittering crystal staircases. There were layers of people dancing. One man would swing a woman around onto his layer, and then lift another man from below him and swing him upward. There were lines of people entering the dance floor with mime gloves, dancing in synchronization with each other and to the beat.

"Sometimes, individuals bring a choreographed dance to the club and they allow others to download the dance onto their gloves. The one who made the dance is leading in the front, as you can see. It's a great way to show off your dancing creativity to others while letting them experience it themselves."

"That's something I would like to try, but at another time. I have to meet up with whoever this is." Sebastian followed the light through the back exit. Citlali followed closely behind, making note of how quiet the streets were compared to the club. The sun was setting, making the line of light on the floor appear brighter and the realization he was about to meet someone special that much more exciting. The streets were calm as Sebastian ran through them. Everyone looked on with a gentle vibe as he pursued the light.

"Oh, I can't wait for the sun to go down," Citlali said, kicking both her legs into the air in opposite directions like a ballerina.

"Why is that?" Sebastian asked. Running and jumping over a bench. He stopped to look over at the sun. It was moments away from setting.

"Something is supposed to happen today when the sun goes down. You'll see." It was dark now, with the only lights coming from the glowing U-ITS light bugs moving slowly through the air like white dust. "Aaaaand cue the music …"

Suddenly, the streets were filled with music and everyone started dancing as if they were at the club. For blocks, the once-calm people were now enjoying the beginning of their nightlife with dance. Sebastian continued onward, wondering whether they were dancing with people they knew or strangers who happened to be next to them.

"I like this music," Sebastian said. "If I had a soundtrack to my life this would be in it."

"This is something that could not have been done decades ago," Citlali said admiringly. "I'm going to stay here."

"What?" Sebastian asked shocked.

"You're about to meet her. She's near, and you're going to want to meet her privately," she said sadly as she disappeared bit by bit. "I'll be around enjoying this if you need anything."

"Okay. Thank you, Citlali. For everything."

Sebastian turned around and kept his pace, jumped over a bench as the light on the seashell-colored ground continued onto a silver path. Following up a ramp, he heard footsteps heading away. He walked forward, and after turning a corner to look for the trail of footsteps, he saw no one. His eyes met the sandy beach in front of him. Then the ocean. The light continued into the sand. Nearby was a spherical pavilion. He followed the light around the pavilion until it led up to its round surface.

Before he even had a chance to look up, a woman slid down the pavilion's smooth surface. She landed on top of Sebastian as they hit the cool sand. While on his back trying to figure out what happened he looked at the woman he had been lured to. The woman who was now seated on his stomach. Her silky brown hair made its presence known on his face and out of reflex he bit onto a lock of her hair. She smiled, showing off her white teeth and convincing Sebastian to do the same.

"So, we were meant for each other?" Giselle giggled, raising an eyebrow.

"Looks like fate likes to take a jump at life." Sebastian stroked her hair. "Why the surprise at the end?"

"Why not? I wanted it to be more fun." She poked the tip of his nose while he softly pressed his fingers against the pillow that was her cheek.

"I knew your skin was as soft as the clouds," he said gripping her waist. "I had been missing something since I was brought back."

"Shh, you can't talk about certain things," Giselle placed her hand over Sebastian's mouth.

"Oh, right, I forgot," he managed to mutter through her hand. "Private conversation—" but before he could even finish there was a holographic confirmation that the two were now in a private conversation. "I knew I was missing something. Well, someone. You see, I was with someone in my previous life. And I had a family."

"So did I," she said guiltily. Giselle slid off his body and sat on the side quietly. "I had a family and someone special in my life, too. I don't know what became of them. I can only hope they lived good lives. To be honest, I considered running away from the line leading me to you, because I wasn't sure if I was ready to move on. I'm still not sure."

"You're not the only one who isn't sure," he said. "But we can't change the past. We were led to each other. I think we can help each other. Let's at least start somewhere and see where it leads."

"Why do you look so familiar?" she asked, gazing into his eyes, still a little unsure of what to make of the situation.

"From the moment I first laid my eyes on you, I thought there was something about you. But I couldn't figure out what it was."

"If it has something to do with the past, maybe we'll figure it out as we get our memories. Your last name is Ramirez, but my last name is Garcia, so we weren't married."

"Maybe we did know each other from before," Sebastian said. "I know Alice from my past life. That sounds so weird to say out loud."

"You do seem familiar though," she whispered.

He cradled her into his arms and kissed her cheek. She enjoyed that more than she dared to admit on their first night together. They lay there quietly, with Sebastian on top holding her as if to not lose her. They listened to the constant flow of waves splashing onto the beach. She turned her cheek against the sand and looked beyond into the white and dark-blue horizon. The moon's silver gaze glittered into her eyes. When she looked up at him, the stars seemed to reflect her mesmerizing soul. Her eyes and smile made it clear what she wanted. Passion more aggressive than the moon's force on the oceans and love as delicate as the sand. Harmonious love moving like wind brushing against a fluid stream. He leaned into her and began kissing her lips. With each kiss he attempted to block out the noise from every rush of wave.

They paused and stared at one another. Excited, Giselle brought her head down to his neck. Even with her head pressed into his neck, Giselle was still having trouble holding in her chuckles. After catching her breath, a beeping noise interrupted them. Over her bracelet, a miniature hologram of Charles appeared.

"Giselle, you're needed back at the institution," Charles said. "Something came up."

Giselle kissed Sebastian on the lips.

"Don't move!" she said, frustrated. She stood up and walked a few steps away. Her conversation moved toward a mutual understanding between her and Charles as she calmly ended the chat, reassuring him she was on her way back. She walked back to Sebastian and knelt. "Look, my team and I have a lot of preparations we must go over for our crucible. After that, we can pick up where we left off."

"Not an excuse on behalf of Charles to separate us, is it?" Sebastian joked with his head against the sand wishing he had more time with her.

"I have to—as they say—drop everything that I'm doing to go make the world a better place. What can I say?"

"This is, after all, the life we chose. Good luck, Giselle."

She raised an eyebrow at her last remark and winked. A vehicle appeared in the distance, stopping near the two. She leaned over and kissed his lips. Giselle then walked over to the hover car and was gone. Sebastian lay on the beach with a smile on his face, remembering the smoothness of her skin. He could not have been happier. He stood and walked around where he had last seen Citlali.

"Well?" Citlali said from the roof above, her legs dangling from the edge.

"She's perfect," Sebastian smiled.

"Gotta love algorithms, huh?" she said. "No pun intended."

"Yeah, well I'm ready to head back now." A vehicle appeared from behind him. He jumped in as it hovered above and collected Citlali. "By the way, why did you stay here?"

"I wanted to see everyone dance."

"You said 'this isn't something that could have been done decades ago.' What did you mean by that?"

"You ask a lot of questions," she said, wiping away a tear. "But that's good that you're curious."

"I didn't know you could cry," he said wiping away her tear.

"Yes, I'm an artificial intelligence, but I'm programmed to be as human as possible. I'm not just a compilation of information. I have feelings and react to memories like everyone else. Sebastian, I've been around for quite some time. Like you remember the world in a different way, so do I. It was so different; so vile. There was shelter, but no one had a home. There was food, but few were well fed. There was desire, but no one loved. There was only darkness and lost paths. A world torn in war, famine, climate change and hate. But I'm glad that's over. That's why I sometimes get so lost in moments when people who don't know each other can comfortably get along with one another."

Citlali left Sebastian for the night as he made his way through the dormitory halls. Ryan was on his way to his room from the gym. He had learned an incredible amount of fighting techniques while Sebastian was away. Sebastian recalled his story of Alice with Ryan in the privacy of his room, not yet wanting to bring up the intimate moments he shared with Giselle. He preferred having their romance kept a secret at least for the time being. Rosa passed by the room, sharing her newfound wisdom in controlled simulation environments through a technology called Mastermind Stratagem. The librarian recommended the subject to her at the front desk. She wanted to talk more about it but thought it would be best to go to sleep, as curfew was about to come into effect. She left, but not before she suggested they visit the library together the next time they were free. Ryan said good night and went off to his room. As Sebastian lay on his bed he thought about his son. He couldn't be there for his son. Couldn't see him grow or watch him do well in school or bring him to a soccer game. He couldn't watch him go off on his adventures. How did he do? He didn't know, and he might never know. Then the comforting words of Citlali echoed in his head: "That's why I sometimes get so lost in moments when people who don't know each other can comfortably get along with one another."

CHAPTER 10 – CRUCIBLE

The trio was isolated from the rest of the people at the institution, told their obstacles wouldn't give them any time to rest. The three had on their simple clothes: white T-shirts, khakis and brown boots. They matched the bright moon and ground below them. They were told to be there by eleven at night, but their training would begin at midnight. They stood there in anticipation for an hour, waiting for their crucible to begin. Marching and yelling echoed in the distance. They did not expect twenty other personnel, all dressed like Drill Sergeant Taylor in camouflage uniforms and rolled-up sleeves. They formed a circle around the three recruits. Charles, Citlali and Taylor stood in front of the trio.

"Who stands here in front of me!?" Drill Sergeant Taylor yelled out.

"Ryan!" Ryan yelled out.

"Rosa!" Rosa yelled out.

"Sebastian!" Sebastian yelled out.

"Why are you here?" Taylor asked.

"To start our crucible!" The three said in unison.

"I want a different answer," he responded.

"To become peacekeepers!" The trio shouted. Their bodies became tense as rushes of tickling energy soared through their hands. After all, this was the moment they had waited for. Their crucible was here. They would either prove themselves worthy of being peacekeepers or continue their basic training for a few more weeks.

"Why are you here!?" Taylor shouted again.

"To become peacekeepers!"

Charles, Citlali and the military personnel remained unfazed. They had seen many crucibles before. They've seen teams pass and many teams fail. Charles took a few steps toward the three.

"Rosa, Ryan, Sebastian," he began, "you three have learned and grown much since I first met you. It's amazing how three strangers can become so close to each other. It's also inspiring to see that you all want the same thing: to defeat the Orderkeepers. You three are here tonight because of the brute dedication and teamwork you have shown the past two months. You will need that not only to complete your crucible but also to take on the conniving individuals we will put you up against. You will encounter clever and hardened criminals. We know you have the potential to take them on, but before you do, you will have to complete this grueling crucible."

Citlali took a few steps forward next to Charles.

"It is now five minutes to midnight," Citlali started. "In many missions, you will not have me to assist you. At times you will be expected to fight behind enemy lines. I am not able to enter that territory. Therefore, to mimic that factor, I will not be present tonight. There will be highlighted arrows along the way to lead you on to your first task. Good luck."

The three waited for what felt much longer than a few minutes. It was quiet. But then the clouds, leaves, and branches above expanded to cover the stars and moon that lit their surroundings. It was pitch-black. When they thought it couldn't get any spookier a loud church bell rang, signaling midnight. A dim light appeared, hovering over them like a firefly. When the three could see again, they noticed Citlali and Charles were gone.

"You're trying to become peacekeepers!?" one military personnel said. "Time to warm up!"

"Get in push-up position!" another one said as the three dropped to the floor. "Let me see some push-ups!"

"You think you have what it takes to hunt down Orderkeepers!?" everyone yelled at the same time. They ordered the three to get up and back down into push-up position. When they stood up after a dizzying set of ups and downs, pull-up bars appeared in front of them.

"Pull-ups, now!"

"You think you're ready to take on this world?! You are a disgrace!"

"All of that training and for what?!"

"Are we wasting our time on you?!"

"Jog! Jog! Jog!" the crowd yelled, not bothering to make an opening for them yet. The three got off their pull-up bars and started jogging. The drill instructors jogged behind them, screaming in their ears. Sometimes the three had a terrible time understanding what they were saying, either because they were too loud or because they were giving multiple orders every second.

"I see some cracking! Are you going to crack?!"

"No, sir!" The three yelled.

"You three are slow! Let's get a move on it! Up the obstacle!" Wooden ramps and steps appeared as they ran over them, giving them little time to know where to step. They stomped and climbed up a spiral set of wooden stairs that only appeared as they made their way up. A few of the instructors followed closely behind to the top.

"Jump onto those ropes!"

The three ropes were far ahead, but still they made the long jump. They were still by each other's side as they swung through the air and falling leaves, the roaring from below following close behind. When the three saw the wooden platform ahead they jumped off their ropes and rolled onto it. Another stream of endless yelling was waiting for them as they stood up.

"Keep going! This doesn't end! Who do you think you are? You don't stop until we tell you to stop!"

The three were chased down the wooden spiral of stairs and onto more obstacles.

"Up the net!"

"Down the net!"

"Over the wall!"

"Down the wall!"

"Faster!"

"Too slow!"

"You three better be in top shape by the time we see you again," Drill Sergeant Taylor said, waving for everyone to leave. He left too, but not before wishing the three a grim "good luck." The three were practically bathing in sweat. It was only when the sun came up that they realized how much time had passed.

A white gloomy arrow appeared before them. They slowly walked toward it together. When they arrived at the arrow, it disappeared. Another white arrow appeared in the distance. They began to walk a little bit faster and by the tenth arrow they were jogging. By the twentieth arrow they were running despite already having been through a physical ordeal. They soon arrived at a wooden cabin.

"Let's see what's inside," Ryan said, heading past a white arrow pointing inside. Upon entering they found a tunnel ladder. Around the ladder were dusty shelves with a thick rope. Sebastian tied the rope around his body in case they would need it. After looking down the ladder and seeing it was pitch-black they converted their contact lenses into night-vision mode.

"I'll go first," Rosa offered, descending the ladder. Ryan followed, and Sebastian brought up the rear. After an abyss of steps down, they finally reached the bottom. An arrow appeared, and again the three jogged to their destination. An underground chasm greeted the trio. Once at the foot of the chasm, there was no longer a solid path to follow. They turned off their night vision as the light provided to them was enough to see ahead. Only darkness appeared below and above, with yellow moonlight coming from distant large candles mounted on the sides of the cavern walls.

"The rope!" Ryan exclaimed. Sebastian handed the rope to Rosa's open palms.

"It looks like we will have to figure out how to use this," Rosa said, holding it in front of the other two. They examined it for a moment before Rosa approached the edge of the chasm. As she walked, she tied the rope to form a lasso. She swung the lasso around in the air and threw it into the air toward the opposite side of the chasm. Without any guidance, it extended and glided toward the other side until it hit the ground. It was no longer a few arm's lengths wide. It had expanded to reach the far end of the underground canyon. The lasso end then started moving around as if in search of something. It moved toward a boulder and tightened itself around it.

Rosa gently tugged on the rope to make sure it was secure, then made another lasso and placed it on a nearby boulder. Sebastian led the way on the rope climb, followed by Rosa and then Ryan. The rope became metallic, allowing for an easier grip. It was sturdy and did not allow any ripples of movement. Their breathing echoed as they climbed, but that wasn't the only sound they heard. A faint clicking sound froze the trio's progression. They stopped to get a clearer listen. The clicking sound stopped as well. The three continued, and again they heard the clicking sound. They stopped once more as the clicking sound got louder and more clicking commenced. They looked up into the darkness where the sounds were coming from. Sebastian turned on his night vision and saw a ceiling with giant bats hanging upside down. They were waking up from their sleep and beginning to flap their wings around.

"Bats. We have to move!" Sebastian turned off his night vision and began rushing toward the other end. "Quickly!"

The three were halfway across the rope when the bats swooped down at them. A roaring of screeching violently filled the chasm. Bats pinched at their skin and pounded their bodies. Sebastian made it to the other side safely and started throwing rocks at the beasts. This did no good, as there were numerous bats ready to replace any wounded ones. He wondered if there was more he could do as he looked at the rope. He watched as the creatures piled on Rosa. They were weighing her down, making it harder for her to hold onto the rope. The bats had stopped Rosa from getting any further, and because Ryan was behind her, he was trapped as well. The lasso on the boulder next to Sebastian started blinking red. He knew the rope was trying to get his attention. Two small areas of the rope started blinking red as well. Sebastian realized that the rope knew something was wrong and wanted him to put his hands on the two red areas of the rope.

Sebastian started pulling. As he pulled, Rosa and Ryan were getting closer to him. More and more bats started plunging themselves onto the three. He swung his arms from side to side to push the bats away. After a few more tugs he helped the two cross the chasm and reach the ground. After pushing the last pursuing beasts away, the exhausted three were freed. As if on cue, the winged creatures flew away, and the metallic rope loosened itself from the two boulders and shrunk down to a band next to the three.

"I'm fine," Ryan said getting up and leaning over Rosa.

"How are you, Rosa?" Sebastian asked.

"Give me a few," she said, letting out a light cough.

A white arrow appeared next to a small opening, but the three decided to rest for a few moments to recover. When their breathing slowed down, Ryan led the way into the small tunnel. It was only big enough for one person to get through at a time while lying down. Ryan got on the ground facedown and headed inside. Rosa was again in the middle and Sebastian at the end. They each moved their right arms and legs, then their left arms and legs to move across. Sebastian's breathing became shallow as the corners became smaller. He focused his breathing and kept a constant pace behind his two teammates. They were now in a wide, empty well, allowing them to stand up. The only possible opening in the room was up.

"I'm up for a climb," Rosa smiled, with her hands on her hips.

"Let's use the rope again," Sebastian said, swinging the lasso into the opening above. It made a swooshing sound until it grabbed onto something. "Careful. We don't know what's up there."

Sebastian gripped the rope and started up the wall. Rosa followed Sebastian, and as Ryan tugged on the rope to begin his climb, the opening they came through slammed shut. The three looked at each other, startled. They heard a wave of water approaching in the distance. Not knowing what to expect, they continued their climb. Soon, the wave of water made its way through growing holes above and splashed hard onto the floor. By the time Ryan gained a proper footing on the wall, the water had already reached his ankles.

"And of course, the water is freezing cold," Ryan said. "This water is coming up quickly. We have to hurry."

The three tried to rush, but Ryan soon found himself fully submerged in the water. He had no problem holding his breath, but once underwater he saw it was filled with holographic birds. They exploded onto him in a sticky glue that pinned his body to the wall. Rosa and Sebastian looked down at Ryan, but they could not see what was going on in the dark water. All they saw were dark splashes striking into the air.

"Get to the rope and pull us up!" Rosa said, with the rising water reaching her neck. "I'll check on Ryan!"

She was soon submerged into the dark, cold water as well, as Sebastian continued his way upward. She soon noticed he was struggling to free himself of a gluey substance, and she swam toward him frantically as he let out breaths of air. She grabbed onto the substance, freeing his arms. It was clear Ryan was drowning. Rosa moved closer and pressed her lips onto Ryan's, giving him a breath of air. Ryan looked surprised and relieved. She freed his legs and started again for the top. They wheezed for air once they got to the top of the water, but below them, more holographic birds formed. The birds exploded onto each other and formed a holographic octopus. The octopus grabbed their legs, dragging them below water once again.

Sebastian made it to the top of the well. When he climbed out and brought himself to his feet a mysterious figure jumped from the top of a nearby boulder, knocking him off his feet and back into the well. Sebastian fell a considerable depth but managed to grab a hold of the rope. He looked up to see who had pushed him, but no one appeared. Again he scaled the wall, but this time he stopped just shy of the top, not wanting to make the same mistake twice. He pushed himself off the wall toward another end of the opening and grabbed the edge. He got up and looked around. Several holographic human figures stood around, carrying knives and staffs. On the other side, the metallic rope was tied to the boulder. It blinked red like before. Sebastian knew he had to manually tug the rope on the blinking red lights to get the rope to pull the rest of his team upward, but first he had to make his way past the holographic figures.

The octopus swung Rosa and Ryan into the walls and deeper into the water. Although the octopus's grip was powerful, it was no match for Rosa's and Ryan's strength. The two freed themselves from the octopus, only to find more tentacles latching onto them. They knew if they kept on with this circle of moves they would run out of air before they could escape. Rosa came up with an idea to free herself as Ryan continued to battle the many tentacles. Rosa waited patiently until she was close to the wall. Once the octopus bashed her into the wall, she pulled off the tentacle that trapped her. She grabbed the wall and pulled herself up, leaving a stream of air bubbles behind. Her strength allowed her to move upward too fast for the octopus to catch her. Ryan was bashed into the wall and moved in the same way. He wrestled the tentacles off and pulled himself up the wall, also leaving a stream of air bubbles, to join Rosa above the water.

Sebastian attempted to jump over the opening toward the rope, but a hologram grabbed him from behind and pulled him onto the ground. Sebastian twisted the hologram's wrists to free himself. As soon as he got back on his feet, one of the holograms rushed at him with a knife. Sebastian grabbed the knife-wielding arm and twisted it, breaking off the fingers one by one. The hologram let go of the knife before being thrown to the side. Sebastian picked up the knife and faced the remaining holograms. He knew he didn't have time to take on each hologram. He threw the knife at the nearest staff-wielding hologram's head and took its staff as the hologram incinerated into the air, indicating defeat. He then used the staff to push away as many of the holograms as possible. He now had a clear path to the rope and made a long jump over the rising waters in the cavern below. Using his arms, he managed to keep his balance as he hit the ground. The holograms followed and jumped onto Sebastian, trying to get ahold of him. Two of the knife-wielding holograms ran and jumped into the hole.

"No!" Sebastian yelled out, realizing they were going after Rosa and Ryan. He elbowed the one on his right and twisted himself below the right arm of the hologram to his left and pushed it to the ground. He started for the rope but was tackled into the hole by a hologram who followed him down. Sebastian grabbed the edge, with the hologram securing itself around his knees.

Rosa and Ryan grabbed the rope and began making their way up the wall again. The water was still rising, and with every inch of progress the two made it rose another inch. Just then, two knife-wielding holograms appeared from above and splashed into the water.

"We have to move faster," Rosa said moving up the rope. One of the holograms pushed out its knife-wielding arms from below the water and slashed Ryan's knee. Blood spit out as he grabbed his knee to stop the flow.

Sebastian gripped the edge with his hands as the hologram furiously started swinging around, trying to get Sebastian to lose his grip and fall back into the water. He knew with the amount of resistance from the hologram he wouldn't be able to rise above the edge and onto his feet. He swung his legs back and forth, smashing the hologram onto the wall until it was knocked out and evaporated into the air. He made his way onto the ground on top of the well opening. The holograms were guarding the rope, but there were only four of them left. He picked up a staff left by one of the fallen holograms and walked toward the remaining adversaries, clubbing one in the head. The holograms started to take a few steps away from Sebastian. He pushed them far enough away with the staff that he could make a dash for the rope. He put his hands on the red blinking lights and tugged upward. Then he let go, and the rope began pulling itself up.

As Rosa and Ryan moved farther up, Ryan continued to fight the onslaught of slashes and stabs from the holograms below. The rope started pulling the two upward but disappeared from inside the hologram's grips causing the two holograms to fall and disappear into the pit's rising water.

Once at the top, Rosa pulled herself out and saw Sebastian beating the remaining hologram. The hologram evaporated when Sebastian saw Rosa and Ryan rising onto the ground. Their clothes dripped with water but were soon dryer than the dirt. They used their shirts to dry their faces and hair. Their shirts were wet once more, but soon dried on their own again.

"We're finally at the top," Rosa said, looking curiously at Sebastian's hardened stare. They looked below into the well once Ryan was on his feet and saw that the water and holograms had disappeared. "Are you all right, Sebastian?"

"Yeah, I'm fine," he said, smiling. "How are you two?"

"A little cut up, but glad to be on solid ground," Ryan said, dropping to the earth. A white arrow appeared, pointing at a small steel crate that barely occupied its table. "What's this?"

Inside the crate were three medical patches. They placed a medical patch on Ryan so his legs would heal from the slashing and stabbing he had taken. Within seconds, his leg returned to its previous healthy condition. Rosa and Sebastian placed patches on their shoulders to heal also.

They looked around the large room, wondering what they had to do next. A rumbling noise caught the trio's attention. One of the walls cleared an opening for them. The three started on their path through the newly made entrance.

"Look around; there's no way out except across another chasm," Sebastian pointed out. He grabbed the rope and aimed it to the other side. The other end of the chasm was below, so they would have to zip line on the rope using the staffs they had taken from the holograms. Rosa placed the staff over the rope and pushed herself off the ground and into the air. The swift breeze that passed her only added to her adrenaline. She kicked her dangling legs in the air and landed on the ground. Sebastian followed and then Ryan. They landed safely on the ground and retrieved the rope.

What better way to work off their adrenaline then another marathon through the caverns? There were colorfully lit plants lined up across the floors, walls and ceilings, their numerous colors featuring the various routes through the cave. One could walk through this alien world for nights and not see the same two palettes of plants. When the trio followed the last floating bright arrow into a grotto, they saw plants illuminating the water. The plants' light was so magical you could dip your hands into the water, pick it up, and still see its light radiating in your hands. Upon throwing the water into the air, the water splashed back downward while the glittering light drifted off like little butterflies. The trio's eyes widened in awe. They spent a few moments admiring the lines of glowing paint dancing on the walls and peacefully into the air.

"Quite quaint, ain't it?" Citlali said in the distance, with Charles standing nearby.

"Quite," Ryan responded.

The three ran up to the two and lined up.

"You don't have to worry about formalities when you're around us," Citlali said.

"This place is incredible," Rosa exclaimed, easing up.

"A marvel of both architecture and biology," Charles said. "Ready for your first mission?"

"What about the crucible?" Sebastian asked.

"This mission is part of the crucible," Citlali responded. "You three will at times be placed on missions without a moment's notice. You need to be ready for a mission regardless of what you're doing or how exhausted you are. For this real mission you three will team up with ..."

Charles raised out his hand. Out from the darkness behind Charles and Citlali came Ramon, Arthur and Giselle. Sebastian and Giselle exchanged shy smiles upon seeing each other.

"In order for all six of you to complete your crucible, you will have until the end of the day to obtain the whereabouts of a California cell of Orderkeepers based nearby," Charles said. "This is a real mission with a short deadline. We have reason to believe our enemies in this state may be planning an attack on a high-profile citizen. We have captured one of them. Interrogate him. Citlali will escort you to the man. Remember, you each have special skills to contribute. Work together. Now, on you six go."

CHAPTER 11 – THE INTERROGATORS: INSIDE THE SECRET MIND OF A WARKEEPER

After leaving the cavern, they were brought via aerial transport to a remote location in the icy mountains. They were hurriedly led toward a series of metallic transparent doors before stopping at the last closed door. At the center of a room after the last door, the man who was captured in the city plaza two months before could be seen sitting. Sebastian, Ryan and Rosa gave each other startled glances. They had briefly wondered what had become of the man but now they knew. The top half of his head was wrapped with a crystal helmet. A man and woman with silver hair and orange eyes like Charles stood next to him. Their neatly kept uniforms blended with the white room.

"These two standing guard are part of our military," Citlali explained. "They are watching over him to make sure he doesn't escape. The rocky bit on his head is forcing his brain to simulate certain scenarios. He cannot hear what we are saying, so speak freely."

"Certain scenarios?" Ryan asked.

"Yes," Citlali answered, as a floating screen appeared in front of them. It showed the man in the same room as the one they were in, except he was the only person there. "The two military members specialize in interrogation, but because their interrogation is constantly monitored by public civilian inspectors, they can only take their techniques so far. That is where individuals like you come in. I'm not asking for anything unethical but be creative."

"You want us to use this helmet to modify scenarios in his head to get him to tell us information about other Orderkeepers?" Rosa asked. "Using what? A Mastermind Stratagem?"

"Yes. You'll use reanimation technology and this computer to manipulate the settings into what you want. The 'helmet' and computer are part of a system called the Mastermind Stratagem. I will recall the two military agents, and when they are gone the rest is up to you. For the same reasons as these two, I can't be here to witness this, so I'll have to leave. As for how far you go to accomplish your tasks, I will at least be able to employ plausible deniability if I am ever questioned about this clandestine program. If you need me, exit where you came from, and I'll be there."

Citlali walked into the distance, disappearing pixel by pixel into nothingness before arriving at the door. The two military agents left through another door. The last transparent door opened and allowed the six to enter.

"Any ideas?" Ryan started. "They didn't even show us how to use this."

"That's fine," Giselle said. "I taught myself how to use this awhile back."

"Let's see if he has a fear of heights," Arthur said.

Giselle started moving her fingers along the computer. Various lights flickered on and off on the screen until she paused. The computer made a swift noise and the projected screen showed the Orderkeeper no longer in an interrogation room. He was now standing on the edge of a building under a dark cloudy sky. Various other similar buildings surrounded them seemingly unoccupied. He remained unfazed.

"That's pretty cool," Ryan exclaimed. "Can you put one of us inside there?"

"Sure," Giselle said, pressing more buttons.

"On our first time in the city we saw this man captured by the police," Rosa said.

"Maybe we can ask him about that day," Giselle said.

"I've been curious about that incident," Sebastian started. "I'll go in—"

"Let's stick to the mission," Arthur stated. "I'll go in first. I have some experience with interrogation."

The rest of the crew looked worriedly at Sebastian as he stood there quietly. A seat animated itself as Arthur dropped into it. One of the crystal helmets reanimated itself onto him. It covered his hair and then his eyes as he drifted off into a trance.

"Afraid of falling?" Arthur said, appearing behind the Orderkeeper on the screen.

"What?" the Orderkeeper asked in confusion. "Who are you?"

"I think the question is, who are you?"

"I know who I am," the man said wearily.

"Can Arthur hear us?" Ryan asked.

"Yes, he can hear us," Giselle answered.

"I'm an Orderkeeper," the man said.

"Do you have a name?" Arthur continued.

"No."

"Why are you out here in California? Warkeepers are supposed to be south of the border."

"I—," he stopped, realizing something. He didn't say anything for a few seconds. "I don't remember."

"Of course you remember!" Arthur said, grabbing the Orderkeeper by the collar and holding his back against the edge of the roof. The interrogee remained unfazed.

"If I were to fall off this roof, the world would go on."

"Don't let your life be in vain. Help me with something."

"What to know something? Things are about to change for the worse."

"How so?"

"Those in charge of this world will make it worse. Haven't your superiors told you?" he said with a weak laugh. "It's already happening!"

"Just tell me what you were doing here!"

"It seems as if he is about to tell us something," Ramon said. "But Arthur is too aggressive."

"Place me in one of those seats," Sebastian urged.

A seat appeared next to Arthur. Sebastian jumped in with a crystal helmet animating on his head as he slipped out of consciousness. Sebastian appeared next to Arthur in the simulation as the Orderkeeper looked over at the hauntingly empty buildings.

"Are you here to interrogate me, too?" the Orderkeeper asked softly.

"I'm here to see if you can work with me," Sebastian said.

"Good cop-bad cop?" the Orderkeeper smirked. "That's the best you got? What do you think the other two with orange eyes did?"

"We don't need to work with him," Arthur interrupted. "He is our prisoner now."

"Forget the warkeeper, it's these two who need to work together," Rosa said.

"Let's have some faith in them," Ramon said.

"Can you work with me?" Sebastian asked.

"Maybe. Maybe not. Do you want to hear what I have to say?" the Orderkeeper questioned. "I already told the other two interrogators this, but they didn't care. They only wanted to know about other *warkeepers*."

"What do you have to say about the world getting worse?" Sebastian asked.

"There's a handful of individuals who control what goes on in my area of the globe. I'm sure you know this. The rundown violent society your peaceful side of Earth has been avoiding for some time. But that handful of individuals works for another group. A group that operates on this side of the globe."

"I wonder what he's talking about?" Ryan pondered.

"Well he's talking now, so I think we should just get any intel we can," Giselle suggested.

"What are you talking about?" Arthur asked.

"Why should I tell you anything more?" the Orderkeeper said, widening his eyes. "Why should I help *you*?"

"Why are you suddenly not telling us what you had to say?" Arthur asked.

"We need to gain his trust," Sebastian said, walking away for a moment to speak privately to the team. "Can we poke into his memories?"

"I've been trying to access his memories, but I've come up empty," Giselle said. "Normally with this technology we should be able to, but since he is an Orderkeeper, I'm sure he's had training to suppress those memories from us."

"Do you think there's something we can do to trigger them?" Sebastian said, staring into the distant night skyline. Giselle looked at Sebastian's projection on the screen. Despite not being able to see outside his realm, Sebastian was unintentionally staring into Giselle's eyes through the screen.

"It's possible, but what can we try?" Giselle asked.

"What do we know about this specific group of Orderkeepers? Where are they from?" Rosa asked.

"They're from the southern tip of what used to be Mexico," Giselle said, pointing to a floating holographic file she had been reading. She tossed it toward the main screen, which magnified the file's words. "What's something that would trigger his memories?"

"Smell is a strong sense," Rosa said. "If we can get something to simulate all the different smells found in the Yucatan Peninsula and monitor his brain activity, we can see which scents have more meaning to him!"

"Let's try it," Ramon said.

He snapped his fingers and a thin metallic bar appeared. It gravitated toward the Orderkeeper's unconscious body and positioned itself next to his nose. It moved under his nose from left to right and back again several times. Everyone watched in anticipation. Soon, a beeping noise on the screen identified a strong cognitive reaction to the smell of cleanliness with a mild mix of desert plants. The bar read "75 percent cognitive reaction expected."

"Giselle, can you pull that scent into the simulation?" Ramon asked.

"On it!" Giselle responded. She continued to type onto the screen and wave her hands around as she adjusted the settings.

"Do you smell that?" Arthur said in the simulation. He and Sebastian had overheard the conversation going on in the interrogation room and knew what to expect. The Orderkeeper looked startled. "Brings back memories, doesn't it?"

"I don't know what you're talking about," the man shouted.

"Increasing the smell strength," Giselle said.

The interrogated man began to struggle with himself. He balled up his hands until bones began snapping. His teeth were clenched so hard they started chipping and falling out of his mouth.

"No, I can't go back there!" the Orderkeeper cried, unable to contain himself.

"Back where?" Sebastian asked.

"Look at his stress and heartbeat levels," Giselle said pointing to a chart. "They're rising."

"Keep going," Ramon said. "We're getting to him."

"Back to the training camp," the man whined. "I can't go back!"

"I'll make sure you don't go back there," Sebastian said. "But you need to trust me. Work with me. Can you do that?"

"I don't know," the Orderkeeper answered in desperate confusion.

"He said training camp," Ryan said, sliding over holographic photos and videos of a desert warehouse and its office space. "Here are some visuals of warkeeper training camps. Let's see how he feels after we replicate this environment in the simulation."

"I'm trying to help. I really am," Arthur said, looking around as the dark, cloudy sky turned into a brightly lit ceiling. The concrete ground of the roof was replaced with a dark marble floor mirroring their feet and faces. They were in the warehouse shown in the picture Ryan was holding.

"I'll tell you everything if you can get me out of here!" the Orderkeeper pleaded. "Please!"

"The warkeepers. Where are they?" Arthur asked.

"They're east of Long Beach," the Orderkeeper squealed.

"We got him," Ramon cheered. "Okay, let's set it to a neutral environment."

The warehouse now became a grassy field with sparse trees. The Orderkeeper kneeled over a pond and splashed his face with water.

"Deep within its mountains," he said catching his breath. "The headquarters is under a small wooden house. You'll find three of them."

"Give him control of the simulation and let him replicate the scenery of the area," Rosa suggested. "Arthur and Sebastian will be okay."

With a few more adjustments made by Giselle, the Orderkeeper took control. The simulation shifted into a line of mountains, and adjusted according to his memory. The high rocky cliffs were greeted gently with specks of snow, and a small wooden house appeared in front of them. A figure from his memory appeared. It was him looking at a map of Long Beach. It detailed his trip from the city to the wooden house.

"We're losing him!" Giselle shouted. The Orderkeeper's nose started bleeding and his eyes became bloody.

"What? How!?" Sebastian asked.

"I don't know, but his body is being hacked," Giselle said. "I'm trying to override it."

"Hacked?" Ryan asked.

"When a body is hacked it's similar to a computer being hacked," Rosa started explaining. "If you find an open door to a system and enter it, you can exploit the system and do whatever you want with it."

"Get them out of there!" Ramon ordered.

The simulation of the cool breezy point turned into a molten lava apocalyptic scenario. Volcanoes exploded in the distance as earthquakes trembled the hot darkening floor. Giselle frantically prepared for their consciousnesses to return to their body.

"You mentioned something before about a group of people who 'operate on this side of the globe,'" Sebastian said. "What did you mean by that?"

The man cried out as blood began pouring out of his eyes and ears. His actual body in his seat did the same. The dirt ground below them cracked in all directions, with lava revealing itself in the rifts. Arthur and Sebastian disappeared from the simulation. Their crystal helmets disappeared as their eyes in their actual bodies opened widely. They nearly fell out of their seats when they woke up in sweat and panic. Giselle hurried toward Sebastian, wrapping her arms around him. The crowd watched the couple with gentle curiosity.

"I'm okay," Sebastian said, placing his arms around her. Ramon was trying to shake the Orderkeeper awake when his body made explosive noises and his vital signs dropped to a halt.

"He's dead," Rosa confirmed, looking at the projected screen.

"Citlali!" Ramon called out as he ran past the door to reach her.

"What happened!?" she asked Ramon from a distance.

"His body was hacked," Ramon informed her. "He's dead. But we have the location of the three remaining enemies."

"Can you relay that information to the military now?" Sebastian asked.

"I can't do that," Citlali said. "The Department of Ethics will inquire as to how we came about such information. Our military interrogators only got so far, but they were not able to go the extra mile like the rest of you. The military has the capabilities to hack this man's mind, but we can't do that because the Department of Ethics forbids it. We also have clandestine peacekeepers that can human-hack, but we wanted you all to get experience in using the Mastermind Stratagem. With this man dead, we can't use our military to find the remaining Orderkeepers, or there will be questions. Questions that can lead right back to us and our clandestine operations. Questions we can't answer. Remember, these operations *do not exist*. We don't exist for a reason. We conduct work that would otherwise be condemned as unethical."

"What happens now? What do we do with this information?" Sebastian asked.

"You six will handle the three Orderkeepers."

CHAPTER 12 – WHERE ARE OUR MINDS

It was difficult to not slip on the icy slopes of the mountain as they approached the aircraft, their clothes transitioning from khaki pants and black shirts into loose forest-green camouflage uniforms with sleeves already rolled up. Bubbly nanotech protective suits appeared over them before fitting onto their bodies and disappearing. The teams took their seats across from each other in the red, dimly lit holding area of the aircraft. Their seatbelts tied themselves around the six quiet recruits while Citlali remained standing. A jump in their stomachs indicated they had taken off, while verifying their uneasiness. To distract themselves from the mission, they carefully broached the subject of "human hacking."

"How does someone get 'hacked'?" Sebastian asked.

"It can happen through nearly any means of reanimation interaction," Citlali started. "Simply using U-ITS can get your mind hacked, but a human hacker needs high-level administrative access to U-ITS and be within sight of the person to manipulate their brain. But even being within sight of someone, hacking them is still no easy challenge. Few people or computer programs are capable of hacking people. The U-ITS is sophisticated because it is protected by military grade software. But when they do hack someone, they will do so by sending a sort of electric virus to your brain, corrupting it so there is a permanent path from the brain to the hacker."

"I think I got it," Sebastian shrugged. "Should we be worried?"

"Maybe," Citlali said. "Human hacking can't happen to those of us on the peacekeeper side unless we are captured by Orderkeepers. What happened to the Orderkeeper back there wasn't preventable. Who knows what the other side has done to him? We must only worry if we're near a human hacker. If a human hacker is close enough, they could cause us great harm."

"Great, so nothing to worry about," Ryan said sarcastically.

"Remember not everyone is a human hacker," Citlali reassured. "It takes a lot of practice and skill to become one."

"Looking back at what happened in the interrogation room, it may be that these Orderkeepers have been hacked by their own also," Rosa commented. "What if their organs explode also?"

"Then they die," Arthur said in a rough tone. Sebastian looked from Arthur to Giselle curiously, wondering why he was in a bitter state of mind. She shrugged her shoulders playfully. Here they were on this shaky transporter, about to risk their lives and not knowing what they were getting into. Possibly the most terrified ones were Sebastian and Giselle, who were now avoiding each other's eyes. But they were more worried about one another. Why? They had just met each other. They had spent only one night with each other, and even that was brief. Still, in this new life of theirs on this vastly populated twenty-billion-person planet, they were the only ones they truly felt connected to, and they still did not know why. They barely knew each other.

"Sixty seconds before we reach our destination!" a voice announced over the speakers. Sebastian and Giselle looked at each other again. This time, they saw the concern in each other's eyes.

"You six have been given reanimation bars as well as anti-detection transponders," Citlali said. "If these Orderkeepers have anything scanning the area for possible trespassers, these devices will hide your presence. You also have your clear, bulletproof armor suits protecting you from most physical harm. You will be dropped off one klick away from their hideout. Move quietly and enter it."

"Thirty seconds!" the pilot said.

"All you have to do is capture them and collect their intel," Citlali said. "Do this and then report to us. Do this and your crucible is over, and you are all one step closer to calling yourselves peacekeepers."

"Five seconds!" The aircraft made an abrupt stop as its doors slid open still two stories above ground.

"Good luck," Citlali yelled as she disappeared. The six jumped out together, turning their reanimation bars into floating platforms. In mere seconds, their boots touched the ground. The aircraft took off, leaving the group on a grassy plain surrounded by a forest.

"Let's go," Arthur said, turning his reanimation crystals into a metallic rifle with everyone else doing the same. He led the team through the ruby and sapphire trees. Their ankles brushed against the crispy exotic plants on the ground as their boots crushed the purple dirt road entering the nearby mountains. "We're near. Let's scope out the place and meet back here in five."

Everyone agreed. Rosa and Ramon continued along the purple road to get a better view of the wooden house from a cliff. The area looked exactly as the Orderkeeper had shown in his interrogation. Mountain cliffs with bits of snow and trees encompassed the bottom of the mountains. Ryan and Arthur went into the top of the cliffs to scope for possible enemies or exit points on any of the other mountains. Giselle and Sebastian went off into the forest to scope it out the same way Ryan and Arthur had. She used a small bit of her reanimation bar to make insect drones to help scout the area. After some walking, Sebastian decided to break the silence.

"Hey, do you want to talk?" Sebastian asked.

"About what?" Giselle asked curiously.

"Well … us? We're on a mission. Aren't you concerned about one of us getting hurt? I mean I know we just met, but …"

"We're on a mission; let's stay focused and we'll be all right." Giselle looked at Sebastian before looking down at her satellite bracelet. Giselle refocused her attention on scouting around and examining the ground they were standing on. Giselle's insect drones reported no signs of tunnels or other disturbed terrain. She turned around to make her way back as Sebastian followed slowly, neither one of them saying another word. He was hurt that she didn't even acknowledge their still-short relationship. Since they were on a mission, Sebastian decided to follow her lead and focus.

"Nothing in the forest," Giselle said to the team.

"Nothing around the mountains," Arthur said, retrieving the last of his bird drones.

"We've scanned the cottage house and here are the schematics," Rosa said, using the reanimation bar to make a hologram projector. It was a small, one-story wooden house from the outside, but underneath that, there was the enemy lair. It was a four-story catacomb with spiral pathways on the outer ring that stopped at each floor but commenced on the opposite end and then were connected by a corridor. At each floor were rooms running down each side. The bottom two floors contained a large room. It was unknown where in this catacomb the Orderkeepers were. They must have been using anti-detection transponders as well.

The team's nerves showed on their faces as the realization that they were about to take on an aggressive enemy settled in even more.

"We don't have to worry about any traps in the forest, mountains or in the house," Rosa continued. "It looks like the Orderkeepers didn't place any, perhaps to avoid making this area look suspicious. I can't say anything about their underground lair. We were only able to make out the hollow areas of their base, most likely because they've blocked all other sensor-detection methods."

"If there are only three of them, why is there so much space?" Ramon asked.

"Maybe they were anticipating a platoon of reinforcements," Giselle said.

"Looks like they won't be needing all that space after all," Arthur said. "Let's get moving."

The six moved through the trees close to the house. Arthur waited to the right of the door with Ryan behind him. The rest lined up around the corner of the house to the left. Ryan animated a battering ram and slammed the door down. The door hit hard against the floor, clearing a path for everyone to enter.

"Move, move, move!" Arthur said as they cleared the first floor. Only steps away from the entrance, they moved toward the basement stairs and battered down its door. They moved tightly down the stairs in fast unison. Still no sign of the enemy. They moved around the basement and cleared its rooms. Nothing but dusty tables, chairs and construction tools from the early twenty-first century. Rosa moved toward the table in the corner. "According to the schematics, the entrance should be right here."

She pointed underneath the table. It was heavy, but Ryan and Ramon managed to slide it over. As it moved, the floor underneath revealed an opening. Arthur again led the team down the tight spiral of stone steps. It led to the first dark underground floor. It was empty, but the team kept its vigilance. After a few moments traveling in silence, Ramon used an insect drone to scout the path. It went into every room, relayed video of what was there, and then returned. Still, a careful Arthur suggested everyone clear each room again. At the opening of the first room to the right of the hallway, Arthur held out two fingers and pointed them to the right. Ramon and Rosa immediately went to the right and cleared the empty room. He held out two more and pointed left. Sebastian and Giselle went quietly to the left, clearing another empty room. Arthur and Ryan moved forward through the middle with the others reassembling at the rear. With no Orderkeepers in sight, they moved toward the next descending spiral pathway. They moved against the walls, down the dim trail and to the next floor, which was also empty. They passed the hallway, clearing each room they encountered, and continued down another spiral hallway and onto the third floor, which contained a spacious war room with holograms spread around. The group stared at the large hologram at the center of the room. It was a map of North America, with red dots sprinkled around on it. Most of the dots concentrated in the southwest region.

"What is this?" Rosa asked.

"I'm not sure," Arthur said. "Maybe their hideouts? We'll come back to it and collect the intel, but first we need to clear the area."

They came to another dim spiral hallway, but before they could enter it, a bullet bounced off Ramon's bulletproof armor.

"I'm fine," Ramon said nervously. His insect drones scrambled in the direction of the bullets. "To the sides!"

They all moved away from the opening and against the walls.

"There's no one there," Rosa said, looking at her satellite bracelet. The hologram projected on her bracelet showed the tunnel but no one in sight. They descended farther into the floor to another spacious war room. "Hey! I've lost feed from the insect drones!"

Once at the center, Rosa stopped. She began fidgeting, and blood began dripping from her nose. Her head forcibly tilted back with her eyes staring at the ceiling, as if yanked by some unseen force.

"Hey! what's wrong?" Arthur asked. She remained still and quiet. "Ramon, check on her."

From across the room, Giselle looked more worried than everyone else.

"Rosa?" Ramon asked. "Hey, there's blood coming from her nose and eyes! Rosa, can you move?"

She swung her elbow back, hitting Ramon in the forehead. A man across the room with his arms and hands stretched at Rosa accidentally revealed himself. Giselle and Sebastian immediately swung their weapons up, aimed at the man and shot. His body slammed to the floor now no longer moving.

"She's been hacked!" Giselle cried out, running to her. "Quick, hold her down! Now!"

"Ryan and Arthur, stay focused on that opening!" Sebastian yelled. "No one gets out!" Ryan fell into his post while Arthur grimaced at Sebastian. "Now!"

Arthur then moved to secure the opening with Ryan. Rosa landed two more punches and a rifle swing at Ramon before being restrained by him and Sebastian. Giselle used her reanimation bar to make a syringe and a cylinder-shaped chemical-maker, connecting the two to make a tranquilizer. She stabbed Rosa's arm, putting her to sleep. Shots flew around them as Arthur and Ryan exchanged fire with the suspected Orderkeepers.

"Don't worry, Sebastian," Giselle reassured, staring into his eyes. "She's going to be fine. Ramon and I will use a Mastermind Stratagem helmet to help ease her mind. Who knows what she's experiencing in her mind right now?"

Ramon turned his reanimation bar into a crystal helmet, placing it on Rosa.

"Go help them," Giselle said, modifying settings on a projected hologram.

"The more reanimation bars used, the better the grade of shield I can make," Arthur said as Sebastian made his way to the shootout. "This default armor can only get us so far."

Sebastian threw his reanimation bar to Arthur, who combined it with his own to form a thick see-through shield. Sebastian used Ryan's remaining bar to make a small gun. With Arthur's shield leading the front of the pack, he was followed closely by Sebastian and Ryan.

"There's no way out!" Sebastian yelled. "Stop shooting and surrender!"

Bullets continued to fire in all directions. Arthur continued onto the last floor of the underground lair. The rapid shooting increased, but it was still no match for the shield. Sebastian changed his bullets to bouncing bullets. This allowed his ammo to bounce off the walls and ceilings until they hit flesh and blood. With his contact lenses creating precise computations, he aimed at the wall and shot several bullets. They hit one of the Orderkeepers, causing him to fall to the ground, startling the other Orderkeeper. Ryan and Arthur took this chance to aim with their hot lead bullets. After a series of shots, the two targets were on the ground and detained with newly animated metal rope and tranquilizers. The recruits began downloading the information systems from the war rooms onto reanimated hard drives.

"Why did their armor not protect them?" Sebastian asked.

"Warkeepers don't have the same level of technology as us," Arthur huffed. "You should know that."

"All right, relax Arthur," Ramon said coming down the tunnel. "You don't seem prepared for everything, either. They hacked Rosa. Did you not think the warkeepers were capable of hacking? You didn't see that coming, did you? I saw the look on your face when she was hacked. You were as surprised as we were. That is why Giselle intervened, and Sebastian had to tell you what to do."

Arthur didn't answer. He and Ramon stayed at the bottom level, downloading the information systems, and standing guard over the unconscious enemies.

"Don't worry about him. Arthur clearly has an ego problem," Ryan said, as he and Sebastian went back upstairs, where they encountered Giselle, already going through one of the Orderkeeper databases. "You did great."

"Find anything interesting?" Sebastian asked.

Giselle smiled but remained concentrated on the visuals in front of her. "I take it from the lack of gunshots that the warkeepers were captured?" Giselle asked. "And by the calm looks on your faces, everyone else is fine."

"Yeah, we have them in custody," Ryan said. "What are you looking at?"

"Look at this. Remember all those red dots on the map in the southwest of North America? It's where all the covert warkeepers are currently located. They're expanding their operations and working with other warmongering nations to expand simultaneously against the peacekeeper coalition of nations. According to these records, there's also been a few attempts by other peacekeeper nations to make the same expansion into warkeeper nation territory."

"In other words, things are escalating between the two societies," Sebastian said, worried.

"What's going on here?" Arthur interrupted. "We're supposed to be collecting intel, not analyzing it."

"No one has to know," Giselle said.

"Well, rules are rules. Let's get what we came for and head out."

"Yeah? And who made you leader? If anyone is the leader, it's Sebastian. He gave out orders when no one else did. He is the one who remained focused on what needed to be done and made sure it was done."

"And now I'm giving out orders and making sure what is needed to be done is done," Arthur barked back.

The relief that they were on their way to concluding their first mission was enough to convince them to avoid further tension. They decided to wrap up their mission and head back to the institution. With their unconscious captives strapped to floating stretchers they made their way to the extraction point in the forest. Rosa was on another stretcher, still reeling from being hacked. The three captives were whisked away on an airship. While jumping into a separate airship, the six broke their silence when Citlali asked if everything was okay.

"Yes, everything is fine," Giselle said, stealing a look at Sebastian, whose frown turned up into a tight smile. "What happens now?"

"Well, I will take care of the… *package* and data you've gathered. They will be brought to a secured location. I'll also report to the warden. Get some rest and enjoy yourselves. The human hack was, albeit a brutal one, only an amateur attempt. Rosa will be back to her normal self by the end of the night. I will see you all soon."

"What happened?" Rosa asked, sitting up from her stretcher as she regained consciousness. It wasn't long before they were on the roof of the institution.

"We did it, Rosa," Ryan told her. She released a silent, joyful smile. "Save your strength. We're on our way back to fix you up."

"How are you doing?" she asked Ryan, embracing his hand. "Are you okay?"

"I'm fine. Focus on getting better."

"All I remember was a high-pitched ringing with the sound of a motorcycle engine revving."

"If the Orderkeeper was only hacking you for a few seconds, then I am sure no information was taken out of your mind," Charles said. "For now, rest and you'll soon be back on your feet."

"You all should go out and celebrate," Rosa said.

"No, no I'm going to stay here," Ryan said.

"Fine then, but you two should go out and enjoy the rest of the day," Rosa said to Sebastian and Giselle. "We did good today. Go on and enjoy the remainder of the day for me, please?"

After taking Rosa to the medical station knowing their teammate would get better, and with excitement running through their veins, Sebastian and Giselle walked hand in hand out into the field. Their clothing transformed into matching scarlet clothing, letting everyone know they were, indeed, a couple.

CHAPTER 13 – ROOTING FOR US

After many more days of training, the happy couple was now commonly seen together in the cafeteria, lounges, and at times walking out of the training grounds. They were not yet officially peacekeepers. They still had to wait for their graduation, which would take place when a few more recruits attained the status after completing their crucibles. Upon exiting the institution on one late afternoon after training, Giselle playfully shoved Sebastian and took off running. She laughed behind every tree she used to hide from him until he eventually caught up, embracing her from behind. Their laughter only stopped with a kiss. Then she pushed him off and began running once more.

"Come on, Sebastian," Giselle playfully called out as she dashed up the small mint hill. "I've been meaning to try that mind-transfer technology. Let's go, slowpoke!"

"Wait, so you haven't tried it either?" Sebastian called out.

"Nope, I've been, uh, too busy," she said nervously.

"Too busy?" he asked. "That's the reason?"

"Yeah," she said, looking away. "And I've felt a little uneasy about using it."

"Same here," Sebastian said excitedly. "Citlali wanted me to experience it. Let's go do it. Hey, by the way, what's up with Arthur? Why is he annoying sometimes?"

"It's his memory incursions," Giselle said, stopping on top of the mint hill. "He's been getting bad flashbacks."

"I'm sorry to hear that."

"I think he just needs time."

"You know you gave out orders too."

"Huh?"

"On our last mission. You said I should be leader because I gave out orders when no one else did. But you gave out orders too. Why didn't you give yourself credit?"

Giselle looked towards the city skyline and then turned to eye him who stood steps away from the top.

"He was starting to get on my nerves so I was in the mood to annoy him. He sees you as a 'threat'. And to propose you as the leader for the mission would agitate him to world's end. And I think it did. Anyways given his flashbacks I'll try not to bother him again." The wind brushed by carrying a few small birds. "You know many of us see you as a leader. Partly because among the many history lessons out there one of them is that some of the best leaders are those who don't obsess over power and accolades."

She waited as Sebastian climbed the hill. With a smile she brushed shoulders with him. She let out a "ha" and continued off, Sebastian not far behind.

Through the plains and onto the streets, under the clouds passing metallic fleets, their hearts let out beats that could turn anyone sweet. Exploring the underground clubs of dark neon-lit lairs, their mesmerizing stares could bring anyone up the surrounding heavenly stairs and into the hopeful air. Dancing their way through the club, they made their way to the roof and entered a newly animated hover car, which delivered them to the wishbone-looking building. Once Sebastian was out, he put out his hand for Giselle. She grabbed hold and stepped onto the ground. It was as if nothing could take the smiles off their faces. But then they entered the wishbone-looking building.

"Now what?" Sebastian asked, looking around the lobby.

"Glad to be of assistance again," Citlali said as her hologram appeared in front of the two. "Follow me. It seems you two are undecided as to what kind of bodies you want to try out."

"We know what we're getting ourselves into," Giselle said, then quickly countered herself. "No pun intended!"

"Really?" Citlali said as she stopped and turned around. Her left eyebrow sliding unusually high.

"No, we don't know whose bodies—" Sebastian started.

"—we're going to try out first," Giselle said, finishing the sentence.

"Ah, I was worried for a second," Citlali said, beginning her walk again. "I thought for a second there was something wrong in my programming, since I couldn't figure out what you two were possibly thinking."

"Right, you can read minds," Sebastian said.

"No, I can't, so I can respect people's privacy. But based on your physiological and historical history alone I can take an accurate guess as to what your preferences are. I hope that eases your perception of me. Hmm … I don't think it has."

"What are your recommendations, then?" Giselle asked.

"It's always recommended to be in an unfamiliar body," Citlali suggested. "If you two were to swap bodies with each other, things would get awkward fast, especially if you're looking to let's say kiss."

The sudden thought of kissing while looking at their own body through another person's eyes made them incredibly uncomfortable. Thanks for the thought Citlali.

"We did not think that part through," Giselle said.

"We just wanted to try out the experience of walking in another person's shoes," Sebastian said. "No pun intended!"

A surprised Sebastian and Giselle blushed and looked away as they were about to embark in a new experience. They had made it all this way in overcoming their nerves. They were not about to back down from a new arc in their life story. They wanted their young relationship to take another bold step.

"Switching bodies with a close person does not always work but sometimes it does in a way," Citlali said.

"When would something like that work?" Sebastian asked.

"It works in the phenomenal cases of transfer twins."

"Transfer twins?" Giselle and Sebastian asked.

"Let's save the story of transfer twins for another time." Citlali led them into a room with two adjustable chairs. "Here we are. I sense you two would not like anyone walking around in your bodies, so I've arranged for a pair of bodies with no consciousness. The bodies have already been chosen, and your minds will be transferred over. Once you two are seated, we can begin. Don't worry, this process is quick."

Sebastian and Giselle sat in their chairs and placed their heads back. In the blink of an eye their minds transferred to two bodies on the other side of the wishbone building, and the two woke up in their new bodies. They slowly rose from their chairs and began examining their new figures. They looked at one another, startled at not being able to recognize who they saw.

"How do you feel?" Citlali asked. Sebastian smiled at the sea-blue woman across him. He stood up as a mirror animated itself next to him. He looked at his sunset-colored body, extending his hands and then his biceps.

"I'm not sure if I can get used to this," Giselle said, stretching out her legs.

"You still look incredibly beautiful," he said, gazing at her.

"I'm blue," she said, blushing yellow. He placed his giant arms around her waist and looked down into her eyes. The sun gleamed through the windows, creating surges of euphoria throughout their bodies. "This is definitely not my face."

"Those bodies were specifically designed for pleasure," Citlali said. "The skins absorb sunlight like a plant would and converts it into energy."

Without a moment's notice he picked her up from the ground and burst out of the bubble window. The blue woman gave a small wave and smile at a surprised Citlali. A reanimated vehicle hovered below as he safely landed atop and slid her gently into one of its seats.

"You two could use an activity to burn off all that energy," joked Citlali's voice from inside the vehicle. The two laughed through their psychotic smiles. "Maybe several?"

The two were flown to a fake cemetery with fortified ruins, where they played competitive survival games of zombie apocalypse with hundreds of others. Afterward, they moved to a pool club. Inside the pitch-black building were brightly lit clear blue water paths and floating trays of glowing alcoholic beverages and patches. They moved past everyone in their bathing suits and found a lounge. Rainbow bubbles began appearing all over the water and in the air. They waved their arms in the air, popping as many as they could. After drying off, they made their way into a library, where they decided they would pick out a book together. They walked up to a glowing wall of streaming letters and numbers. Sebastian brought one hand into the wall and took it out, bringing forth a holographic book. Giselle dug her hand into and out of the wall as several children's books animated into her hand.

"*La Vida* ..." Sebastian read out loud the title of his book, stopping as he looked over at what Giselle had chosen. At the top of the books was a cover depicting cartoon kids exploring the many kinds of frozen fruit treats. It reminded her of the family she had left behind. She held it out, flipping through the first few pages. Sebastian went back to his book, not wanting to bother Giselle, who seemed to be enjoying her book. He knew she was thinking about her family, and now he was thinking about his as well. She placed it back into the wall of digital letters and numbers.

"No doubt there are a lot of good books here," she said, turning to him. "Let's come back another time."

"Yeah, let's get some fresh air."

"Now what?" Giselle teased as they stood under the warm white fireflies floating above.

"There's somewhere I want to take you."

"So where to?" She leaned in closer looking at him without blinking. "Looking to finish the night off?"

She winked as he maintained his composure.

Giselle jumped on a newly animated bench. She turned Sebastian around and wrapped her arms around his shoulders. Sebastian grabbed her legs and ran off with her into the distance.

Later that night they made their way to a nearby roof and entered a hover car, quietly embracing each other's warmth as they drifted off into the sky. They were dropped off at the top of one of the tallest skyscrapers around. After briefly admiring the view of the city, reanimation technology built a stairway into the sky. He scooped her up and carried her, running up the stairs, which ended in the clouds. He took steps on them and found that they were as sturdy as any ground, but soft, like cotton balls. With no one else around, he gently placed her on one of the warm clouds creating a mist surrounding them. Blue cushioned grass then manifested itself beneath her.

They were hidden in the clouds watching small flickers of light from the stars above. With her on him, he moved his hands closer to her waist but stopped, unsure of himself until she took his hands and moved them around her waist. He looked at her, unsure what to do next. Her soft hands moved around his neck as she moved closer to his eyes. He kissed her, starting with her soft lips and then to her neck. She clasped her hand against his chest and slid the other up and over the firmness of his head.

He slid his fingers along her neck tickling her. She opened her mouth, letting out soft giggles. Even high up in the air the wind was calm, but their hearts pounded. The moonlight bounced off the sweat and cloud dew on their bodies. As their love for each other continued they realized they did not want to stop, and it was as if they could not.

Later that night, he held her in his arms while she cradled her hands in his. Sebastian kissed her forehead as the two tightened each other's grip of one another.

"What are you thinking about?" Giselle asked. "Don't you wonder about your past life?"

"Yeah, from time to time. But I try not to think about it."

"I've left loved ones behind, and you have too. Doesn't that bother you?"

"Of course it does, but like I said, I try not to think about it. I wish I could change things, but I can't, and it haunts me when I think about it."

"I'm sorry to hear that."

"Maybe in time I'll be able to talk about my past."

She had no words. She wanted to talk about the things she wished she could have told those she had left behind, but he was a closed door. How could she be with someone who didn't want to be open about their past? After seeing a concerned look on Giselle, he slowly leaned forward and planted a kiss on her forehead.

"It's getting late," she said, turning away. They walked to the end of the cloud as clothes reanimated onto them. Via hover car, they made their way back to the Mind Transfer Administration building. Citlali waited in the room, holding back a smile as they casually walked through the window and into the room. She knew something was wrong but pretended not to notice. They took their seats and laid down. They tilted their heads to look at each other one more time. The transfer process happened once more, teleporting Giselle and Sebastian's consciousnesses back into their original bodies.

"So?" Citlali asked with her usual smile. "How was it? How did it feel to switch bodies?"

"Interesting," Giselle said wryly, slowly getting up and making her way back to the institution. Sebastian opened his eyes but remained lying down. He stood up when he realized Giselle had left the room. He ran out the window and into the hover car.

"Look, I'm so sorry if you wanted to talk about your past," he said as they were piloted away. "I'm not good at talking about this stuff. But I promise you I will listen to you and talk about whatever you want to talk about."

"You know what I want to talk about!?" she shouted. "You! Today confirmed I hardly know you!"

"That's not fair. You know that's not fair. I hardly know myself. I've only had two memory incursions."

"Well then, that's something! Now tell me something about you I don't know. Maybe tell me a little about your past?"

"And what about you!? You haven't told me about your flashbacks. That's a bit of a double standard, isn't it?"

"That's not the point! I was trying to bring it up, but you wouldn't let me!"

"I'm sorry," Sebastian said as he fought back his frustration. She was right. He needed to share or risk losing her. The ride back gave them enough time to talk, but she didn't want to pressure him to talk about his flashbacks. Instead, they talked about their experiences of waking up into their new lives for the first time. The vehicle became less noisy as they let one another talk, and even quieter by the time they finished. They hugged each other, thankful they were able to salvage the night.

***

The following week, the institution's saloon on the fifth floor was filled with peacekeepers. Ceremonial music now filled the blue halls, but who was playing remained unknown.

"Where is that music coming from?" Rosa asked looking out a giant window overlooking the city. Chatter accompanied the music as peacekeepers stood around waiting for the master of ceremonies. Everyone was dressed in traditional peacekeeper dress attire: black slacks, white gloves, dark-blue stand-collar button-down shirts with navy-blue-and-white blazers over it, followed by blue bandannas tied around their necks and blue berets on their heads. This was the first time Sebastian, Giselle and their teammates were wearing these. It was also their first time in the saloon. The past four months, since they were brought back to life, had been spent mostly in the gym or courtyard, as well as in the city. After completing their first mission, they had earned the right to this celebration. Like Sebastian, for some it was their first time in the chapel-looking room.

Everyone was happy, but not as happy as Giselle. She was happier than Sebastian had ever seen her. He assumed it was because of the celebration. Everyone was now lined up in rows. In the first row were the new members of the institution being initiated: Sebastian, Ryan, Rosa, Giselle, Arthur, Ramon and several others.

The walls of the saloon altered until they had carved designs. A stage animated in front of the peacekeepers as a man with a serape scarf over his shoulder made his way forward. Sebastian recognized him as the first person he had seen when he was first resurrected. He hadn't given much thought to the man with the scarf since then, but it was clear now that he must have an important role in the institution. The music grew quiet as the man made his way to the podium.

"Greetings, ladies and gentlemen," the man said. "For those I haven't had the honor of meeting, let me introduce myself: My name is Ishmael, and I am the regional director of this covert program under the peacekeeper military. As director, I am responsible for ensuring this program is sufficiently ran with the latest state-of-the-art technology and training, while maintaining secrecy from the public. Why the secrecy? Because we operate outside the law to end crime, corruption and inequality. We all chose this line of work. No one is forcing anyone to be here. You know what is at stake. Our lives. Yes, even mine. And you're all more than willing to risk it all for the betterment of everyone out there."

He pointed his hand out the giant window in the direction of the city. The room was still and quiet as the group anticipated his next words.

"Now, we are here to commemorate the progress of our new peacekeepers," Ishmael continued. "Please give a round of applause to our courageous volunteers in the front row. Join me in welcoming your new teammates!"

Soon the applause and musical chimes were followed by a surrounding group of peacekeepers encircling their new brothers and sisters, welcoming them with two-handed handshakes and smiles. Among them were Alice and her team. Some of the first peacekeepers were somewhat reluctant to shake the new peacekeepers' hands. No matter, the high spirits would not go away so easily.

"As part of the celebration, we will all be attending a gala with all the other peacekeepers in the United States of North America," Ishmael said. "You've earned it. I'll see you there."

After the congratulations, Giselle grabbed Sebastian and ran off to look for a quiet hallway on the fourth floor of the institution. Their teammates respected their privacy and told them they would wait for them to return so they could all leave together for the party. The couple made their way to the windowsill where they had had their first conversation. Sitting by the opened windows with their backs to one another, they looked out toward the city. A few smaller buildings of the institution were hidden under the shore of trees that cradled the view of the city skyline in their branches. Few clouds moved freely allowing for the sun to emit its orange glow onto everyone below.

"I can't wait to meet the peacekeepers from the other institutions," Giselle said in excitement.

"Yeah, I wonder what kind of stories they'll have," Sebastian said.

"Apparently the celebrations will take place in San Francisco," Giselle said, looking at her satellite bracelet. A hologram showcased videos of past galas. "Look, there's going to be dancing! Oh, I haven't danced since, well, I can't even remember." Giselle smiled tilting her head towards Sebastian, who was looking at the nearby city. "What is it?"

"I'm thinking about those out there in the city. You know what he said about secrecy. They might never know what we do."

"But *we'll* know." With hope of talking about something more personal, she changed the conversation. "You know, we will have to go back out there to complete more missions."

Their hands closest to the windows made it into each other's grasp.

"With all this training, we should be fine," he comforted.

"Do you wonder why we were chosen for each other?"

"Well, we've only known each other for a short time, but we certainly have great chemistry."

"Maybe we've known each other for much longer than a short time," Giselle said quietly. As she turned around, their hands let go of each other. He moved to face her not knowing what to expect. Sitting on her knees while leaning towards him, she gazed into his eyes. "I never told you about my new flashback because it occurred today. I had my third memory incursion. But before I tell you about it, let me tell you what caused it. I

119

was reading earlier today trying to pass the time when I stumbled upon a quote."

"What was the quote?" Sebastian whispered as Giselle took a moment to prepare herself.

"Love be bound no more," Giselle started, followed by a pause. Sebastian looked at her with a sudden realization.

"I put this smile on her," Sebastian added, almost hypnotized.

"I help him to his feet as," Giselle continued.

"Purpose is fulfilled at last," they said together. "We have found our greatest treasure. One once sought by our ancestors."

"Why do I know that quote by heart?" Sebastian asked.

Giselle nodded, still staring into his eyes as if to wait for something other than time. She placed her hands behind his neck and grabbed his hair. She leaned into him, and as her lips met his and parted, Sebastian had a flashback. It wasn't like the memory incursions from before. This one was a vague collection of memories Charles had described to Sebastian earlier on, except now Sebastian was seeing them for himself. There he saw the pier through his eyes. He was ready to commit suicide. Yet, like Charles had described, he stopped himself when he heard a woman being attacked. When he went to see what was going on, he saw it was Giselle. The woman who was staring into his eyes. The woman who would be the mother of his child. His lifelong partner in that life and in this new life they had been given. There they were, on their first date, buying their first home together and raising their son.

After reliving bits of the terrible scene of the car crash and last view of his son, he awoke with Giselle crying, hands clutched to his collar. Their tears rolled down on each other's pressed cheeks. Sebastian took hold of her and embraced her, never intending to let go. They had lost their son and through the graphic flashback had lost him once again.

"I remember more of my memories," she whispered coldly. "But this time they included you and our son, too."

"It is you," Sebastian said, breaking the silence and looking at her. "I can't believe it is you. You're still with me. You were ... in the past life and now in this new life."

"Yes, it's me," Giselle whispered. "I've only told you so far. I didn't know how to tell anyone except you. Seeing our son again ... what happened to my boy? My baby boy."

Sebastian embraced her again as her voice began to crack and she wept. She choked trying to come up with words but nothing came.

"I was driving during the car crash," Sebastian confessed quietly. He could not move. He couldn't even blink. "Giselle. It's all my fault."

CHAPTER 14 – GALA PART 1: DANCE, SEBASTIAN, DANCE!

The peacekeepers assembled in the courtyard, using temporary platforms to see who could get to the rooftop first. They playfully pushed each other around, trying to be the first ones on the aircraft so they could get to the gala. Ryan and Rosa eagerly waited for Sebastian in the empty simulation library. They hadn't danced in half a century and were eager to practice some moves. They did not know how much time they would have before Sebastian and Giselle were finished with whatever they were doing.

"I can't believe you haven't been here before," Rosa said, welcoming Ryan into the library with open arms. She held out a hand as if to catch something. Immediately an orb of lit up letters swung itself into her hand.

"Well I'd much rather spend my time in the gym," Ryan said, looking around curiously. The floors and tables held rays of digital knowledge. Seats were spread out for those looking to go into a holographic experience, while large, empty spaces went down the halls for anyone who needed space to practice simulations. "But this place looks amazing. What can I learn here that I'll need when fighting warkeepers?"

"First aid, combat engineering, piloting," Rosa said. "A lot of that is automated in cities with an abundance of reanimation technology, but you never know. You might end up in a place without that gray crystal magic. But today, we are going to learn how to dance."

A ribbon appeared on Rosa's free hand. She placed it into the orb of light and carefully attached it to Ryan's arm, feeling his bicep and looking up at him before pulling away. She reanimated another ribbon and did the same, this time tying it around her own arm. Without even thinking, he clicked arms with her and began moving in circles. They kept their eyes on each other, not bothering to look down to avoid stepping on each other's feet. This was their first dance, and already they were mastering the moves.

"How do you feel about this new life you have now?" Ryan asked.

"Grateful," Rosa responded. "I remember being so angry and frustrated with the world back then. The world was such a mess. It's sad to think about it because so many people didn't think they could do anything to change the wicked world."

"But you did something about it. More than anyone I know. In this life or in my past life." After a few quiet turns and steps, Ryan decided to break the silence. "Did you want a family?"

She blushed, embarrassed at the question. "I did, but not in that world."

For the next few minutes they danced, until they received a notification that Sebastian and Giselle were on their way to the aircrafts.

While in the courtyard, Charles looked at his digital checklist to make sure everyone was on their way. He noticed Sebastian, Giselle and a few other peacekeepers were still not checked off as "heading to gala." He walked away from the courtyard to look for them using his satellite bracelet. He was able to reach a few of the peacekeepers to tell them to get on the aircraft so they could arrive at the gala together. Sebastian and Giselle did not respond to his satellite call. A concerned Charles went off to look for them.

"No. No," Giselle pleaded. "I know … I've always known you needed help. But that didn't stop me from loving you. You told me what you were experiencing because of the war. It's not your fault. There's nothing you could have done. Don't take this out on yourself."

Sebastian had become silent, his eyes tearful and red.

"Ah, there you two are! We should be going now. We don't want to be late!" Charles said, entering from across the room and watching Sebastian wipe away the tears that slid down his cheek leaving behind damp trails. The couple did not bother to look at him. Charles quietly waited for them to say something, realizing what he had walked into. "Is everything all right?"

"No, everything—" Giselle shouted before stopping herself.

Down the hall were two peacekeepers leaving their rooms and chatting about the gala. No one needed to know their business. Charles gestured for the two to follow him to his office. Though most peacekeepers were outside readying themselves for the party, they still did their best to avoid as many as possible while inside.

"What is it?" he asked cautiously, as his office door closed on its own.

"You knew. I bet you knew," Giselle said shaking her head. "Sebastian and I were together in our past lives."

"Wait! Hold on, you two?!" Charles said happily, almost not noticing her heated temper. "This is great! But why do you seem upset with me? I told you your files were corrupted, and I could only see fragments of your information. I was telling the truth. This is a surprise to me, too!"

"I'm sorry," Giselle said, lowering her voice. "I'm sorry. I can see you're telling the truth. I'm just overwhelmed. We had another memory incursion."

"That's how you two found out?" Charles responded. "But I'm thankful you're all right. It looks as though your bodies are handling the incursions well now."

"Their medical charts indicate their bodies are fine," Citlali chimed in, animating like a wave coming from above. She leaned against the wall to their side with her arms crossed. "But if you don't want to go to the celebration because you need the evening off, we understand."

"I'll go if Sebastian goes," Giselle said, looking at a quiet Sebastian. "I understand if you don't want to go, but don't beat yourself up with this. I'm sure our son had a good life. Please tell him it wasn't his fault that the car crashed and brought us here."

"You couldn't control your flashbacks back then, Sebastian," Citlali said. "Not even with our technology can we control anyone's memory incursions."

"How are you feeling?" Charles asked Sebastian.

The three looked at him, noticing he was still absent from the conversation. He had cleared his face of tears and was now doing his best to hold himself together.

"I'm just glad to have Giselle back," Sebastian said, almost scripted and still showing restraint.

"Will you still be able to attend tonight's festivities?" Charles asked. "Maybe it can ease your minds a bit."

"Yeah, that's a good idea," Giselle said. "But only if Sebastian is feeling okay enough to go. Maybe it'll help us all."

"That does sound good," Sebastian said. "I don't want anybody asking us why we didn't show up. I don't think I'll ever be ready to tell anyone about this."

The two made their way to the rooftop, which echoed with footsteps from the peacekeepers and training personnel from the institution. Giselle and Sebastian forced cheery expressions as they met their teammates, who were not aware of the couple's recent memory incursion. The floating aircrafts took the peacekeepers to the nearby city of San Francisco, a metropolis of glowing sights. It was one of a few North American cities competing in developing innovative technologies for the asteroid-mining conglomerate. Here, millions of people were studying the various STEM fields to create new transportation and mining techniques to bring over the immense shipments of minerals from space. A newly found metal called transelementum was the main component from which reanimation crystals were built. Although reanimation technology seemed abundant in the urban hubs, it was still unexposed to some of the sparsely populated areas of North America. Reanimation crystals were also constantly being stolen by those working for the Orderkeeper nations, which did not have an asteroid-mining organization to bring back the metal.

Among the first things the peacekeepers saw were rows of kids in a crowded neighborhood that nested inside an airport style stadium. They were leaving a science museum and marching on their way to a school aircraft. Citlali gloated that the kids of this city were among the most academically and mentally prepared in the world. It was also said that kids nowadays were given rapid human growth hormone to age faster both physically and mentally. It took about two years for the kids to grow into teenagers, and another year to become physical adults. Then, they would stop aging in their twenties.

"Is this ethically moral?" Rosa asked.

"I don't know," Ryan said. "Brave new world."

One would think they had shrunk upon entering the white marble floor and blue-and-gold halls of the California peacekeeper headquarters. It was not hidden at all but restricted anybody not affiliated with the military from entering. The hallways led to a crossroads with spiral stairs extending around to the sides and numerous elevators leading up. A neon-blue arrow led the peacekeepers to one of the elevators, where they rapidly ascended past many openings. They stopped when the arrow disappeared, indicating they had found their floor. It was filled with chatter from other peacekeepers who were already filling their bellies. Music filled the ears of the recently arrived peacekeepers as they wondered what they should do. There were many on the dark dance floor, illuminated only by their flow as streams of light formed following their feet, hands and hips.

"Go on, do a twirl, Giselle," Citlali appeared, encouraging them to have fun. Sebastian grabbed her hand and swung her around. Immediately, her peacekeeper outfit converted into a purple sparkling dress that touched the ground and exposed the sides of her legs. Sebastian's peacekeeper uniform changed into a suit and purple bow tie with a white button-down shirt and purple flower in his blazer's top pocket. Their hair became nicely shaped, too. But Sebastian's newly done combover was not as mesmerizing as Giselle's loose braided updo, which had white and purple ribbons woven through the braids. He was tempted to embrace the locks of hair, but he did not want to mess them up, even if reanimation technology would redo her hair in an instant.

"You look great!" Sebastian told her.

"There must be more than a hundred peacekeepers here," Ryan said, as everyone's clothes reanimated into long dresses, suits and ties.

"There will be more coming soon," Citlali responded, gazing at the dancers and getting into their rhythm. "Anyone care to join us? If you don't know how to dance, you better learn quick."

She snapped her fingers and did a slow 360-degree turn, moving ever closer to the dance floor. Giselle grabbed Sebastian's hand and ran off with him to the dance floor, hoping to ease their minds.

Sebastian grabbed hold of Giselle's waist. After spinning around each other like coins they stepped away from each other holding on to the other's hand kicking their feet backward and forward. They did not know that they could dance like that. Was this a skill that they had learned in their previous life and could now use?

Mime gloves appeared on all the dancer's hands. Their dancing was now synchronized. They all mirrored their partner's moves taking a step back and forward together. Each time echoing a united stomp like a marching army. Then while still holding on to their partner's hands everyone spun and stretched out their leg backward letting out one last stomp in unison. The mime gloves then disappeared. Sebastian and Giselle were astonished at the sudden and brief dance.

"Look," Giselle said smiling at everyone. "Some people are swapping partners."

He spun her as she winked at him. Her figure glittered around him as she moved out of his sight from one side and reappeared on his other. He lowered her on one arm as golden sparks and teal rays twisted into the air and then into nothingness. The more they moved, the more lights continued to form around them, their harmonic side to side continually expressed by the stalking lights animated in their presence.

"Those moves, Sebastian!" Giselle cheered. "Look at you!"

"Thanks, you're pretty good yourself," Sebastian said. "Some of the dancers are switching partners."

"When you get to the next peacekeeper, see if you can get any information about their personal lives and missions," Giselle said.

"Why?" Sebastian asked.

"To help us."

"You're always one step ahead," he said, calmly scouting the room. Giselle smiled. Here came the spin and partner trade. A woman threw herself into Sebastian's arms, her purple body brushing firmly against him with her cyan-colored eyes innocently staring into his.

"Couldn't help but notice you haven't embraced this world's new interpretation of... *body art*," she said, she looking him over curiously.

"I did embrace it once with my girlfriend when we used the mind-transfer system," Sebastian said. "I see not everyone here has. I guess we'd like to stay in the bodies we were born into. Call us traditionalists. Nothing wrong with that, is there?"

"No, of course not," she said, smiling as she looked up at him.

Sebastian could not help but avoid her eyes. They were captivating, and he knew he might stare into them longer than deemed appropriate. He looked over through the dim lighting at Giselle, whose eyes tracked them from over the shoulder of the gentleman she was dancing with. She couldn't help but let out a chuckle at Sebastian's awkwardness. Sebastian gave her a look as if to say, "Look what you got me into."

"Don't you think it's great that there's no more loonies and toonies?!" she said, changing the topic.

"Loonies ...?"

"Loonies and toonies. Currency! Nobody uses currency anymore! Don't you think that's great?"

"Oh yeah! That's great!" After thinking what her name could be, her first and last name appeared through his contact lenses. "So, Ms. Miller, how are you adjusting to life? Are you enjoying your new line of work?"

"Call me Chloe. Can't complain. It's fascinating. I had to go through a long walk into the deep blue sea in my last mission."

"*Into?*" he asked.

"Yeah, with reanimation technology you can create a giant air bubble so you remain dry and can breathe underwater. You should try it sometime with your girlfriend," she suggested. "There was some sort of boogeyman terrorizing an oceanic city. My team and I had to explore the ocean floors to find clues to locate this man. Another interesting mission I've been on was safeguarding an Alaskan town from warkeepers across the Bering Strait. We were caught in a nightlong firefight with them. A lot of my colleagues tell me the warkeepers in the Far East are becoming more aggressive. Apparently, our enemies up there are eager to invade."

"Do you think they'll invade?" Sebastian started.

"Not so fast. You're going to have to try harder next time if you want to know more, Sebastian Ramirez," she said. "Well, this was interesting, but I think it's time we switched. Maybe someday us Canadian peacekeepers can show you what we're up against in the north."

Sebastian spun her off to Ramon. The two seemed rather pleased with each other's random dance partner selection. He requested in his thoughts for more information on her. Through his eyes an image of her appeared with her name, Chloe Miller; her residence: Vancouver; her peacekeeper status: completed twenty-five missions. Another woman came into his view, bumping into Sebastian in hopes he'd catch her. He dropped to catch her painlessly, almost splitting his legs and jumping up. It was a quick save that impressed everyone.

"Nice one," she said. Her pink cotton-candy hair swung lightly as he lifted her up. She pushed up her clear aviator shades and smiled at him.

Sebastian mentally requested her info. Name: Jaylyn Amaya; residence: Mexicali; peacekeeper status: completed forty missions.

"New to dancing, right?"

"Yeah," Sebastian said, holding back his astonishment at her mission record. "How are you liking this party, Jaylyn?"

"Great, it's always nice to meet other peacekeepers, like yourself. After my first peacekeeper gala it isn't required I show up to any others, but I still

128

come to see the fresh faces. You're new to everything. I see you only have one mission to your name. Everyone starts with one. You'll get a lot of experience soon."

"Yeah, I see you aren't new. How do you feel about the peacekeeper program? Do you think we're making a difference?"

"Yes, of course. You'll soon see that since they first started reviving, training, and giving us peacekeeper missions there has been a great impact on life everywhere. It's rewarding. You see news on the screen and know you or someone here was personally responsible for that happening. Now people are less concerned about incoming warkeepers because we covert peacekeepers are pushing them back by hindering their operations in our land. Before us covert peacekeepers there was a lot of crime conducted by the enemy in our territory. The public doesn't know about us. They assume the warkeepers are giving up and abandoning their operations. It makes sense since they come from rogue nations that do not have the same resources as peacekeepers. For instance, they don't have access to the Asteroid Belt's resources like we do. People think our enemy nations are about to collapse under their extractive system, like the Soviet Union in the 1990s. I think you already know, but most people living in their territory are either put in strict government-run labor programs or placed in the military. Because of this, their military is exceptional."

"Why don't they have technology like us?" As the two flowed in circles, the floor became slippery like ice, causing them to breeze easily around the long stretch of dance floor. Sebastian smiled nervously and hoped he wouldn't slip. Fortunately, they gracefully moved around the room along with the other dance couples as if ice skating. When it was time to switch partners, Jaylyn grabbed Sebastian tighter to let him know she wanted to continue dancing with him. The two remained in each other's arms. She smiled up at him, resting her chin against his chest.

"They're missing something important, which is reanimation technology. Reanimation technology is made from a mineral called transelementum. You can only get that from asteroids! Without it, they must resort to old factories to build their equipment. But the warkeeper dictatorships only survived for so long from peacekeeper nations because they did not have covert peacekeepers to deal with. This peacekeeper program has only been around for three years. Before the program, they stole resources from naval and aerial ships and kidnapped some of our most gifted minds. There have been many setbacks, but the general population thinks it's unwise to go to war with them because if we do, the warkeeper dictatorships might use its people as human shields when they fight us. That would be a nightmare. That's why it's best our program remain a secret, so we can begin a silent invasion of the enemy territories."

"How long do you think that'll take?"

"Here. Come with me," she said, halting to grab his hand. She slid off the dance floor, bringing him along. Giselle looked over her dancer's shoulder curiously as Jaylyn and Sebastian disappeared onto the balcony, which revealed they were dozens of floors above the ground. Once outside, Jaylyn waved her hands and out appeared a map of the globe. "Take a look. Peacekeeper territory is in blue, and Orderkeeper territory is in red. It's roughly divided between the southern and northern hemispheres, with some areas in South America in the Global Peacekeeper Alliance. It looks like both sides have roughly the same amount of territory, right? When you asked how long it will take, the answer is as long as it takes. Now, we're in the first phase of this operation, which is to end the sabotage from warkeepers. After nearly three years, we have brought it to an all-time low. After we end the operations here on our side, we will get the green light to start the second phase: sending handfuls of our peacekeepers into their territory. We will launch our own sabotage campaigns and rally the local populations to overthrow their dictators. But we will train them, of course."

"I thought we didn't want innocent people to get hurt?"

"Well, we won't force anyone to fight, but if there are those willing then it is our duty to help them fight for a better life."

"True. Fighting for freedom definitely sounds better than being used as human shields."

Jaylyn pointed at North America and South America on the map.

"We peacekeepers in this part of the world will be launching clandestine operations in Central and South America."

"It looks like the United States of America, Canada and most of northern and central Mexico are part of the United States of North America."

"Or U.S.N.A. for short. Similar to the European Union in the east."

"Is there a third phase?"

"That's all I know for now."

"Why didn't Charles or Citlali tell me this?"

"They probably would have but would rather have you focus on training and catching up on current events in North America. It was the same for my team. We weren't told this until a few missions in," Jaylyn said, moving her back toward the edge of the balcony and resting her arms on the parapet. "That's pretty much the basics of it all."

She was still, but suddenly looked alluring. She was quiet, focusing on Sebastian. The wind that embraced her with love now met Sebastian. His heart pounded as he looked at her, hypnotized. Why was he suddenly attracted to Jaylyn?

She turned around, focusing on the city skyline, and started humming. "Sometimes, I feel like he isn't awake. When we both have something incredible to create. Why do we keep on with the ignorance and lack of faith in our fate? We did not go this far just to wait to be great."

As Sebastian moved closer to hear her, she turned around. Her hands glided farther out, stretching her arms and grabbing his hair. Sebastian stared at her with his hands in his pockets, wondering if she was trying to seduce him. Sebastian moved to her side, looking over at the horizon.

"Do you have someone?" Jaylyn said, looking through the corner of her eye at Sebastian.

"I'm sorry if I gave you the wrong impression," Sebastian paused taking a few steps back. "Giselle. Her name is Giselle and she's back there. And that's where I should be."

"Sorry, I didn't know," she frowned, looking over at Giselle in the party's saloon. Although Giselle had a view of the two at the balcony, she pretended not to see them. "I see her. She's a beautiful woman. I think you should go back in there."

She pointed with her eyes. He rushed into the room and walked straight to Giselle, who was standing quietly next to Rosa.

Without saying a word Rosa walked away to give the two privacy.

Nearby peacekeepers looked over a bit startled, but soon went about their own business.

"What was that?" she whispered, avoiding his eyes and gripping her drink. "Look, I understand you're not feeling yourself after that flashback, but the last thing I need right now is someone being careless."

"I know." He looked at her, not knowing what to say. "Nothing happened."

"Look, I understand that a lot is going on, but if you need to talk to someone you can talk to me." Giselle finally looked at him. "It doesn't even have to be me."

"Sorry. You saw that nothing happened and nothing *will* happen. Not with her and not with anyone else. It's only you and me."

"I trust you so just forget it."

Not sure what to do but heed her advice he decided to change the conversation.

"Listen. I found out some interesting things about the program. Do you want to hear them?"

"Another time. Let's go somewhere more private. Some of our friends are going to hang out in a theater down at the far end of one of the halls. Let's go."

CHAPTER 15 – GALA PART 2: NOT-SO-WICKED GAMES!

Sitting around the semicircle of cushioned chairs were the newly inducted peacekeepers. They had found an unoccupied theater and decided to use it to pass the time. Among Sebastian and Giselle were Ryan and Rosa, who were now commonly seen together. Ramon and Paula were there as well. Jaylyn and her teammate Patricio sat down beside them, with Patricio leaving his tan blazer folded across the back of his seat. Giselle had already had the pleasure of meeting Patricio from their dance earlier. Name: Patricio Gonzalez; Residence: Mexicali; Peacekeeper status: completed thirty-nine missions.

"Are these the lovers you almost broke apart?" Patricio asked. His biceps were well defined through his button-down shirt. His forest-green-and-white scarf reached down onto his crossed arms as his cowboy boots crossed each other while extending outstretched onto the floor.

"Patricio!" Jaylyn said, her voice echoing through the theater.

"Well, while we're in the privacy of this auditorium, why don't we play a game?" Patricio clapped his hands together.

"Is it that game again?" Jaylyn asked, looking over at the others apologetically.

"Truth or dare," Patricio said. He jumped up from his seat and popped himself on top of the stage in front of the semicircle of seated audience members. "Ask me to do a truth or dare."

He pointed at Paula, who looked confused.

"Me? Okay, truth," she commanded. "Tell us your most ridiculous story since being brought back."

"Off to a good start, I see. Where to begin with this story? Okay! This one time I was in the demilitarized zone in southern Mexico. It's on our side of the skyscraper-tall border. If you don't know, the demilitarized zone is where no military presence can be shown. Yet, there are still many people living in that area, and it is ravaged by clandestine warkeeper hideouts. You must be careful there, even though it's ruled by neutral artificial intelligence martial law. I'll explain what that is throughout my story. Now, I was there delivering supplies to an underground safe house that provides shelter to those who managed to escape from the south and are making their way up north farther into peacekeeper territory. It's my first time doing this. I arrive there mid-afternoon, but little did I know I'm dropping off the materials to a paranoid old lady. She has me wait there until midnight while she inspects everything to the littlest detail. I'm thinking, 'Okay, this is fine, I can stay here and wait for the sun to rise so I can safely leave the area.' Now, with A.I. martial law, all reanimation technology ceases to work, and unreliable transportation becomes the only way to get around. I cannot travel through the zone safely for fear of encountering warkeepers. Being in a safe house, I'm assuming I will get a room for the night. All the rooms were filled with families of refugees. Sad, really. I'm thinking I'll sleep in their lounge. Turns out, on Fridays, as part of its cover, the lounge turns into a pop-up club! Yeah, who would have known? I guess they left that out of the report."

"You stayed, right?" Jaylyn said, raising her eyebrow and mimicking dancing with her arms.

"No," Patricio continued. "Anyway, with no room to stay in, I decided to leave the place. I look at my satellite bracelet, and lucky for me there's a school bus picking people up two blocks away, and it's only five minutes away. I tell the old lady, 'Hey, I'm going to leave and catch the bus.' She said before I leave she wanted me to help throw out the trash. I patiently wait for her to get up from her chair, she grabs two garbage bags, hands me one bag, approaches the balcony, and tosses it over! I cannot believe she had me wait to help her do what she could have easily done herself. I was dumbfounded. We say our goodbyes and I leave. Anyways, I rush down the stairs and get an update from my bracelet that the bus is a minute away. I make a run for the bus stop, and as I get to the street, it zooms right past me and the stop it should have stopped at. I'm running in the middle of the street, with the few cars at night passing by me, trying to stay in sight of the bus, but after a few blocks, it disappears over a hill. I stand in the middle of the lanes as cars pass by. The next bus won't come for another two hours, so I decide to walk through the demilitarized zone toward the only train station that would get me out of there. I open a map on my bracelet, and it leads me down a route through the residential complexes. Now, these buildings are huge, so you would think since they're housing thousands of people that there would be people outside. No. It is dead quiet, and I'm all alone on these streets. A few blocks in and a dark-tinted vehicle drives slowly through the cul-de-sac and stops close in front of me. I pretend not to notice it and continue walking through the block. It eventually drives away. Who was in the vehicle? I'm glad I never found out. On the next block I hear shouting. I look forward and back. I look left and right. I see no one. I continue to hear people shouting. I forgot to look up. And there they are on the balcony of their apartment near the roof. You know you're loud if someone on the ground hears you from your thirtieth-floor apartment. I ignore it and move on. After a mile of walking through this neighborhood, I make it to the train station, and of course the station in the area isn't working. There was a wanted person poster casually stating something about certain people stealing metal off the tracks to make tanks. Crazy, I know, right? Another poster said I had to take a shuttle bus. I look around, wondering which direction to go for the shuttle bus, and then I see one pass right by me. I must have looked out of place walking around that neighborhood at night because when the bus driver saw me, he looked like he saw a ghost. As the driver passed by he tilted his head so he could keep his eyes glued right on me. Mind you, his eyes were off the road, and he was still driving the bus! Anyways, I make it to the shuttle bus, which takes me to a nearby train, which takes me home to friendly territory! The second I'm in Veracruz I use reanimation technology to create a hover car to zip me back to Baja California. What a wonderful night."

"Next time do dare," Jaylyn mock-whispered to Paula.

"That was a good story," Giselle said, as a light clap commenced among the peacekeepers.

"Now it's your turn," Patricio said, looking at Paula again.

"Me?!" Paula asked, startled.

"I should have warned you," Jaylyn teased.

"Yes, you, since you asked me for a truth, now it's your turn," Patricio said, getting down from the stage. Paula sat herself on top of the stage's edge, dangling her legs and rubbing her thumbs together.

"I'm going to dare you," Jaylyn said, stopping to look around with an inquisitive eyebrow.

"Have her sing us a song," Patricio said.

"Yeah, let's have at it," Jaylyn said politely. "Sing us a song! But not any song! A new song no one has ever heard before!"

"What!?" Paula asked, surprised. "You must be joking. I can't sing, nor do I have any experience writing songs. At least, I don't think I do."

"Don't worry," Patricio said. "The reanimation technology in the air offers stimulants to get your creative juices flowing. Here, I'll help you."

"I breathe, and I can create a song?" Paula asked, looking motivated.

"Does that mean anyone can sing a new song?" Ryan asked.

"Here, I'll help out," Patricio said.

"That's right," Jaylyn insisted, as a guitar animated into Patricio's arms. "Nowadays you can easily write a new song, and lyrics will flow through your mouth and into everyone's ears."

"Whenever you're ready," Patricio said, lightly tapping on the guitar. Paula sat up, beginning with a hum.

"When I woke up, the first thing I saw was light," she began. "I was alone. Past not known." The crowd's spirits were immediately lifted as they followed along with her soothing voice. "Lost in a world between night and delight surrounding my head. Before I woke, I was dead. Wondering what would reach me instead. Had to look in a certain light, just to see that things were all right. We were given a second chance just to do this one simple dance." Patricio moved closer to Paula while shaking his hands over the strings of the guitar. "Now here I am in what I always hoped a dream would be. I left a city of broken streets. But who knew I'd be greeted by light and glee? But was still lost in a world between night and delight surrounding my head. Before I woke I was dead, but now I'm here. Looking at you and the life in your eyes. We'll be like when the oceans touch the skies." She brushed her hands against her legs as the crowd lightly cheered in excitement. Then, the two performers sang the last bit together. "How could we say no to such a high? When we are no longer capable of saying goodbye. Here in each other's soul. Lost in our new world. How could we say no to such eyes? When we are no longer capable of saying goodbye."

The crowd let out an applause. Patricio's smile widened at Paula as she winked at him. The guitar disappeared as he moved closer to her. She moved her knees to the side, inviting him to get closer until the space between their lips disappeared. Everyone was quiet as they watched with warmth. He widened his large hands around her waist, picking her off the stage and bringing her to the floor.

"When I heard you sing, I thought, 'If this is heaven then I'm glad I'm dead,'" Patricio said as they both smiled and let out a quick laugh.

"I didn't know it was going to be that intense," Paula said as the two made their way back to their seats. "That was fun."

Paula crouched down on the seat next to Patricio, putting her head on his chest as she was embraced by his arms.

"I guess I'm next," Jaylyn said, taking center stage again. "Giselle, dare me!"

"Tell the person you're *most* madly in love with that you're most madly in love with them," Giselle requested in a hawkish tone. "In those words, exactly. And I emphasize *most*, because it's obvious you're interested in quite a few people. Hey, not judging you. Just saying."

"*Most* madly in love with?" Jaylyn said letting out a small breath and overlooking the sly comment. "Truth! I choose truth!"

"Can she do that?" Paula asked.

"No," Patricio said.

"I can!" Jaylyn interrupted.

"Fine, truth," Giselle said. "But you're not getting away that easily. Who are you most madly in love with?"

"Ishmael," Jaylyn said, defeated. "I know it's crazy. It'll never happen."

"The director?" Rosa asked. "Why?"

"Yeah, him," Jaylyn said. "I'm not sure how many of you got to know him, but he is a sincere man. He used to be my warden when this program began, and so I got to know him well. The things he's done."

"What things has he done?" Giselle asked.

"Well, it's not my place to tell someone's personal secrets," Jaylyn started. "But what I can tell you are some things you can look up on his public profile. For instance, like me, he also never got to know his parents. They died in an accident when he was young. It's not recorded how exactly, but it's tragic nonetheless. After high school, he joined the Army and made it his home for the next several years, working in intelligence. In my past life, I too was without a family until I joined the military and worked in intelligence on the cyber operations side. Our close similarities in life were the reasons why I was one of the first people resurrected to become a peacekeeper. He trusted I would be a great addition to help lead the charge against the warkeepers."

"Oh, you're one of the first peacekeepers at your institution?" Rosa asked.

"Patricio also. And one of the first ones in the North American region," Jaylyn said.

"You're nice compared to some of our first peacekeepers," Ramon said.

"Yeah, we don't all have inflated egos," Patricio said. "Sorry to hear some of your first peacekeepers are still like that. I thought they would have been more welcoming by now."

Sebastian and Giselle both started thinking about Ishmael. He had lost his parents in an accident. Sebastian and Giselle were separated from their son due to a horrible accident, but they didn't remember their son's name. They couldn't even recall his name after their earlier flashbacks. They could barely make out their son's face from the memories they had recovered.

"I even got a scarf exactly like his," Jaylyn continued, as a serape scarf with the same color patterns as Ishmael's reanimated around her neck. "But please don't tell him. It's kind of embarrassing."

"It's not embarrassing at all," Ryan said.

A colorful serape scarf cradled around her neck, and at that moment a critical switch triggered itself inside Sebastian and Giselle.

***

"These hurricanes are getting worse," Sebastian said, grabbing his son's coat from the coat stand at the end of the hallway to the apartment's door. "Aren't they, dear?"

"Yeah, it's unfortunate," Giselle said, coming out of the living room and into the hallway. "Maybe we should move?"

"I think that's a good idea," Sebastian said, looking up at her, worried. He moved to her and kissed her forehead.

"Ewww, that's gross, dad," their son said, covering his eyes.

Sebastian patted his son on the head. "How about somewhere warm? Somewhere where it's warm and breezy all year 'round?"

"California," Giselle and Sebastian said together. They weren't surprised by their answer. They had been considering it ever since their short vacation there nearly a year before their son was born.

"California?" the young boy asked.

"It's a big state, like New York, but on the other side of the country," Sebastian explained.

"And it's warm and breezy all year 'round, sweetie," Giselle added, pinching her son's cheeks as he looked out the window at the fluttering rain bursts outside.

"Let's go there now," the boy said, looking back up at his parents.

"We can't now, but we will," Giselle said. "Your dad and I promise."

"We promise," Sebastian reassured. "We will go."

"Why can't we go there now?" their son asked.

"Because we have to go to the shelter now, son," Sebastian said, trying to keep his smile. "The shelter is the safest place for us now. The hurricane will flood some of the streets in our neighborhood, so we're going to the shelter where they can make sure we stay dry. Okay?"

"Okay!" the boy said excitedly. "I don't like getting wet."

Giselle tugged at the serape scarf around Sebastian's neck. She gazed at his scarf and then into his eyes. He knew what she was asking of him. Their son was beginning to be terrified of the storm. He needed something to raise his hopes up. Sebastian knelt in front of his son and took off his colorful serape scarf. The wonderful pattern of green, white, red, blue, yellow, sky blue and many other colors were now tied around his son's neck. His son smiled with a finger next to his dimple, innocently avoiding eye contact.

"Isn't this your and mama's lucky scarf?" the boy asked.

"Yes, but now it's yours," Sebastian said. "This special scarf has the ability to bring happiness and hope to whoever wears it. Just believe, okay?"

"Okay!" his son said. "What should I believe in right now?"

"California, and a happy life there with us," Giselle said, kneeling to hug her son. The parents stared into his innocent eyes, wondering why they had brought him into a collapsing world. A tear almost rolled down her cheek. The window shattered open as a pot from outside flew into their kitchen.

"I thought you boarded the windows!" Giselle exclaimed.

"I did!" Sebastian said, running into the kitchen. "I used steel nails and reinforced the wooden boards with metal sheets!"

"Come on!" Giselle said, grabbing her son's hand. "We need to go before the storm picks up even more!"

Giselle opened the door and with her son ran out, followed closely by Sebastian carrying a duffle bag of essential emergency items and food. Their frantic echoes of footsteps down the stairs were soon dominated by the screeching sounds of the soon-to-be-nightmarish hurricane.

***

"Give them some air," Jaylyn said. "They'll be all right. Give them a moment to recover."

Everyone was quiet as they waited for Giselle or Sebastian to say something. The two were now on their backs on the floor, their flashback still sinking in like a dying vessel full of hysterical souls.

"We need to see Ishmael, now!" Giselle shouted, getting up and looking at Jaylyn's scarf.

"Whoa, there," Patricio said. "Breathe. Why do you need to see him?"

"He can be selective in who he meets," Jaylyn said.

"The flashback," Sebastian managed to get out. "We think he might be our son!"

"No. No, there's no way," Jaylyn said, looking at the two. "Wait, your son?"

"We found out we were together in our past lives earlier today," Giselle said. The room grew quiet and still. "Sebastian and I had a kid together."

"Giselle and I never married, which is why we have different last names," Sebastian said, looking a little shocked and avoiding everyone's gaze as he stood up with Ryan's help.

"And that serape scarf is the same as the one in our flashback!" Giselle pointed at the same wonderful pattern of green, white, red, blue, yellow, sky blue and many other colors around Jaylyn. The exact same pattern the couple saw in their flashback. "If he has it, then—"

"He is here at the gala," Jaylyn said as Giselle began choking up.

140

Giselle got up and charged for the exit. Sebastian, still a bit drowsy, followed as best as he could. They made their way through the hallway when Citlali appeared.

"I overheard, and I know what you're thinking, but I want to tell you two to not get your hopes up," Citlali pleaded.

Giselle and Sebastian halted.

"What are you trying to tell us, Citlali?" Giselle cried.

"Ishmael isn't your son," Citlali admitted.

"But how do you explain the scarf?" Giselle asked. "It has the same exact pattern as the scarf we saw in our flashback! How many serape scarfs have the same exact pattern?"

"Giselle," Sebastian whispered. "If Citlali says it's not him, then it isn't."

"How could you give up just like that!?" Giselle shouted.

"I'm not giving up," he said, approaching her. "But we need to accept how things are."

Giselle wept against the wall with Sebastian trying to comfort her. Citlali disappeared, deciding to give them privacy. She reappeared in front of Ishmael, who was in a private booth overlooking the dance floor. Ishmael stood at the one-way window alone watching the peacekeepers.

"What is it, Citlali?" Ishmael said.

"It's about Giselle and Sebastian," Citlali said. "They had a flashback of their son."

"Did they think I was their son?" Ishmael asked, standing still and grabbing firm of the threads on his serape scarf.

"Yes."

"And you told them I wasn't? Right?"

"Yeah. Giselle didn't take that particularly well. Don't you think maybe we should tell them the truth?" Citlali paused. "I'm pretty sure they would want to know that you're their grandson."

"I'll let them know eventually. Right now, my mind is focused on someone else."

"Who are you staring at?" Citlali approached Ishmael's side and stared down at the peacekeepers below.

"Take a look down there. Do you see what I see? There's a peacekeeper down there who is actually a warkeeper."

CHAPTER 16 – GALA PART 3: SOCIOECONOMIC TRANSGRESSIONS

The gala was in full swing as everyone danced, drank, and told stories. While in the private booth, Ishmael remained calm at the sight of the Orderkeeper below. The weary man with cocoa skin and Inca eyes blended in and casually walked through the peacekeepers while holding a glass of tequila.

"Why is he here?" Ishmael asked. "More importantly how did he get here without us noticing?"

"Do you want me to find out?" Citlali asked.

"Yes, but don't get too hasty. The fact that this agent is walking about without anyone noticing him shows he has a lot of skill. I want to find out all I can from him."

The mysterious man made his way off the dance floor and into the hallway. Using reanimation technology, Citlali made floating specks of cameras that watched him from all angles. He walked into a secluded lounge and sat down at the empty bar. He held out his hands as another glass of tequila appeared in his empty hand.

"Would you like a drink?" the man asked. "Can an A.I. even enjoy the benefits of alcohol?"

Citlali approached with caution. Although she knew she couldn't be harmed, she didn't want to endanger the peacekeepers nearby. She grabbed hold of the glass and held it in front of her chest, not drinking it.

"You're not a peacekeeper," Citlali asked. "Who are you?"

"I'm a warkeeper. Former warkeeper. Believe it or not, my name's Angel. Twisted, given the fact that I was trained to hurt people. Feel free to pronounce it the Spanish or English way."

"What are you doing here, Angel?"

"Would it be hard to imagine I changed my whole outlook on life and decided to be good?"

"Yes, it would be. War agents are hardwired to do nothing but destroy whoever they're told their enemies are."

"As far as your people know, this is true. But don't you think it's possible for someone to change?"

"I've never seen it happen."

"Just because you haven't seen it happen doesn't mean it isn't possible. You're trapped in the peacekeeper hemisphere like all those living here, Citlali. How do you know what it's like living on the other side of the border? I've seen warkeepers have a change of heart from time to time, but they don't ever get to see another day once they convince themselves they want to escape to the north. I'm sure you know warkeepers are closely monitored by our own artificial intelligence."

"Yes, I know of this malevolent artificial intelligence. If it is true Orderkeepers have changed in the past, then how come they didn't make it out of Orderkeeper territory like you did?"

"I simply learned from their mistakes. I blocked out sudden thoughts of deserting to avoid triggering any alarms from the A.I. After years of quiet planning, I perfected my escape strategy. On the day I had my opportunity to escape, I used my hacking skills to hack into my own mind and deprogram any malicious mindware that would cause me to die if I went into peacekeeper territory without authorization. I can show you how I did it."

"How are we supposed to trust you?" Citlali asked, keeping a straight face. Angel took a mouthful of his tequila, shook his head, and turned to her.

"I have intel on the warkeepers. And a lot of it. I can help the peacekeepers, if only given the chance."

"Okay, Angel," said Ishmael, who had entered the lounge escorted by several military guards. "We'll give you the chance to help us."

A confused Citlali looked from Ishmael to Angel. Angel held his glass in the air in a sort of weak toast and waited patiently for her to do the same. Citlali clinked her glass against his and they drank.

"I promise you, I won't let you down," Angel replied hollowly as he picked up his glass for another sip. "Because of how tired I am from my recent escape, it may not seem like I'm grateful, but I am."

"For now, you will be escorted back to an institution where you will go through tests to gain our trust," Ishmael said, nodding at his security detail. Reanimation crystals restrained a tired Angel's wrists as the guards escorted him away.

"Are you sure about this?" Citlali whispered. "Since when has a warkeeper been known to change? And did you take a good look at him? He looks like he's been through hell. He is clearly in no shape to help us."

"He has been through hell. Living on the other side is horrifying, even for warkeepers. Let's see what kind of intelligence he has to offer. It might turn the tide. And with recent events, we could use all the help we can get. Now we must update everyone on what's changed. Let's conclude tonight's event."

The peacekeepers assembled in the war room around the holographic screens. Many of the new peacekeepers were impressed by the one-story wall with quantities of data zipping all over it. On the other side of the room, Ishmael and Citlali took their place on the balcony.

"I'm sure everyone has had an exciting time today," Ishmael said, receiving smiles and laughs in return. "But now it is time to go back to our mission. Life of a peacekeeper, huh?" He was greeted again, this time with humorous approval. "Now, I'm going to have all of you go into the peacekeeper virtual information program via your contact lenses." For the peacekeepers, everything went dark. "I will be debriefing everyone on our next step in our peacekeeper initiative. As many of you know, we are dedicated to ending the Orderkeepers' terror, but what none of you know—until now—is that we have another problem. We have another front to deal with. The two individuals you are looking at are examples of what humans can become. They are what we call socioeconomic criminals.

"Now you are not from this period. You are all immigrants of time and a border of time has been raised separating you all from your original home era. In your past lives, there were thousands of people like this who forced regions of innocents to live without food, water, shelter, peace or prosperity. A relatively small portion of the population controlled most, if not all, the planet's wealth. They turned the system of socioeconomic forces against humanity and nearly ran this world into ruin. Thankfully, the people of the world had enough and took power away from them. Although we were able to put on trial some of these socioeconomic criminals, there still remain many who have escaped trial and are living their lives to this day without answering to their crimes against humanity."

They saw information on two socioeconomic criminals, and everyone was shocked when they found out the current president of the United States of North America was one of them. The other documented criminal was the dictator of the Orderkeeper states of Central and South America.

"They have once again sought refuge in positions of power and are harming others by working with the Orderkeepers. Now, before me, I see you all. You are people from that time who were affected by them. I know you will put these criminals in your own trial and carry out the justice that has been delayed far too long. I wish I could say we can simply bring them in, but because of how powerful and well protected they are, we cannot do that. As you can see, they have climbed through the ranks of society using new identities to avoid being flagged by U-ITS. Even with Citlali, it has taken a lot of hacking effort to get this information. Our method of getting this information will be deemed by the Department of Ethics as evidence that cannot be used in the high courts. Also, in the process of penetrating such deep levels of security, we did trigger some alarms on the enemies' deep-web corner, which means they may already know we have this information."

Gasps and chattering filled the room, but only briefly before Citlali hushed everyone.

"It will take the covert work of our peacekeepers to end the reign of socioeconomic criminals and Orderkeepers once and for all," Ishmael continued. "Do not be troubled. This is a task we can handle. Soon you will all be given your new missions to tackle these individuals. Good luck to you all."

Once their virtual reality session ended, the chattering resumed.

"Tomorrow starts a busy phase in our efforts, so get a good night's sleep," Citlali said. "The aerial vehicles by the balcony will take you back to your respective institutions."

Sebastian grabbed hold of Giselle's hand, noticing she was still overwhelmed by her earlier memory incursion. She was looking at Ishmael and studying his facial features until he walked away. They walked with Rosa and Ryan to the balcony and said their goodbyes to the peacekeepers they had met. The newly initiated peacekeepers remained quiet the entire way back.

***

"Pay close attention to what I have to say!" Drill Sergeant Taylor yelled out. The peacekeepers were up at the crack of dawn, sweating from their morning physical training in the courtyard. "Yesterday, you were updated on the situation with the socioeconomic criminals. I am disgusted they are still around, and by the looks of it, so are all of you." He pointed at the mud-covered faces and uniforms. "I know the training you received here will prove its worth today on the field. I'll see you all soon. Dismissed!"

Each group followed a set of arrows that led them in separate directions across the institution. Sebastian, Ryan, and Rosa rushed down the arrowed path to a quiet studio.

"Welcome," Citlali said. "As of now, you three will be focused on domestic issues involving the socioeconomic criminals that were discussed at the gala. Chief Vanessa has given us intel about a secret meeting between a U.S.N.A. government official and an Orderkeeper. Don't worry, we also work closely with high-ranking law enforcement officials. People like Chief Vanessa can be trusted to know about our covert operations. You will infiltrate an area where Kliment, the president's aide, will be. Once inside the secured location, you will need to make your way to Kliment. This aide is aware of the past crimes the president has committed. We will use him to assassinate the president. We also need to find out what he knows before we program his mind to perform the assassination. You'll be using the Mastermind Stratagem to absorb any information. Here, Rosa. This bandanna can be converted into a Mastermind Stratagem."

"What kind of information are we looking for?" Sebastian asked as Citlali tied a blue bandanna around Rosa's neck.

"We need the identities of the remaining socioeconomic criminals," Citlali said. "We've only identified two, but we believe there are more out there thanks to our collective international artificial intelligence reports."

"Collective international artificial intelligence reports?" Rosa asked.

"As I am the central artificial intelligence managing the Universal Information Technology System here in the United States of North America, there are other unique artificial intelligences across the globe managing their region's U-ITS," Citlali said. "Those of us in peacekeeper territory work together to find patterns on individuals who raise red flags."

"Sounds like an espionage program," Sebastian said.

"It basically is," Citlali said, holding out a silver cube. "Once you use the Mastermind Stratagem, place this cube on the back of his head. It will dissolve into his head, rewiring his next move to be to kill the president. Careful with it and don't touch it with your skin! Use gloves to hold it. Here I'll put it in a plastic cube for you. Also, you can only carry this small block of reanimation crystal. For now, I'll turn it into a card and attach it to this necklace." She pulled out a brown necklace with the reanimation block melted into a clear container attached to it with the metallic cube tied next to it acting as pendants. Rosa took hold of it and placed it around her neck. "We don't want anyone to suspect you're there on peacekeeper business. Now, off you three go into the city."

Soon the three were back in the bustling metropolis following the arrows leading them into a philosophical sect deep in the alleys of the city. This area was a cauldron of new religions that, although they did not align with one another, were more than able to peacefully practice their ideologies steps apart. Passing an arch of flowers, the three were literally thrown into the air by nothing but music. As they fell back down, they were caught by hooded men and women. Their skins and eyes had various combinations of colors and tattoos, and they danced along with their harmonic humming. The newly arrived individuals were cradled in their arms. Citlali appeared in front of the peacekeepers, unbeknownst to the religious cult.

"Don't look at me," Citlali said. "Only you three can see me through your contact lenses. They can't know I'm here working with you guys. Don't say anything; go along with what they're doing and follow the rest of my instructions." The three peacekeepers uncomfortably went along with the ceremony. "This religious cult is a front for criminals. The religious participants unknowingly work for the socioeconomic criminals who use their little-known religion to hide their meetups with other criminals. Right now, this group thinks you three want to join their religious organization.

Once you get through their introductory ceremony, they'll teach you their philosophy and practices. Go with it, and you'll soon be inside their chapel."

The trio was carried through another arch of flowers that turned into a waterfall after they passed through it. Looking back, they saw the entire area had become a glass dome, with a newly formed waterfall splashing from above and blurring the scene from outside.

"The waterfall is meant to maintain privacy. Not even Citlali can see what happens inside here," one man said, winking. Three orange cloths were tied over their foreheads with soft gold ribbons. "All potential members wear orange cloths."

The chapel was filled with other religious followers and newcomers with the same orange cloths tied around their heads. The trio was led to the front with the newcomers.

"Please give a warm round of applause for this amazing group of individuals," a man said, standing from behind a podium on the stage. "All of you are about to embark on an incredible journey. I know many of you are here because you have lost a sense of meaning in life. Here we can offer to help you with that. You already know the goal of our philosophy is to live life to the fullest, but how we do it is not so common. We go in depth into the various religions and philosophies that have helped many others. We applaud you for taking the first step to delving into this open-minded way of thinking!" The chambers echoed with energy. A row of robed individuals lined up in front of the newly committed members. "Please follow those in front of you, and they will lead you through the catacombs to your first sermon."

"This is our chance," Ryan whispered. After being led through the catacombs, they snuck out of the group and quietly ducked into a corner and out of sight.

"Since we do not have access to Citlali down here, we will need to be creative in finding our target," whispered Rosa, for fear of her voice echoing. Everyone used a little of the reanimation block to convert into anti-detection transponders and scanners to map out the catacombs. The distant chatter of the group they'd slid away from was now beginning to fade. Rosa used a tiny bit of reanimation technology to manually configure a sonar detector. "Using this, we can detect vibrations from throughout the catacombs. We will use it to find any vocal activity, and once we do, that's where we will head."

The sonar detected sound in the far distance, leading the trio toward a private praying session deep in the catacombs. There was no sign of the president's aide, so they moved on to the next sound the sonar found. It was security guards looking for the trio. They must have caught on that the three had ditched the group. The three turned back and hid.

"I'm surprised it took them this long to start looking for us," Sebastian smiled. They activated the sonar again, but this time it detected many different noises in all directions. "Looks like many search parties are looking for us now. All the new noise is coming from the security. Calibrate the sonar to ignore all the noise that has suddenly popped up."

Rosa narrowed down the search to a few locations. While avoiding the security, they made it to their next destination. It was a well that led into darkness. With no more reanimation crystal left, they were forced to convert their transponders into rock-climbing gloves.

"Hey guys," Rosa said, shakily looking at her sonar detector after climbing down the well. "All the sounds in the catacombs are getting closer."

"Let's move," Sebastian ordered as he scaled down the well. His contact lenses adjusted his sight to the darkness as they turned their gloves into anti-detection transponders once again. The sound they followed began pacing away from them. "We have to hurry if we're going to catch this guy."

After a series of small hills going up and down and in zigzagging turns, they spotted the president's aide. He was alone. Sebastian charged the man, grabbing the last bit of reanimation crystal from Rosa and converting it into a taser. A jolt pierced the man's body, shaking him violently. The aide was knocked out and fell to the ground.

"We need to get him away from here so we can finish the mission," Sebastian said, turning his electric weapon into a floating stretcher. "Once we find a suitable place to hide, we'll wait for the search squad to pass us. When we're in the clear, we'll interrogate him."

Using sonar, they made their way through a marathon of endless obstacles to a secret wall leading into an empty tomb. They perched the president's aide inside an opened coffin under a bright chandelier. They converted the stretcher back into reanimation crystals. They remained quiet, as to not be overheard by the passing guards. When their sonar stopped sensing movement within its detection area, they knew security had gone to another area to search for them. Under the center of the room, Rosa took off her bandanna. It reanimated into the Mastermind Stratagem helmet. She placed the headgear onto the unconscious man as lights on it blinked red.

"Should only take a minute," Rosa said. "That jolt of electricity should have wiped out the last few seconds of consciousness. We don't want him remembering your faces." When the Mastermind Stratagem blinked green, she took it off him. After turning Kliment over to his side, she pulled the metallic cube from her necklace with gloved hands and carefully placed it against the back of his neck. The cube melted into his skin. "We can go now."

"What about the warkeepers he was going to meet?" Ryan asked. "Do you think they're looking for Kliment right now?"

"Probably," Rosa said. "Once he wakes up, he should head straight back to his job as aide."

Their sonar searched for sounds of water to find their nearest exit. They followed it to a slurry wall. Their sonar detector and transponders turned into suits that allowed them to walk through cement using technology Alice described in her team's first mission. Their suits would grab dirt from in front and glide it behind the wearer, temporarily clearing a path. Like ghosts, their suits pushed them through the slurry wall, leaving behind a mist of stone dust. They found themselves slowly sinking in an ocean. Their suits automatically turned into scuba gear and three propellers appeared. They held onto each propeller and made their way upward. Once above the water, they were able to utilize communication with Citlali again. They immediately requested a hover car and made their way over the city and back to the institution to report their success.

CHAPTER 17 – THE CELESTIAL WEAPONS CHEST

A panicked Charles and Citlali congratulated the trio on a successful mission, but upon analyzing the Mastermind Stratagem findings, gave them a new task. The two rushed the operatives into a nearby hover car that sped over the forest and into a hangar filled with nothing but empty warplanes. The hangar doors closed behind them as the hover car incinerated into reanimation crystals, dropping the five onto the dark, marble floor.

"Well, you three have had quite a day," Citlali started. "Let me just brief you on what the Mastermind Stratagem has revealed about Kliment's knowledge. It appears that the Orderkeepers are beginning to find out about our covert peacekeeper program. We also learned that all Orderkeeper leaders are socioeconomic criminals. Good job.

"But your day isn't over just yet. We have a new objective for you to complete. Our military is already in battle with the Orderkeepers over what we are calling the Celestial Weapons Chest. This chest contains state-of-the-art technology that has been newly developed by an unknown entity. It contains mainly combative and reconnaissance gadgets, which is why we need it brought back before it enters enemy territory. These weapons are beyond military grade because they are powerful and outside of our capacity to create. We also don't know their origin. Therefore, they are classified as celestial grade weapons! Our military will soon have to stop its pursuit of the chest, since they are reaching the end of our ocean boundary limits. The enemy is out in the Gulf of Mexico, but they will soon make their way into Central American territorial waters. It looks like our military will fail to safely capture the chest, but our covert peacekeepers can still chase them in secret. As of now, the Orderkeepers are still in neutral international waters. At the end of this conversation, you three will air dive from this airfield, and with the help of these reanimation bags, you will retrieve that chest."

"We're in an airfield right now?" Sebastian asked, as clusters of reanimation crystals clamped onto their backs and molded into thin backpacks. "I thought we were still near the institution."

"The second the hangar doors closed, it silently took off and began its route to our destination," Citlali explained. "Time is of the essence, and you need every second you can get to complete this mission. Your satellite bracelets will lead you to the battle. Try to be stealthy, but given the circumstances of the situation, that may be difficult. We can't let the Orderkeeper leaders or public know what we are doing, otherwise this program will be in jeopardy. Good luck! End of conversation!"

The dark, gloomy floor below them slowly incinerated, leaving the endless blue-and-white abyss to swallow the peacekeepers one by one.

The bags expanded from their backs into planes that encased them before diving into the water. They rapidly took off, following the red dots on their satellite bracelets. Their thoughts raced faster than the aquatic life zipping by them. Their faces became covered with black-and-forest-green camouflage paint. Their clothes changed into red-and-black Orderkeeper outfits, and riot masks concealed all but their eyes. They passed beneath the debris and damaged Navy and Air Force vessels that were forced to stop pursuing due to international boundaries. Not far from them was a sinking Orderkeeper airbase that must have come into violent contact with the peacekeeper military.

"With our disguises on, we are going to fly our planes next to their fleeing aircraft," Sebastian said.

"We have enemy underwater militants and bases scattered across this area," Rosa said through the radio. "We will be seen as Orderkeepers to them, but they'll know we're not them once we try to take the chest."

"The chest is located at the center of their aircraft," Ryan said, looking at the blueprints of the enemy airship. The covert peacekeepers were now in view of their lone target aircraft. The three ascended from the waters and into the air. The aircraft headed in the direction of Orderkeeper territory. It made an abrupt sharp U-turn, moving away from its original destination and came dashing toward the trio.

"What is going on in there?" Rosa asked. The three guided their planes out of the path of the bulky airship.

"Is everyone ready?" Sebastian said. "We need to fly next to the aircraft!"

"Ready," Ryan and Rosa responded. They turned around and glided next to the airship, slowing down their speed to access the situation. To their surprise, they spotted familiar faces on the side deck of the massive aircraft. Despite their black-and-green face paint and semi-covering face masks, they recognized Ramon and Arthur. The two were fighting Orderkeepers, trying to stop them from reaching the ship's bridge, where Giselle with her disguise was manning the turn wheel.

"They're hijacking the ship!" Sebastian shouted. "Follow closely!"

They moved closer to the bridge, hoping the peacekeepers on the ship would see them. They got up from their seats and stood on the wings of their planes, making their swift jump onto the enemy airship as their abandoned planes reanimated into a stream of crystals onto their backs. They rolled behind a startled Ramon and Arthur, who thought the trio were enemies. The Orderkeepers they were fighting also hid behind the same uniforms and masks as the newly joined trio.

"It's us," Sebastian said, holding up his hands hoping his voice was still audible and familiar to them through the mask.

"What took you guys so long?" Arthur shouted, instantly taking reanimation crystals from Sebastian's bag and creating a whip to push back one of the Orderkeepers.

"What do you mean?" Sebastian asked, turning part of his reanimation bag into a levitating orb and throwing it at another foe, who was pushed into several more foes and eventually the water. One of the Orderkeepers who fell off grabbed hold of the side of the ship and used his red reanimation technology as a lasso to latch onto Ramon's arm. Using Ramon as support, the Orderkeeper began scaling the airship.

"You're our reinforcements, are you not?" Arthur asked, slicing the lasso off Ramon with his whip. Using jetpacks, a few enemies flew from below to the deck of the ship. "They don't give up!"

"No, we were sent here to retrieve the chest," Rosa insisted.

"The chest?" Arthur repeated. "You were sent here to get a chest but not help extract us?"

"You mean you're *not* trying to retrieve the chest?!" Rosa asked.

"What chest!?" Arthur repeated. "We need to get back to peacekeeper territory. We took this ship because we were stranded in warkeeper land after our mission was completed. We barely have any reanimation technology left to bring us back home. Most of it was destroyed by their insane artificial intelligence. We can't use their reanimation technology because it isn't programmed to work for us. Those red reanimation crystals can only be used by warkeepers. But we managed to escape into the ocean with what little reanimation technology wasn't corrupted by that insane A.I. Are there enough crystals to make planes for the six of us?"

"No, but anyway, we need to get the chest first!" Sebastian shouted. "Whose plan was this?"

"Your girlfriend!" Arthur said, nodding toward the bridge she was in. "We're holding off these warkeepers until we are in peacekeeper waters, then the military can bring us back north."

Sebastian made his way through the trembling ship and onto the bridge. "Incredible," Sebastian said, walking to Giselle. "You thought about this?"

"Not now, Sebastian," she said, concentrated on the path and several screens. "Can't you see we're busy?"

Sebastian went back outside to join the fight. Giselle's view became clogged with birds swooping down from above and onto the front of the ship. Fish from below managed to damage the ship's engines, causing the ship to rotate in various angles and gradually slip in altitude.

"I can't keep this ship steady," Giselle shouted at the peacekeepers. "Hold on to the floor! The ship's about to rotate!"

As the ship turned, the birds in front of Giselle's view flew off. The peacekeepers used their reanimation bags to create magnetic boots and gloves. Arthur and Sebastian were not quick enough to grab hold of the floor with their magnetic boots as the ship turned upside down. They were forced to use their magnetic gloves to hang on to the floor with their hands, with the floor now becoming the ceiling and their feet dangling in the air. The Orderkeepers were able to create guns and stay grounded on the floor with their magnetic boots. They aimed them at the peacekeepers, but before they were able to shoot, Arthur and Sebastian kicked the guns out of their hands and began kicking their heads. Ramon, Ryan and Rosa, who still had their feet flat against the floor, began punching and interlocking arms with the remaining Orderkeepers. Sea creatures continued to pummel the airship, except this time the peacekeepers were in direct range of the ocean. Whale sharks aimed closely at the peacekeepers and brought down wrecked debris from the airship with every strike. Arthur and Sebastian continued to hang by their gloves and kick at the enemy soldiers until the ship began turning again. As soon as the ship was facing the right side up, the two were motivated to do a backflip to be on their feet again. It wasn't long before the ship made a ninety-degree turn and forced everyone to use their magnetic gear to cling to the side of the ship. The Orderkeepers persisted and began shooting at the peacekeepers. Ramon tried using the reanimation technology to block every bullet like the other peacekeepers were doing, but because he was closest to their opponents, his legs and arms were pierced by several bullets. Once again, the ship turned right side up. Ryan used this chance to bring Ramon into the bridge. The ship continued its gradual descent into the waters, now coming close to skimming the water.

"We're almost there!" Giselle yelled. "Hold on, Ramon!"

"We need to get out of here," Arthur said.

"We can't leave yet," Sebastian argued. "We still have to retrieve the chest!"

"What chest!?" Arthur asked, clenching his teeth.

"It's our mission to retrieve the Celestial Weapons Chest," Sebastian explained. "It contains powerful weapons that will help us win the war against the warkeepers. It's at the center of this ship. Will you or will you not help us take it?"

"Fine," Arthur said reluctantly. "What's the plan, boss?"

Sebastian turned his reanimation technology into ground-moving gloves, like the suit he had used with the slurry wall in the previous mission. He clawed away at the floor as smokey dust drifted from the top of the gloves. A hole expanded until it was big enough for the two to jump in. "We're going through these walls and fighting our way through it."

The now ninety-degree-turned ship forced Sebastian to jump toward the next level of the ship and hang on it with his magnetic boots while scraping away another hole into the next floor. Enemy soldiers stood at the end of the hallway, shooting at Sebastian. Arthur covered him with bits of reanimation shields generating around his body as the bullets tried to hit him. He reanimated a gun and shot at their clinging feet, turning parts of the red glue keeping them steady into dust. The bullets stopped when the ship was upside down again, throwing the soldiers against the ceiling and knocking them out. Sebastian finished making the hole and moved toward the next floor. He looked once more at his satellite bracelet to see they were at the center of the ship and close to the chest. Sebastian pulled himself up through the hole and jumped, grabbing hold of the next floor with his magnetic gloves. He pulled away at the remaining steel to make another hole. More Orderkeepers walked toward him shooting, only for their bullets to be repelled by Arthur's reanimation defenses. The ship then unexpectedly leaned forward. One of the soldiers lost consciousness when debris from the assaulted ship slammed him to the bottom. The other soldier used the momentum to dive toward Sebastian and grab hold of his waist. Arthur issued several kicks to the man's face, but it did no good, so he formed a baton and swung it at his neck, striking a nerve and forcing his foe to join his fallen comrade at the bottom of the ship. The final piece of metal withered away. A blue-and-gold chest illuminated the dim room. It could easily be carried with one arm.

"Get it and let's go!" Arthur ordered.

With the chest floating near them under the support of floating crystals, they jumped through holes to make their way to the bridge.

"We got it," Sebastian said, standing up from the first hole he'd made. The ship was now right side up again. Sebastian, Arthur, Giselle and Ramon were holed up on the bridge, with Orderkeepers trying to break their way inside. Rosa and Ryan were nowhere to be seen.

"Good, now hand it over," a man in a dark trench coat said over an intercom from outside the glass windows of the bridge, with several Orderkeepers standing silently behind him.

"Don't do it, Sebastian!" Rosa yelled from outside. Several soldiers had her and Ryan restrained. "We're almost there!"

"Do you want them to die?" the man said.

He raised his charcoal-banded arm at Arthur. Arthur fell to his knees and began coughing up tar. Giselle wanted to help him but did not want to move from her command of the ship's controls. Ramon wanted to help Arthur but was too badly injured to even move. Sebastian was stunned but did not show it. He remained still.

"I don't go by a number name like so many other Orderkeepers do. My reputation has earned me the name Viper. Do you know what I can do to you? Especially with this celestial weapon. Now hand over the chest,"

Viper said chillingly as he glanced with admiration at his charcoal band. He waited another moment, but Sebastian didn't budge. "Very well, then."

Sebastian, too, fell to the ground and started coughing up tar. He dropped the chest onto the floor, causing the lock to click open. Beams of light came out of the chest, flying through the window panes and into the sky in numerous directions beyond the sea's horizon as the chest evaporated.

"Look what you've done!" Viper said again in his chilling voice.

A chain of military sea and aircraft lined up across the sea as they approached. They were entering peacekeeper waters. Now able to use reanimation technology, Ramon and Giselle pushed the enemy soldiers off the deck. Viper and his Orderkeepers took off in the nearby red planes, but Arthur and Sebastian remained on the floor in coughing fits. The ship could no longer hold itself in the air and crashed into the waters, causing a story-high splash. Giselle ran to Sebastian to see if she could help him breathe. Splashes of water rained on everyone as they waited on the sinking aircraft for the approaching military ships.

CHAPTER 18 – HOME OF ALL

The following week, clusters of peacekeepers were gathered in the war room below the institution. Although the friends of Giselle and Sebastian were concerned about the two, they knew they shouldn't push the couple to reveal anything they didn't want to. Although none of them had left behind a kid in their past life, they knew it must have been difficult to live with and dared not bring it up unless the two were ready to talk about it … if they ever would be. They looked up from their seats at Charles as he rushed to take his place at the podium. The room was smaller than the one at the California Peacekeeper Headquarters, but it still had enough room to hold everyone who trained at the institution.

"Listen everyone!" Charles said, gesturing with his hands for everyone to settle down. The mutters about all of the enemy hostile activity died out until only Charles's heavy breathing echoed in the room. "I know how unusually busy our week has been. We have done incredibly well here in our North American region in fending off the war nations in the south. Unfortunately, not all peacekeeper regions have been as successful as us. It appears Orderkeepers have launched a campaign on our bases and outposts across the globe. We are not in possession of the Celestial Weapons Chest but neither are the Orderkeepers. The weapons are scattered across the globe, but we will soon be out looking for them. As you all know, thanks to Rosa, Ryan and Sebastian, we have been able to get additional information on the other socioeconomic criminals."

A round of applause commenced as the smiling three received approving pats on their backs.

"Like we have developed a plan with phases that involve repelling Orderkeepers, scouting their territory and liberating people, it appears the Orderkeepers have entered a new phase of their own," Citlali stated. "There is no need for alarm though: I have gone through trillions of scenarios. We will recover the items from the Celestial Weapons Chest and begin taking out their most elite Orderkeepers, such as Viper. All is unusually quiet at the border, but we will continue to send a few of you on whatever missions come up."

Citlali took a breath and smiled.

"Now, it is also that time of year again," she continued, followed by gasps and bits of excitement from the crowd. "It's time for our regional gladiatorial tournament, and this time it will be held in the Mexicali Peacekeeper establishment. For those of you who don't know, this is a friendly but fierce competition where all the peacekeepers from the North American institutions show off their skills. With contests ranging from stealth to melee, you'll be able to show you have what it takes to go on future high-level missions. At the end of the competition, military commanders and I will assess the victorious gladiators and decide what missions they'll get to go on. If you want that prestige, fight like hell in these contests. If you don't, feel free to watch from the sidelines." Light chuckles broke off for a moment. It was clear everyone wanted to show off their competitive side. "As you all know, this is a chance for all of you at this institution to work together and learn from other peacekeepers. You will have until the end of the month to prepare for these events. Good luck!"

There were excited slams and roars as energy soared throughout the room. The new members of the institution didn't know what to expect from the games but were still excited. Later that night, the trio talked in Sebastian's plain white room, the roaring of their fellow peacekeepers still ringing in their ears. The excitement was contagious and had now infected the three. Ryan leaned on the wall overlooking his two teammates sitting on the bed.

"I can't wait," Sebastian said, smiling widely. "We'll be able to see Jaylyn and Patricio again."

"I'm sure Paula can't wait to see Patricio again," Rosa smiled, raising her eyebrows. "Jaylyn and Patricio are fun people. I can't wait to see them again, too."

"I can't get this competitive feeling out of my system," Ryan said. "I wonder what kind of challenges they'll have."

"I'm sure some of the older peacekeepers here will tell us," Sebastian said. "That makes me wonder, though. Why haven't we tried making more friends *here*?"

"Speak for yourself," Rosa teased, throwing a pillow at him. "I've been meeting people at the simulation library. We should be going to sleep, though. I'm not tired, but I think I might take one of those sleep patches."

"I can't sleep either," Sebastian said. "I actually want to go to the gymnasium and practice with the others."

"We can do that in the morning," Rosa said. "I'm sure those guys will be up there all month punching bags."

"They'll be fine. Probably get some sleep the day before the tournament," Ryan joked as Giselle and Alice walked in. The two looked around at the walls in confusion and then in suppressed laughter.

"I knew I should have come in here earlier," Alice said. "Not even Jaime's room is this plain. What did I tell you, Sebastian? Don't be boring like Jaime! I would wave my arms around and redesign this little room, but only you three can do that since it's your space."

"You know, I never thought about it," Sebastian said, looking around at the dull setting.

"It's okay, Sebby," Giselle said, sitting on Sebastian's lap and patting him on his head as if he were a baby. "We'll fix this."

"Sebby!?" Everyone exclaimed at the nickname as Giselle winked at the room of guests.

"You can use the space going into the forest to expand the room into a sort of tower or even a backyard with a slide or firefighter pole going down!" Alice suggested excitedly.

"Firefighter pole?" Ryan and Rosa asked in unison.

"Why not? Others have them. But you three should have more than this," Alice said, looking around. "If you combine Ryan and Rosa's adjacent rooms, you'll have luxurious quarters. And since there is no floor above, you can expand upward as well. Unless this is what you all want. Nothing wrong with living in a simple room, but with you three risking your lives out there, don't you think you deserve a more fitting dorm?"

"No one told us we could do that," Rosa sighed. "Okay, let's do it!"

"All right," Ryan said, putting his fingers together and cracking them as he pulled them away. "Three floors. This will be the second floor, but more like the lounge and living room."

He clapped his hands together and the wall with the window and the adjacent walls disappeared, revealing the two neighboring rooms and outside.

"Facing where our dorm windows were, we'll have stairs on the left and right sides curving up to meet on the third floor," Rosa added. "The third floor will have our rooms. Between the stairs we will have a few steps of stairs going from the second floor into the first floor."

"The first floor will have a bar, pool table, and holographic televisions," Sebastian chimed in. "Behind the bar will be countless colorful bottles of who knows what. On the other side of that room will be a long trophy set of treasures and relics from around our planet."

"And neon lights with glowing flowers," Rosa added.

As they said this their rooms were no longer boring, white barracks but a dormitory of their greatest fantasy. The first-floor living room was filled with red-cushioned sofas and pillows, long silver mirrors and empty art frames.

"Is it all right if I invite Paula and Jaime to your new apartment?" Alice asked as she and Rosa began throwing pillows at each other. The hosts happily agreed, wanting to show off their new place to others.

"Can I invite Arthur and Ramon? Arthur especially could use more uplifting memories right about now," Giselle asked, whispering the last part to Sebastian. "Oh, and let's invite Ezekiel, Abigail and Gabriel!"

They consented as he took her to one of the empty frames. Sebastian looked down at Giselle's blank expression. Sebastian snapped his fingers. The frame was now filled with a brightly colored Mexican folk painting with happy men and women dancing in traditional garments. Giselle became overjoyed with his appreciation of their culture.

"Nice place you have here!" Ramon shouted, holding the wooden door open for Paula, Jaime and Arthur. It wasn't long before another group had joined the get together.

"Oh snap! This is your place?!" Ezekiel shouted, his eyes moving from the chandelier at the lobby's center to the artwork on the walls to the sides. Abigail and Gabriel followed, shadowed by his tall stature. They all shook hands with their hosts and other guests.

"So, what will we be having?" Ryan asked, walking down the stairs and behind the bar, followed by everyone else.

"Oh, so you're a bartender now?" Giselle questioned excitedly.

"Bartending was a hobby of mine in my past life, so yes," Ryan said. "I've also been learning some moves in my free time."

"I'm already impressed," Rosa said with a wink.

"Any special requests?" Ryan asked.

"Surprise us," the girls said in unison. As if he had been preparing for this moment his entire life, he swiped his hand in the air and out came twelve empty glasses. He began slicing up mangoes, strawberries, pineapples, apples and kiwis as they appeared out of thin air. He crushed ice and placed it in the glasses. Simultaneously, the fruits spread across the glasses. He moved bottles of vodka, tequila and other liquors over the table, not spilling any of it anywhere but in the glasses. Soon their drinks were filled to the top, and they had a rich assortment of colorful beverages in front of them.

"What should we toast to?" Arthur asked, stopping everyone from taking their first sips.

"To good health!" Paula suggested as everybody clanked glasses. "To us and to the struggle to free our fellow Central, Caribbean and South American brothers and sisters to the south! To the liberation of all people! To all those showing kindness despite their circumstances. And to all those just trying to live a better life!"

"To the United States of North America!" everyone cheered.

"To our beloved beautiful world and all its beloved beautiful people! To the beloved beautiful animals, plants and to all that life has to offer!" Arthur yelled. Giselle smiled, intertwining her arms with Sebastian while Rosa and Ryan did the same.

"¡Salud!" everyone cheered. They drank as if they were in a desert. The sweetness had powerfully overcome the flavor of alcohol.

Everyone but Giselle demanded more. She sloppily grabbed hold of Sebastian's arm and stood up from her barstool.

"Too strong?" Ryan laughed.

"You nine or ten … I can't tell … keep enjoying your drinks," Giselle said playfully winking. "Sebastian and I are going to explore the third floor."

"Explore?" Alice asked. "Tell us what it's like when you're done *exploring*."

Giselle wasn't drunk from the drink alone but also from the excitement of their missions and the announcement about the upcoming tournament. These were certainly factoring in her sudden youthful playfulness. They stumbled onto the first step up to the third floor. Sebastian sat against the stairs as Giselle sat on the step below him. She rubbed her head against his chest and looked up into his eyes. "I still have to thank you for saving us on that airship."

"You can thank me upstairs," he said, winking. He stood up, keeping a gentle hold on her hand as he led her upstairs. Their footsteps echoed down the hall of rooms on the third floor and stopped after a stiff wooden door closed. The ten remaining friends continued their small party with drinks. The first peacekeepers told stories about past tournaments, and Alice gave an oration of impressive things technology could do nowadays. They caught up on past soccer games that filled the holographic screens around them. Games played of their favorite national teams winning the World Cup. Their tales of current lives and past eventually led them to ruminate about how most of Central and South America was under authoritarian influence. They did not let it bother them, instead reminding themselves that the day of liberating their ancestral continent would soon come, and they were part of making that day come sooner. The group left the bar long after Giselle and Sebastian were asleep. They moved to the new bedrooms with Rosa sharing her room with Ryan and some of the remaining guests claiming rooms or sofas on each of the floors.

***

"You two look like you had a good night's sleep," a man said to Giselle and Sebastian as they entered the industrial gym. The couple smiled at the memory.

"They sure did," Alice said behind them. "I don't think we've met."

"My name is Angel," he said. "I'm a new staff member here, but I must disclose that I have experience working in warkeeper territory ... as a warkeeper."

"Yes, it is true," Citlali said, appearing next to Angel as everyone else froze. "He is a former Orderkeeper, but he has proven himself trustworthy."

"A warkeeper!?" Alice asked, confused. Her voice echoed throughout the complex as everyone turned their heads to the scene. She wasn't the only person startled. Rosa and Ryan overheard what Angel said and had come over.

"We can trust him," Citlali explained.

"I know what it looks like," Angel interjected. "But like the peacekeepers, I also want what's best for all people. Please accept my help."

An uncomfortable atmosphere opened as other peacekeepers watched silently in the gymnasium. Ezekiel, Abigail and Gabriel, the remaining peacekeepers, gave worried looks to last night's hosts.

"If you can trust me, you can trust him," Citlali said loud enough for everyone to hear. The spectators went back to their drills, exercises and sparring with a hint of uneasiness. "Many peacekeepers may not want to work with Angel, but maybe by training a few of you, he can gain everyone's confidence. He will be training some of our new peacekeepers for the next few weeks until the tournament begins. Any objections?"

"None at all," the crowd agreed.

"Good. Please don't hesitate to ask him about anything," Citlali said, vanishing.

"Thank you for this opportunity," Angel said timidly as more peacekeepers approached. "Let me give a brief introduction. I have been a warkeeper for eight years. I was born with a number as my name, but that name is not important. I was only given the ironic name Angel once I gained the reputation as one of the most successful fighters to come out of my region. I may have been trained as a warkeeper, but I have doubted my nation's regime. Not all of us are bad. Many of us have tried to cross over to peacekeeper territory in hopes of fighting alongside the peacekeepers. I may have been the only one to escape. As part of my service to the North American nation, I will teach you all I know. I will teach you the weaknesses of warkeepers, their style of fighting and even their culture so you know how best to take them on. I was briefed on your mission histories. I know some of you have dealt with the elite warkeeper Viper. Before I train you in dealing with such opponents, I will need to assess what you are capable of. Line up here and face the wall on the other end. Prepare yourselves. I bumped up the difficulty of these holograms."

The nine trainees did what he said. Sebastian, Giselle and Alice's teams faced the other side of the gym, where nine holographic people appeared. One for each contender charged them. The men and women stayed in place, using reanimation technology to hit their respective targets. They continually missed their opponents and it wasn't long before the holograms reached them, evaporating once the peacekeepers were smacked to the ground.

"A common theme will appear as you progress through your training," Angel said as the defeated soldiers rose to their feet. "And that is to be creative and work as a team. Stop thinking linearly. Literally. You were all concentrated on your own targets when you should have worked together. Sebastian! Instead of focusing on your hologram, you should have been aiming at Giselle's hologram. Arthur! When you were aiming at your hologram, you should have hit Paula's hologram. When in a group fight, those in the fight tend to focus on individual targets. It is the team that consistently strikes blows to unsuspecting targets that will win! Yes, that sounds like a cheap shot, but in the field it is your lives and those around you that are on the line. And if your life is on the line then get out of line! Let's try that again."

Lined up once more, their holographic opponents appeared again. This time, without fail, the heroes attacked the holograms at all angles, with waves of metal slicing across the room like a fierce painter at work. The peacekeepers shared impressed glances at their newly acquired techniques.

"Good, good. Now let's put your knowledge to practice. Let's test out your teamwork and creativity," Angel said, snapping his fingers. A dark abyss swallowed them. Soon their dark descent turned into a skydive freefall. Around them, Orderkeepers with axes, hammers and knives appeared, grabbing hold of the peacekeepers. The peacekeepers tried turning what little amount of reanimation bar they had left into a weapon or a parachute. It was not enough to turn into a plane, nor was it enough to turn into a small hover car. Immediately, the peacekeepers turned them into orbs and waves of metallic dust and shot them at the Orderkeepers, knocking a few out. It soon became clear that the Orderkeepers were not trying to kill the peacekeepers but were after the reanimation blocks. An enemy grabbed hold of Rosa's reanimation bar and popped it into oblivion.

Their enemies continued reaching for the reanimation bars, popping each one they got their hands on. How would the peacekeepers survive the fall without any reanimation bars? The last of the Orderkeepers were pushed away and disappeared into the distance. Only Arthur and Ramon had their reanimation bars left.

"This is only enough for two parachutes!" Ramon shouted through the roaring wind. "Now what? We're going to hit the ground real soon!"

A large broccoli tree stood out from below. Sebastian pointed at it. Everyone linked arms and dove directly at the tree. The last two reanimation bars were used as a giant hook to cling to the tree in hopes that their fall would be broken by the centripetal force. One of Arthur's arms was linked to Sebastian's and another held the hook strapped with leather around his torso. Arthur used all his strength to maintain a grip on the hook as it pushed against the top of the tree and nearly dislocating his shoulder. The tree forcibly shivered from side to side as their weight balanced off its sides.

"We made it!" Paula shouted in relief, looking at her injured teammates. "With minor bruises. Is everyone—?"

But before she could finish her sentence, they were teleported back into the gymnasium. They continued the rest of their training in the gym that day with armlocks. The next week was filled with firearms scenarios mixed in occasionally with hand-to-hand combat and more spontaneous simulations to test their resourcefulness in life-and-death situations.

CHAPTER 19 – THE PERFECT HACKER

Inside the industrial gym, a dozen men and women performed basic boxing combos as Drill Sergeant Taylor yelled at them. The mime ribbons around their arms forced their bodies to move on their own, triggering uneasiness in their faces.

"Take a look over there at instructor Taylor," Giselle said, pointing at the uniformed man training recruits in the gym.

"Those are the new recruits," Alice said. "Aren't they cute? Look at them learning how to make a fighting stance."

"We were all new once before," Sebastian said rolling around the mat with Arthur as they tried to put the other one in a submission.

"Focus!" Arthur shouted from under Sebastian, transitioning to get Sebastian in an arm bar.

"I know," Alice said, gazing over at the newer cadets. Paula surprisingly gripped her hands onto Alice's neck. Alice swung her right arm between Paula's elbows, turning her arm counterclockwise while simultaneously twisting her hips, unbalancing Paula, and sweeping her onto her back. Paula grunted as she hit the ground. "Nothing wrong with being new. Their innocence is adorable, that's all."

"Going to make an introduction?" Jaime asked calmly, as he was gently flipped over by Rosa.

"I don't see why not," Alice smiled. "Who knows? Maybe they'll be as good at fighting as these two gladiators."

She looked over at the two giant men sparring as Ramon and Ryan struggled to get one another in any sort of lock. Ryan's headlock on Ramon quickly turned into Ryan being thrown over Ramon's leg and onto the mat.

Ramon's *kimura* failed when Ryan stretched out his arm, causing Ramon to slip to the side and providing Ryan the momentum he needed to roll over onto Ramon. The struggle continued for these two.

"How often do we get new recruits?" Giselle asked, practicing clinch fighting with Angel.

"No one knows for sure," Alice said. "Sometimes we get a dozen one week and sometimes none for several weeks."

"All right, switch partners," Angel said. It was clear that those training under him were now comfortable having him around. At times it was as if Angel had never been a 'warkeeper' at all.

"Hey, where are you from, Angel?" Alice asked.

"Bolivia," he responded.

"That's pretty deep in warkeeper territory," Paula stated.

"I've been wanting to ask," Sebastian said. "While in Orderkeeper waters, they had more reanimation crystals at their disposal than we did. So why were they so easy to push away?"

"One, because they were low-level warkeepers," Angel started. "They were not so well trained. And if I recall, you guys didn't fare so well with an elite such as Viper. Two, it is possible the low-level warkeepers may have wanted you to win. Like I mentioned before, not all warkeepers are bad."

This shocked the peacekeepers to the point that they remained quiet for the rest of the training session, choosing instead to process the information they had come by. After two weeks of combat training, Angel and Citlali decided to introduce them to human hacking.

"You all have learned much, but if you wish to increase your chances of victory, you're going to need to learn how to hack human minds," Angel said, standing next to Citlali. He took them to the war room below the institution. Their training was going to require network hacking, and the systems in the war room offered such software to practice with.

"In your days, there was an incredible amount of computer hacking," Citlali said. "I know personally because I was around at that time. Human hacking is similar, except the targets are people instead of computers. Through your contact lenses, you can see a request has been made asking if you want to download the Basics of Human Hacking Application program. Download it. This top secret software program cannot be shared with anyone outside the peacekeeper program. It is essentially a back door into the U-ITS network system, which leads to the database of everyone registered under its network. This software will allow you to hack anyone using U-ITS through the North American central network."

"You won't learn how to hack a member of my former warkeeper nation until you have mastered how to hack someone in this peacekeeper nation," Angel said. "Complete as many tasks as you can by the end of the week. And to be clear, just because you're getting this special training, don't think that you can get out of physical training. I still expect all of you to meet me every morning for PT. Now begin."

"Welcome to the Basics of Human Hacking Application program," the narrator started. Streams of words appeared on one side of their vision, and a drawing of a body appeared on the other side. "The Universal Information Technology System creates a connection between the human user and the U-ITS central intelligence network. To hack a user's mind, you must first exploit the U-ITS. With this download, that part has already been taken care of. Using the following scene, pick a person from the crowd you would like to hack by raising your hands and circling the target with your fingers. It is not enough to *think* of who you want to hack. For safety precautions, we've added the necessary hand gestures so you don't hack anyone by accident. Now that you've focused on this person, you can begin."

A picture of the target's brain and body appeared on the side in red.

"Red means areas that still need to be hacked," the narrator continued. "When all red turns to yellow and then to green, you will have completed this course. Look at the brain. Activate program Frontal Lobe Brute Force. You must always choose this program first. By controlling this part of the brain first, you can shut down the person's ability to move and call for help. Attack any other part of the brain first, and the target can call for help, jeopardizing your objective and potentially your cover. To complete this program, you must first highlight the frontal lobe. It's as simple as painting with your fingers. Every single program requires absolute precision. If you are off even by a millimeter, the program will fail and the target will call for help and flee, jeopardizing your objective and potentially your cover. Good! Now you must connect and disconnect the neurons you believe will activate your favored results. Please try again. Do not stress. Look carefully at the meter. When neurons are turned off or on, and the meter gets closer to green, leave those neurons. If the meter gets closer to red, change those neuron connections back. This requires practice and patience. No need to rush."

"Good thing I was a brain surgeon in my past life," Jaime said. "This is a cakewalk."

"Your perfect hand movements are probably why they resurrected you, Jaime," Alice said in frustration. "Or did you think it was because of your personality?"

"Well they clearly didn't resurrect *you* for your personality," Jaime responded. "Just be glad you have a team member who is going to excel at this."

"You're right, you're right," Alice said, backing off.

"I'm already making my target hear things by hacking his temporal lobe," Jaime announced.

"What are you up to, Giselle?" Paula asked curiously. "I heard you're good at the Mastermind Stratagem thingy. How are you managing here?"

"I was able to get past the frontal lobe," Giselle said. "I'm analyzing the brain stem now to see how I can make the body do what I want."

Sebastian grew nervous as he remained on the first task, struggling to shift the neurons into his favor. His palms began to sweat, and he hoped no one would ask him how he was holding up.

"Hey, Sebastian," Rosa called from across the room. Sebastian prepared himself for the dreadful spotlight. "How are you doing?"

"I'm still on the first task," Sebastian admitted.

"Thank goodness I'm not the only one!" Ramon shouted in relief.

Ryan and Paula joined in approval as they shrugged in slight frustration at their nearly impossible tasks.

Even Arthur let out a quick sigh of relief. "Hey Angel, why isn't there a program that does this for us?"

"Because you all need to learn the basics," Angel responded, leaning against the front desk as he overlooked his students. "To be honest, the basics are all we've discovered about human hacking. I am sure there are more advanced procedures after this program that we haven't cracked yet. We are hoping for others like yourselves to add to our human hacking library. Brains can also be modified. Believe it or not, many people you encounter on your missions will have morphed brains to increase their defenses against being hacked. It will be up to you to determine what part of their morphed brains does what. You will have to pay close attention to the MRI for certain brain activity when flipping the switches of the brain. We haven't developed a program that accurately detects each part of the one thousand trillion synaptic connections in the brain. Maybe with a few more brain surgeons, we might get that upgrade soon."

Everyone looked over at Jaime as he continued to breeze through the programs. There was no longer envy of the man; it was replaced by hope that he could potentially bring simplicity to a challenging yet imperative skill. The days went by much the same. The only ones progressing through the Basics of Human Hacking Application program were Giselle and Rosa. Jaime, of course, was already asking about the Intermediate Human Hacking Application program, which, for the reasons explained by Angel earlier, did not exist. Everyone but Jaime began looking more and more forward to their physical training.

It was morning again, and almost all the peacekeepers were given the day off. A few of those who were still made to train now had the industrial gym to themselves.

"You all have progressed beyond my expectations," Angel started. "One of you is exceptionally gifted in the ways of human hacking. Jaime, we will have you spend much more time exploring your hacking skills. You will learn how to extract specific information from a mind. Others are well versed in the Mastermind Stratagem. Some of you have near-perfect marksmanship skills and incredible combat techniques. Then there are those with remarkable leadership skills. With your progress, I trust you are all capable of this next challenge. I will put you through someone's past memory. Trust me and trust yourselves."

From the gymnasium, they were thrown underwater and slowly sank as they looked over at each other. As usual when in water, they had on their oxygen masks and clear waterproof suits.

"Now, all of you will replay a historical mission of a Chilean town takeover," Angel's voice echoed through the blue water. "Your role is to assist in the coup d'état. In this scenario, you will portray the operatives who have been working with the local population."

Still underwater, the aspiring heroes made their way to the opening of an underwater cave. Once passed the entrance, they swam a few meters straight and then up. There was no more water there, as if they had walked into an air bubble that held back the encroaching ocean. It was a town below sea level. It even had its own beach with swaying water. Due to rising sea levels, it had become submerged late in the twenty-first century, and those living there were able to build a rock-and-steel cenote around the land to hold back the water. They looked up and saw a well of light shining down on what used to be a town—part of the mainland—but was now an island overcome with restless foreign aggression. The heroes made their way through the low level of water and onto the beach, pushing through the adobe houses. The scene soon became chaotic with protests and military presence. The ground tremored at uneven intervals. Floors of buildings exploded on one block after another. The streets were colored in red and angry shouts and desperation raged everywhere. Angel's students followed their satellite bracelets and made their way to the capitol, where the enemy's de facto leader was hiding.

"Let's eliminate our target, confirm the hit, and move out," Arthur ordered. It was clear he was as uncomfortable with the mission as everyone else.

Although it was a simulation, it still felt real to everyone, especially since this was someone's memory. The capitol's center was filled with enemy combatants. Sebastian noticed a small group gathering on a nearby rooftop, sneaking into an attic. He nudged Ryan and pointed over at them. The two stealthily led the way to the attic. A civilian spotted Sebastian and his team and told them to hurry inside. They dropped to the attic's floor and spotted an armory around them.

"Thank goodness you're here," one man said. "It's time we reclaimed our land. We've recently finished a series of tunnels heading across town, including one underneath the capitol. But with this earthquake, we're not sure how long they can hold, even with reanimation support. It's an artificial earthquake they created to scare the townspeople. Will you help us?"

"Show us the tunnel that leads under the capitol," Sebastian said.

"Yes, of course," the man replied. He led them down the trembling building to the basement's tunnel. Dust and rocks fell erratically onto them as they made their way through the narrow tunnel. It scraped at them, causing bruises and cuts, especially on their heads. Once under the capitol, the guide went up a wooden ladder and quietly slid open the door to the basement. He pushed himself through, followed closely by the soldiers. They moved up the stairs of the empty basement, rifles in their arms. Arthur went to the top of the stairs and creaked open the door slightly.

There were distant conversations, and the guide they were with verified the voices they heard were those of the enemy. Arthur continued to slowly creak open the door as to not make too much noise. Quietly, and with hand movements, they moved from room to room on the first floor. Using their silenced weapons, they took down the soldiers several at a time. The dead soldiers lay on the floor in their black uniforms with blue lining. Soon they were standing in front of the enemy leader, who was still sitting by the time all her soldiers were on the ground.

"Why?" the woman asked. Her orange eyes and silver hair looked oddly familiar. "Why do you warkeepers do this?"

Sebastian and the others looked at each other confusingly.

"We're peacekeepers," Arthur said.

"Not in this simulation," the woman responded. "I'm the peacekeeper and you are all warkeepers."

Shivers made the heroes hesitate as they lowered their weapons and looked at each other. Before Arthur could shoot from his raised weapon, he and everyone else were warped back to the gymnasium.

"What was that?" Arthur asked angrily.

"A memory of mine," Angel said. "Of me leading a mission as a warkeeper. And those artificial tremors were caused by warkeepers, not peacekeepers. I was following orders. It shouldn't be an excuse, but do know that I didn't want to do any of that. I was already reevaluating my place with the warkeepers. I wanted you to understand that there are warkeepers who want to change. We *can* change if given the chance."

"You didn't have to show us that, Angel," Arthur said as everyone quietly stood up.

"Don't blame him," Citlali said, marching between the group. "We had him show you that memory. We understand he was our enemy once before, but if we are going to win against the Orderkeepers, we are going to need to start trusting some of them to help us. You also need to prepare yourselves for what it will be like when we move into enemy territory. I'm sorry we made you do that, Angel."

She turned to him and placed her hand on his shoulder. Varying degrees of guilt reigned on the peacekeepers. It was difficult to not replay the simulation they went through and not feel resentful toward Angel. At the same time, they too believed he had changed. Now that it was dark out and time for bed, Sebastian and his friends thought it would be nice to talk about the day's events in his team's quarters.

"I'm not saying I hate him, but I know it bothers everyone here what he's done," Arthur said, leaning against the bar with a drink in his hand. "I'm still not sure why anyone thought we should be shown that."

"I believe Citlali is right. We do need to prepare ourselves for what it will be like on the other side of the border," Alice stated hastily. Arthur remained quiet, taking another sip from his beverage. "Was it hard to watch? Absolutely. But that was only a taste of what we will be exposed to out there."

"Well, if he's truly changed," Arthur said and stopped for a second to think, "then that's all that matters."

"Let's talk about something else, shall we?" Rosa intervened. "The games? They're in a couple of days. Have you guys decided which games you'd be best at?"

The night took an uplifting turn as they exchanged what they had heard from the experienced peacekeepers about the competition. The remaining days until the tournament were filled with group combat exercises taking place in simulations of erratic settings such as rain, earthquakes and volcanic eruptions.

CHAPTER 20 – A LONG AWAITED INTRODUCTION

The city of Mexicali was known for its reanimation crystal and aerospace technology exports to most of North America. It handled nearly all the transelementum that came from the asteroid-mining conglomerate and processed it into usable reanimation crystals. It was also responsible for manufacturing the hardware orders for the asteroid-mining conglomerate's future space explorations. Residential skyscrapers spread throughout the metropolis with many emerald buildings on one end, crystal white buildings in the center and ruby buildings on the other side. At the center where most of the white buildings stood were round, chocolate-colored facilities with streaks of gold highlighting the edges. Golden eagles seemed to be the city's favorite bird. They floated around gently, sometimes flying by the peacekeepers in the hover cars as the peacekeepers flew past the city and into the forested mountain region nearby.

Despite the site of the tournament being deep underground away from the public's prying eyes, everyone was still under the illusion they were outside. A faux sky was erected, and a breeze entered the area to add to the feel they were out in the open. From the entrance, they were greeted with excited commotion. The raised flags and banners littering the area gave it a carnival-like feel. Charles went over the rules and goals of the tournament for the new peacekeepers. They were only to enter competitions approved earlier that day by Citlali and were to spectate as many different contests as possible.

"We're entering Jaime into the hacking competition," Alice said. "Paula's going in the marksmanship contest, and I'll be in the search-and-eliminate maze game. And your team?"

"Ryan is going in the weightlifting contest," Rosa said. "Sebastian and I will be going in the agility obstacle race."

"Sebastian!" Jaylyn said, popping out from the crowd, grabbing his face and giving him a kiss on the cheek that caught everyone, especially Giselle, off guard. Jaylyn's mouth opened and closed as she chewed on a patch. "Oh, hey!" Jaylyn was too quick to even give Giselle a chance to open her arms. They hugged while Giselle's arms were locked between their torsos.

"So, how's the team coming along?" Jaylyn continued. "First-timers, right? Well, no matter. You'll do fine if you don't enter the fighting pits."

"Fighting pits?" Jaime asked.

"Yeah, that's where most of the fighting and spectating will be," Jaylyn said. "Lots of blood and sweat there. You'll love it."

Rosa quivered as Jaylyn gave an uncomfortable Ryan a joyful wink.

"What are you chewing?" Paula asked.

"It's one of the stimulant patches," Jaylyn said. "Gives you a lot of relaxed energy. You should try some."

"We're fine," Paula answered.

"You sure?" Jaylyn said. "Have you guys experimented with these new stimulants? Almost every peacekeeper does after a few missions. Especially with the things we do."

"Things we do?" Rosa asked.

"All right, Jaylyn," Patricio said, entering the group as he and Paula exchanged smiles. "They're still getting adjusted to this new life."

"And I'm helping them get adjusted," she argued, still chewing vigorously.

"Small steps," he responded. "Come on, let's be good hosts and show them around."

"Hosts?" Alice asked.

"The games are taking place underneath our institution," Patricio responded. "We rotate the venue every year. It's a wonderful way to expose peacekeepers to different institutions. Maybe if Jaylyn stops bothering you two, you'll be comfortable enough to see our dorm."

"That would be nice," Giselle responded. "And she isn't bothering us."

They passed several arches of ribbons and entered the festival. At the beginning, there were large booths for knife-throwing, archery, shooting and reanimation-striking. They approached a crowded pavilion with people on the stage. The announcer asked the audience who they thought was the best liar on the stage. He then asked the judges to put in their votes. A message followed saying the next phase of the contest would consist of the same individuals switching bodies and portraying whoever's body they were in as accurately as possible.

Several booths away from the pavilion was a small, packed coliseum where two opposing teams of ten individuals were the center of attention. These were the fighting pits, Jaylyn explained. Although their holograms were fighting, it was still a chaotic scene of brutal elimination. The two teams fought until one side was defeated, using reanimation technology to their advantage. To keep the fight interesting, the fighters were randomly teleported around the arena, forcing participants to improvise their next moves. One of the fighters had been charging his opponent when he was teleported behind her. Seeing this in her peripheral vision, she stabbed her rear opponent, eliminating him. Sebastian and the others soon realized that one of the teams consisted of the First peacekeepers from their own institution. Sadly, they lost the fight, forcing their heads to hang low afterward.

"Unfortunate," Patricio responded to the turnout.

They moved on to the next competition, which was the agility course Sebastian and Rosa were going to enter. The rules were simple: One teammate would start at the top of a tower and pass through the obstacles below to reach the finish line. The second contestant would be on a nearby floating platform, aiming a turret that would shoot almost anything they wanted at either their teammate—to provide them with a weapon—or the first-place racer, to sabotage them. The only items not permitted to come out of the turrets were guns, sharp items, or anything that would physically propel someone to the finish line. Sebastian took his mark at the starting line with the other contestants. Rosa took her place at the course sideline on one of the many platforms with turrets. They both had the number 8 painted on their chests and backs.

"I'm going to get all of you!" a contestant with the number 5 on his shirt yelled repeatedly, casting a menacing look at those below at the starting line and aiming his turret from side to side in a taunt to them. He only stopped yelling to give a forced, harsh laugh.

"Everyone ready?" a referee asked, holding out a red orb. It turned yellow once in the air. When the orb smashed into the ground it turned green, emitting sparks and loud crackles. "Go!"

Diving off the tower, Sebastian was one of the first to make it underwater. A barrage of small cannon balls turned to sticky liquid when they hit those who weren't fast enough to enter the water first. The few contestants already in the lead pushed themselves through the underwater track. A fight erupted as the first few in the lead headed toward an opening of a submerged wall, each wanting to be the first through the only cylinder opening that led to the next obstacle. Sebastian was hit by a kick meant for another fighter and was stunned for a second. Regaining composure, Sebastian grabbed onto a man. He pushed him facedown and placed his feet on top of the man's back, using him to spring forward toward the small opening. Another man—number 5 —started pushing himself into the small opening. He spotted Sebastian behind him and started kicking his face. The man continued past the cylinder and upward toward the surface with Sebastian close behind.

Once they pushed themselves out of the water, a ball smashed open in front of their feet to reveal a bat. Number 5 scrambled to grab it. Sebastian focused instead on the next obstacle, a water current streaming against them with monkey bars above. As Sebastian opened his arms to reach the monkey bars, the man hit his rib cage with the bat, causing Sebastian to fall to the ground. The man dropped the bat, jumped and grabbed the first set of metal bars. A series of cannonballs flew, aiming at the man as he began moving past the bars. Soon, players were clawing themselves out of the water. Two players—numbers 1 and 3—made their way to the obstacle, jumping onto it and strategically avoiding attacking each other to catch up to number 5. With blood coming out of his mouth, Sebastian managed to stand up and jump to the bar. After pushing himself through a few sets of bars, he saw under him the stream of water carrying number 5 back to the beginning of the obstacle. He had been knocked out by one of the players on the turrets.

"No! No!" said a man on one of the floating platforms. It was the same man who was taunting from his turret before. "Get up!"

Numbers 1 and 3 were now struggling with the bombardment of cannonballs as they jockeyed for first place. After the injury from the bat to his body, Sebastian knew he couldn't keep a lead with those behind him if he continued climbing. He decided to pull himself up the bar with his legs and crawl over it. It was difficult to maintain his balance with all the shaking, but easier now that his hands and feet could do the work. A woman from below grabbed his ankle, forcing Sebastian still. She tried pulling so he would lose balance and fall, but Rosa saw this and aimed a ball that exploded over Sebastian's hands. It was a zip tie, making it clear what Rosa had in mind. He used the cable to tie the woman's wrist and then freed his ankle from her clutch. She placed her legs over the monkey bars in front as she struggled to untie herself with her teeth and one free hand.

Number 1 was now scaling a wall using a rope attached to the top. Number 3 was at the bottom, distancing himself from 1 to avoid the incoming attacks from the turrets. Number 1 was starting to live up to her number, as she led in the race. She bounced from side to side, dodging the turret barrage, slowly making progress up the rope. A man with the number 7 on his back went up to the unsuspecting number 3 and push-kicked him off the platform and into the stream of water, below Sebastian, forcing 3 to start at the beginning of the monkey bars. He smiled at Sebastian as he began climbing up the rope. Upon hitting the ground, Sebastian knew he could not use his arms to pull himself up due to his broken ribs. He grabbed the rope and placed his feet against the wall, walking up, allowing his abs, biceps and legs to do most of the work. Once at the top, Sebastian followed in third place, behind numbers 1 and 7.

The next obstacle was to grab onto one of the ropes and swing to the other end of the course, onto a small circular platform with tall pillars attached to it. The two in the lead met each other on the small platform. They wrestled, each trying to push the other off while getting peppered by the splattering cannonballs around them. This time, though, the balls splashed slippery liquid instead of the sticky substance like before. Sebastian grabbed one of the long ropes and jumped. After several seconds of swinging to the other side, he landed on the small platform. The last person standing would win. The two stopped fighting, and all three waited at the edge behind the small pillars for protection from the cannonballs.

They waited for the remaining contenders with the same thing on their minds. One by one, those trying to land on the small platform were met with punches and kicks by the three already on the platform, ensuring eliminations once the contenders hit the ground. As each player was eliminated, their corresponding partners were no longer allowed to fire their turrets. One by one, eliminated turret players were transported away. Once they saw the trio working together, half a dozen contenders decided to swing onto the platform together. One was pushed off, while the rest made it safely. Number 1 charged into the group of newcomers and jumped into the air, rapidly delivering a 360-degree kick to their heads, knocking them off-balance and pushing another one of them off. One of the other men charged Sebastian. Using a *harai goshi* technique, Sebastian grabbed the man and flipped him over the tower's platform. With all the intense training instilled in him by Angel, it had become second nature to react strategically in group fights. Number 1 grabbed one of the contenders and wrestled with him, inching closely to the edge as Sebastian and number 7 softened their two targets with punches and elbows. The two then twisted their opponents' arms and easily threw them off. With number 1 and her opponent still wrestling, Sebastian and number 7 were left to fight each other. They measured each other with jabs and low kicks before putting each other in a clinch. They tried placing each other in locks but were unsuccessful.

"Where did you learn to fight so well?" number 7 asked in a rough voice.

"I was in the military in my past life. That helps," Sebastian said, not letting his guard down. Once number 1 was at the edge, she swiftly pushed herself away from her opponent and kicked him off. Sebastian glanced over at number 1, giving number 7 the chance to perform a sacrifice throw. Number 7 pulled Sebastian down and over him. Sebastian was thrown to the side but managed to hold on to the edge. Numbers 1 and 7 thought he fell off and was eliminated, so they turned their attention to each other, delivering fierce blows and attempting throws on each other while Sebastian remained still at the edge. Number 7 grabbed hold of number 1 and charged her head into a pillar. He grabbed her again and ran toward another pillar. A dazed number 1 used her feet to run up the pillar and move behind him. She moved to his right side and locked her right elbow into his right shoulder, turned her body, and lifted him off the ground and over the platform. He kept his arm tightly locked into hers as he fell over the edge. She slid off, and arm in arm they were both now hanging off the edge, refusing to let go of each other, as if to say, "If I fall, so do you."

Sebastian used this opportunity to get up from the edge. A small cannonball popped in front of him, releasing a slippery substance. Then another one splashed in front of him. He looked up and saw they were coming from Rosa. The other two players on the turrets continued to hit

Sebastian with sticky balls. Sebastian grabbed the slippery liquid and poured it onto the fingers of numbers 1 and 7, who looked up, shocked to see him. As the slippery liquid condensed under their fingers, the duo began slipping and struggling to grip the edge. In a few seconds, they both had slipped off the platform and were eliminated.

"After an intense showdown, we have our winner!" said the announcer. "Number 8: Sebastian and Rosa from Los Angeles!"

Not the expected climax. Everyone thought it would end with a fight and not a discreet strategy between the turret player and obstacle runner. Still, the audience was impressed.

"Congratulations, Sebastian!" number 7 shouted with a smile. "Let's grab a drink at the after parties."

Sebastian looked up his profile after being released from the Mastermind Stratagem. Name: Liam Roy; Residence: Vancouver; Peacekeeper status: completed fifteen missions.

"You beat us, newbie," number 1 said. Her name was Lydia Fernandez; Residence: Houston; Peacekeeper status: completed twenty missions. "That was a good match. I hope they give you only the most deserving missions in this line of work."

Sebastian said goodbye to the two and left the tent with Rosa. Giselle ran, hugging him and playfully kissing him.

"With that performance, you'll be getting the good missions now," Patricio smiled.

Everyone was impressed with the two and their teamwork. Rosa's cunning thinking mixed with Sebastian's fighting skill and endurance was a powerful combo. Not everyone was excited, though: Ishmael, who had heard about the victory, immediately requested through Citlali that Giselle and Sebastian meet him in his private viewing booth. Despite the astounding victory, Citlali's strict tone made everyone uneasy. The two were nervously led through the festival and waited inside an office venue before being told to enter.

"Do you know why you're here?" Ishmael said, staring hard at the two from behind his desk. Screens of the various performances played out on the side of the office.

"No, sir," the two said, still standing up.

"There's no need for formalities," Ishmael said, his voice getting softer. "Please, take a seat. I see you just won a serious competition, Sebastian. Congratulations."

The couple looked on curiously as he brought out the serape scarf from under the table.

"I'm sure you know that serape scarves have distinct patterns," Ishmael started. "Yes, most scarves follow a similar pattern, but even then they tend to be unique. I know this scarf looks like a scarf you two once possessed. You see, I brought you two here to discuss something personal for all three of us. I wasn't sure when I would tell you two this, but now that you are devoted peacekeepers, I think this would be as good a time as any." He paused, looking at the scarf as he placed it on the desk between them. "This scarf once belonged to your son. He was my father."

Giselle and Sebastian's eyes lit up. A man who looked ten years older than the two was their grandson. And here he was, sitting in front of them.

"What?" Sebastian trembled, breaking the tense silence. Giselle slowly reached forward and embraced the only relic she had of her son. The couple sat there, tears splashing away from their bitter sadness. They touched the scarf as if to salvage any hope of being close to him again. Guilt began to reign at the constant regret of "what if?" What if they hadn't gotten into the car that day? They could have avoided the car accident that would forever open up a border of time, dividing parents from child. The parents wondered how he lived. Was it a good life, at least?

"I never met him," Ishmael said. "He passed away around the time I was born. I wish I could tell you more about him, but much of what was known about his life has been redacted. Not even I know what the records on him once said."

"Why are you telling us this now?" Sebastian asked. Again, Ishmael paused to think of his next answer.

"After winning that last competition, there is a good chance you and your team will be sent to the front lines to complete some challenging missions," Ishmael said. "I believe in you and your team, but I needed to tell you this before you two started going on more dangerous missions."

"You don't think we're going to make it?" Giselle muttered. "Is that it?"

"This is dangerous work," Ishmael said. "We do what we can to prepare you, but we never know for sure who will come back. The reason why more than half of the peacekeepers here are on stimulants is not for recreational use but to help them cope with what they've seen and what they've done!" Ishmael stopped to calm himself down. "Things will only get more treacherous. I wasn't sure when I would tell you the truth. Most of my life I've been by myself. I just always wanted to meet family."

Giselle slowly got up from her seat and walked over to embrace her grandson. A tear slid down his cheek as Sebastian embraced him on the other side. They gripped each other, hoping they wouldn't have to ever let go. Giselle was the first to back away. She told Ishmael she needed to spend some time alone with Sebastian. She walked away, the scarf still nestled against her chest. Sebastian distantly followed her, cautiously watching her every move. The guilt consumed her as she repeatedly thought why she, a mother, had outlived her child. Sebastian and Giselle had each other, but still she wondered. The thought of also losing Sebastian was too wild. With their peacekeeper responsibilities beginning to loom in her thoughts, the realization that something dreadful could happen to him forced her to relive the pain of the car crash all over again. She could not lose him, too.

CHAPTER 21 – NOT ALONE

The two attempted to escape everything by entering the nearby forest. What they needed now was silence and peace. They perched themselves on one of the many large branches of a tree filled with pink Tabebuia flowers. Sebastian kept Giselle in his grasp with the serape scarf gently cradled between them. They stayed there until they were ready to go back to the tournament.

"We can stay here until the tournament ends," Sebastian said. "We don't have to go back."

"If you want to stay, I'll stay here with you," Giselle said, looking up at him.

There were no more tears on her soft skin or on his, but Sebastian could still make out the wet trails left behind. He placed his hand against her cheek, moving his hand behind her ear and onto the back of her neck. They held hands as they made their way back. The sparse and empty tents indicated that they were in the tournament outskirts.

"Were you going to enter a competition?" Sebastian asked.

"I was thinking about it, but I'm not in the mood anymore," Giselle said.

"Psst," a man beckoned from inside one of the empty tents. "Are you up for a challenge? Yeah, you."

"Let's keep moving, Sebastian," Giselle said, grabbing his arm.

"What's the matter? You win that race but you're not willing to test your luck in another contest? Come on. I saw you. You did great. Surely you can beat me. Wager some time, and I'll bet this special bracelet. Do you know what this is, Sebastian?"

184

"We don't want to compete in anything right now," Giselle said. "If you don't mind, we have a lot on our mind."

"What is it?" Sebastian asked, keeping his feet stationed on the grassy mound.

"You don't have to do this, Sebastian," Giselle said.

"It's a weapon from the Celestial Weapons Chest," the pale man said, catching their attention. "It gives the wearer premonitions. You'll be able to see what will happen in the next few seconds. Sometimes you can see within the next few days, but a long-term premonition like that has only happened to me once. Having it will assist the wearer to react in a way that it ensures survival. The challenge is simple. Rip this band off me in less than five minutes and it's yours."

"Is that it?" Sebastian asked.

"That's it," the man said, standing up from his seat to reveal a tall stature. Sebastian's eyes barely met his neck. "Ready?"

His name displayed itself as Elias Seymour; Residence: Seattle; Peacekeeper status: completed thirty missions. This was a chance to win an incredible weapon, and he had nothing to lose. He knew he would need this weapon now that he was sure he would be getting more challenging missions after winning the previous game. He wanted to make sure he came back to Giselle from future missions. She could also use the item for her missions. The clock on their satellite bracelets began clicking as it counted down the time from five minutes. Sebastian charged forward, reaching the smiling man's eyes, blocked his line of sight, then aimed for the silver, silky band. His hand wasn't there anymore. Without looking, Elias had pulled his arm away.

"How?" Sebastian asked.

"I told you," Elias said. "This is a weapon from the Celestial Weapons Chest. No one knows how any of these weapons work, but this one has incredible properties that help the wearer to avoid every single physical attack."

Elias began walking out of the tent with Sebastian still chasing the shiny band. He ran up the crates and on top of a small moving building. As fast as he was, Sebastian could not come within a fingertip's reach of the majestic jewelry.

"Don't worry, you won't be the first person to fail today," Elias taunted.

Sebastian tried throwing Elias onto the ground below, but after each subsequent step it became apparent that no martial art move was going to work on Elias. Speed and tactics were not going to work. But what would work? Human hacking? No, Sebastian had no skill in that area.

"How did you get that?" Sebastian asked, trying to get an idea from him.

"I didn't have the audacious task of having to take it from someone," Elias said. "I found it in the icy Colorado mountains. I was lost and separated from my team."

Hoping Elias was distracted, Sebastian jumped forward to snatch the bracelet. It was no use. Elias was too quick and effortlessly moved out of the way. Sebastian fell to the floor, scraping his arms. He had one minute left to obtain the weapon.

"Now, where was I?" Elias continued. "Right. I was lost by myself and looking for a way back down. We were there tracking down warkeepers. I felt some strange force affecting me. The force was not pulling me, it was more of a gut feeling that I should walk in a certain direction as if I knew where I was going. I kept walking and every time I decided to change direction, it felt wrong. I stayed moving in the direction that felt right. Soon I saw something shining in the snow. It was this."

He glanced at the band, stroking it. Ten seconds left.

"I'm going to miss it," he whispered.

Sebastian looked up, confused.

"Right now, I know it wants me to give this to you. I know because recently I had a premonition of me handing this to you. That was the only long-term premonition I've ever had."

As the clock reached zero, he took off the celestial grade weapon and handed it to a still-confused Sebastian.

"Why?" Sebastian asked, as the silver band wrapped itself around Sebastian's right wrist.

"I don't know," Elias responded. "Listen to it and trust it. It's yours now. Now you have ESP like I did."

"Why did you challenge me when you were going to hand it to me anyway?"

"So you'll know firsthand what it's like to go up against someone using this particular gadget. Like I mentioned before, no one knows how these weapons were made or where they came from. They just started appearing across the globe. There's a theory the government made them in secret and somehow the weapons found their way into the public. Few have even speculated that an advanced alien civilization dropped these weapons down on Earth to see what we would do with them. No one knows for sure; not even Citlali. Look, I don't know why it chose you. Maybe you're going to need it more than anyone. I know why I was chosen to have this. It was so I could give it to you. There are no clear answers, so don't think too much about it. Good luck."

Elias disappeared into the festival. Sebastian went to Giselle, and they looked curiously at the thick silver metallic thread on his wrist.

"Congratulations," Citlali said, startling Giselle as she appeared next to them.

"I knew you were going to appear," Sebastian said, surprised.

"That's how it works," Citlali said. "This has been quite a day for you both. The tournament will be over in a couple of hours, but let's check in and rest in the guest dorms until the after-parties begin."

***

As midnight approached and the blue moon was high, the peacekeepers were seen far and wide. Even though the parties were aboveground, they did not care to be too loud. Throughout the institution was dancing and laughing. Every hall and room Sebastian and Giselle ran through was filled with party, cheers, and bubbling beers. The two did not hesitate to have a quick drink here and there as a series of arrows led them to who knew where. Familiar faces popped up with smiles. Thomas and Daniela, as well as the other first peacekeepers, offered their congratulations to Sebastian as the couple passed by, drinks in hand. Soon they were making their first steps into someone's dormitory. It looked like a paradise and felt like one, too. The creamy floor massaged their feet with endless vibrations and heat. A gentle breeze combed through their hair, and floating crystal plates passed by topped with grails containing food, cocktails, and items from feather fans to silky napkins. Video from the day, including Ryan's debut weightlifting victory and Alice's triumph in the maze game, rolled down the glowing elevator. At the top of the elevator shaft briefly appeared clips of Sebastian's race victory. Patricio and Paula were the first to meet the two at the entrance. Patricio led them to the elevator, and as the two ascended, their clothes changed. Sebastian now had on a traditional suit with white gloves and black tie, complete with a top hat and gentleman's cane with a purple diamond encrusted on the top. Giselle had on a beautiful purple-and-diamond-clustered dress. Her elegant hair did itself into a twisted-back style. Blonde highlights swayed in her brown hair and a golden tiara headband with purple diamonds nestled on top. Sebastian could not take his eyes off her.

"Can't have you dressed in training clothes at the after-party," Patricio said, smiling. "Welcome to my and Jaylyn's home."

"I love what you did with your hair," Paula said, winking.

"Wait, did the two of you think up these outfits?" Giselle asked.

"Yup," Paula said.

Patricio dropped two patches into the elevator. The patches floated upward and caught up to the couple's hands.

"What is this?" Giselle asked, inspecting it.

"Stimulants," Patricio said. "Don't worry; it's safe and nonaddictive."

Paula held out what looked to be a pouch and squeezed out a liquid from it. She poured the syrup into Patricio's open mouth; he drank and looked over at the ascending couple with a smile. Their contact lenses displayed information on the patches. It would take a few seconds for the user to feel its effects, and a calculation showed how long the effects would last in their bodies. They placed it on their shoulders, and by the time they arrived to the last floor, the patches dissolved, and they had begun to get a sense of euphoria. The positivity around the floor was incredible. They saw immense beauty wherever they looked. Whatever they touched felt as if the stars of the universe were tickling their fingertips. They felt warmth and happiness.

The pair congratulated Ryan on his success as he and Rosa braced each other with their arms. Outside was a crystal bridge connecting the dormitory towers. Neon lights moved along this clear glass, sometimes like lightning and other times like waves. Sebastian led Giselle over the glassy floor. As if they were in a dream, a tree moved closely to them, bowing and carrying a pot of soil. A glowing pink flower blossomed in the pot. The tree urged Giselle to pull the flower out, and she did. The tree moved away as she sniffed the flower. Sebastian placed it in her hair, gazing into her eyes. They looked around, hearing the music around them, and stopped to look at each other once again. It was a genre of music they had never heard, yet it was instantly their new favorite. Sebastian took off his top hat and bowed, stretching out his cane to the side. Giselle bobbed a curtsy in return. They braced each other's arms and slowly moved to the music, keeping their hazy eyes on each other.

"Look at you two!" a woman gushed. The couple gently bumped their heads together for support as they turned their droopy eyes to the side. The woman moved her head up so her summer straw hat would reveal her eyes.

Chloe smiled at the two. "Sebastian, this is one of my teammates, Liam."

"Ah, we've met!" Liam said in his deep voice as the two men shook hands. A beer reanimated between their hands as they parted. "He's the one who won the race. Well played!"

"Thanks," Sebastian said, clanging beers and taking a swig with Liam.

"Chloe, Liam, this is Giselle. We were together in our past lives."

"Oh wow!" Chloe said, stunned and hugging Giselle. "That's incredible!"

"You two must be the first couple in history to start over!" Liam said, taking his turn to hug a flattered Giselle. "I don't even mean a bad breakup and makeup. So much for 'until death do us part.'"

"Oh, we never married," Giselle said, struggling to find Sebastian's hand with her hazy senses. "But we are fortunate."

"Well, you two look ready to call it a night," Chloe winked.

"I think so," Giselle smiled, as the couple walked farther down the bridge. Several pet ocelots appeared, walking on the edge. They changed color as the two brushed their hands against the blankets of their bodies.

"I'm sure you've had this drink before," Lydia said, appearing with shots for the pair.

Two large men and another woman held out their shots in the air. "¡Salud!"

"¡Salud!" they all said in unison before drinking their shots.

"Xtabentún?" Giselle said, recognizing the honey taste before her contact lens.

"You're welcome," Lydia said.

Feeling much tipsier now, the two walked off into the dark, private corner of the crystal bridge. They leaned against the back of one of the towers, sneaking kisses from each other before stopping and struggling to keep their eyes on each other. Their eyes felt as if they were being massaged by gentle, warm feathers. He could not get over how incredibly beautiful she was. Even the starlight above traveled for years just to touch her face he thought.

"Jaylyn," Giselle said.

"Yeah, if this is her place, I'm curious where she is," Sebastian asked as she massaged every part of his hair, not missing a spot of comfort. A series of arrows began leading them to the end of the bridge and toward a set of spiral stairs. Still dancing, Sebastian sloppily jumped from the bench to the edge of the parapet, holding out his cane in front of him for balance. He stepped back down next to a smiling Giselle and grabbed her, spinning her around twice before picking her up onto the bench. He kissed her and put her back down as they began their spiral dance down the stairs until they met a silver ramp. They slid down opposite rails, landing flawlessly on the ground. He then circled around her and grabbed her hand. They found Jaylyn not too far away, sitting in a dimly lit room on the first floor. The couple made their way to her as Jaylyn stood up. She went to her opened doorway, blocking it.

"What can I do for you tonight?" Jaylyn said, raising her eyebrow slightly. "You know the party is upstairs."

"Yeah … why aren't you up there?" Giselle asked.

"Not in the party mood tonight," Jaylyn said.

"Does it have anything to do with you chewing that stimulant earlier?" Sebastian asked, concerned.

"Maybe," Jaylyn said. "Not sure how you were able to put two and two together. Must be because of that stimulant *both of you* are on right now! Everybody does them from time to time, you know!"

"You're right, you're right," Sebastian said apologetically.

"How come we never met your third teammate?" Giselle asked. "Isn't everyone grouped into threes?"

"Yeah," Jaylyn said sadly, growing silent and slowly closing the door a bit.

The couple knew they shouldn't press further.

"So, is this your room?" Giselle asked, changing the topic.

"Yeah, until the party is over," Jaylyn answered. "When the last of our guests leave, Patricio and I will change our dorms back to how they were."

"Okay, we hope we weren't bothering you," Giselle whispered. "We'll let you sleep."

"Wait, why are you two here?" Jaylyn said, now smiling.

"We wanted to see you," Sebastian said.

Jaylyn stepped aside, and the couple entered the room as Giselle closed the door and curtains behind them. They talked about the day's events and congratulated each other on their victories. Jaylyn did most of the talking as she discussed her past missions. Eventually they brushed upon her third teammate, Ricardo, who was killed during one of their missions a few months ago. Patricio was absent from it because he was seriously injured from a previous mission. Jaylyn did not want to go into detail, and the couple did not press her. They comforted her until she fell asleep, and then the couple fell asleep beside her.

When daybreak approached, the rested couple left the room to take a relaxing morning walk through the nearby forest. They stumbled upon Arthur, who, sitting on a boulder under a tree's shade, was lost in thought.

"Morning," the couple said as they passed.

"Morning," Arthur responded.

"Is everything all right?" Giselle asked.

"Last night I had another flashback about my wife and kid," he said. "It was a happy memory, but since I'm not with them anymore…"

Giselle moved close to him, wrapping her arms around him and pressing his head against her shoulder.

"I'm so sorry, Arthur," Giselle said.

"I just need some time. Thank you, Giselle. Oh, and I'm sorry for the way I've been since we…" Arthur paused . . . "met. I'm sorry, Sebastian."

"There's no need to be sorry," Sebastian reassured. "Take care of yourself."

They left Arthur sitting on the boulder. Giselle knew him well, and if she thought they should let him be, then it was probably best. She told Sebastian that the reason he was so serious was because he had lived but his wife and daughter had not, like Sebastian had thought he had outlived those from his past. The couple looked into each other's eyes, startled at the commonality between Arthur's past and their own.

***

"Hey Sebastian, help me out here," the man was turned away, but as Sebastian approached him, he saw on his left arm a tattoo that said "John

12:24". Sebastian was back at the end of the first flashback he had, in the field of bodies. Suppressing his emotions, Sebastian dropped the picture onto the grass and continued walking toward the man who'd called him.

"You know what I said about that tattoo!" said the captain. "Get rid of it or keep your sleeves rolled down!"

The man who called Sebastian over slowly rolled down his left sleeve. Sebastian stood next to the man. The name on his uniform's tag read "Arthur". He had a worried look on his face as he looked over at the young enemy guerilla soldier lying in front of him. The young man struggled to breathe as blood streamed over his face.

"Let's fix him up and take him back to the base," Arthur said. The captain immediately went up to the two and without hesitating shot the young man on the ground several times.

"Fix him up and take him back?" the captain questioned. "Look at him. Look how young he is! Even if we interrogated him, he probably wouldn't know much. He looks like he was born yesterday. We don't have time to waste. Keep sweeping."

The captain walked away. The two were left alone and continued walking the field. It was quiet now, except for the few bullets that were fired when their comrades encountered more dying enemies.

"When do you think this will end?" Arthur asked, shaking his head.

"Either when we die or when our contract ends," Sebastian answered.

"I mean for them," Arthur said. "When will we leave them alone?"

Sebastian looked away, choosing to continue sweeping rather than offer an answer.

"Why are we even fighting in this war?" Arthur pushed.

"Because we were drafted," Sebastian said quietly.

"I mean, why are countries fighting? Everyone knows no country started this war; the corporations did."

"It doesn't matter now. Not enough people are willing to do anything about it. I wish it wasn't that way, but it is."

"If you were back home, would you do something about ending all this?"

"What could I, one person, possibly do?"

A wave of bullets rained down on everyone as they all immediately hit the ground for cover. The flashback morphed into another setting. Sebastian, Giselle and Arthur were in a park surrounded by friends, kids and the smell of barbeque. The combined atmosphere of sun and smiles animated the pinnacle of a pleasant experience. He then saw many flashbacks all at once, from his earliest memories of life to his close encounters with death. He remembered his childhood in Brooklyn and being brought by his mom in a stroller to his first day of preschool; his first boxing lesson with his dad, when he learned how to defend himself from bullies; his first fight; the abuse he took from everyone, from the kids at school to family; his first girlfriend and how she knew he was too quiet to make the first move, so she made it for him. She asked him out, and she was the one who leaned in to give him his first kiss. He remembered struggling in school to get passing grades, only to get drafted by the Army weeks after his college graduation. He remembered feeling empty from the war he had survived and the desolated streets that blocked him from reaching any hope. He remembered Giselle, the only love of his life, and feeling whole again because she was in his life and how it gave him a sense of purpose. He was no longer alone. He remembered his child struggling to breathe and play because of the air pollution that had affected his growth while inside his mother. He remembered the day of the car crash and the last thing he said to Giselle. While driving, he told her, "California here we come!" then excitedly looked in the rearview mirror at his son before saying the last thing to him seconds before the car crash: "Our new life awaits us!"

***

Through all the yelling and laughter, through all the bullets firing and cheerful kids playing, Sebastian found his way back to Giselle. She had experienced a multitude of similar flashbacks and instantly stood up, trying to hurry Sebastian to his feet. In tears and in shock, they tried to make sense of what was real. They rushed to Arthur, now remembering they had known each other in their past lives. They received their memory in time like they were told before. They remembered so much and wanted to see Arthur right away.

"Arthur!" Giselle yelled, finding him back on the boulder. "We remember you! We remember you!"

"Yes, I remember you as well," he said looking up at her inquisitively. All their feelings for him changed. He no longer felt like a stranger. It was like waking up from a dream that made you fall in love with someone. Sebastian and Giselle now cared deeply for him as if they had known him all their life. For indeed they had. His appearance even changed. His eyes were warmer and friendlier. "I remembered everything this morning. I was going to tell you guys, but I needed time for myself."

"What's going on?" Jaylyn asked, walking through the path.

"We knew Arthur in our past lives!" Giselle exclaimed, hugging Arthur tightly.

Jaylyn's confused look melted into a smile. Giselle let go of him and looked over at Sebastian, who was standing a few feet away. Arthur stood up, and Sebastian embraced him, tears in their eyes. They had been through war together. They started families afterward. Some of their best and worst memories were together.

Their spiritual reunion was shared with their fellow teammates. Rosa, Ryan and Ramon were pleased to see this happier Arthur, as were Sebastian and Giselle. While in a quieter setting, Arthur was already feeling better as they swapped stories about their past. They talked throughout the afternoon about how strong their kids were and how successful they must have been, even though none of them knew their fates for certain. They talked until Citlali appeared and called on Sebastian and Giselle to follow her. After promising to catch up, they were led to Ishmael's office. They could not wait to hug him again. Giselle was first in giving her energetic hug, nearly shaking him around. Sebastian followed, offering a warm, tight hug that nearly squeezed the air out of the director. They were enjoying their happy moments, partly because they accepted that there was nothing they could do about the past. The fatal car crash still hurt the two, and it was apparent now that these recent flashbacks may have temporarily aged them. But that didn't stop them from trying to enjoy what happiness came their way.

"We did not finish our last conversation," Ishmael said as they all took their seats. "I wish I could talk about your son's legacy, but there are no records of his job history. What we do know is he served in the military. Through my birth certificate, I was able to find out who my father was, and then from there I found his birth certificate, which is how I found out about you two. I chose you to be brought back to life at the same time and at the same institution. I had to pull quite a few strings, but I managed. I knew you two would like to be together."

Giselle nearly jumped over the desk upon hearing this.

"Thank you!" Giselle smiled, kissing him on each cheek and lastly on the forehead.

"The best grandson anyone could have," Sebastian smiled, patting him on the arm. "By the way, should we tell anyone we're related?"

"About that," Ishmael began. "You can tell people but be careful. You'll encounter some ambitious peacekeepers who will think you're getting the best missions only because you know me. In the meantime, only tell those who can keep a secret. I have already told two people. I'd like to introduce you to my son and his wife if that's okay with you."

The two looked at him approvingly.

"We would love to meet them," Giselle said.

"Thank you," Ishmael said. "They don't know about the covert peacekeeper program, but cryogenics programs have been known to the public for a few years now. You can tell them you were brought back to life through a cryogenics program. Well come on, we'll meet them now!"

"Now?" Giselle asked astonished.

"Yes, let's go!" Ishmael said.

The abrupt journey excited Sebastian and Giselle, as they were about to meet their great-grandson and his wife. A hover car took them from the mountains of Mexicali to a marble skyscraper in San Francisco. Along the way, Ishmael's salt-and-pepper hair turned jet black.

"I like what you've done with your hair," Giselle commented.

"I think I'm going to stick with my natural hair color for now," Ishmael responded, placing his boots onto the balcony.

The couple followed, popping out of the vehicle and onto the side of an apartment building, where they were able to enter a living room. "Here we are. Darius? Catalina? Anyone here?"

"Coming," a woman called, appearing a moment later with gold and violet steampunk goggles over her red hair. Her gradient brown and red eyes warmed her guests.

A man poked his head through the opening of the kitchen behind her. "This is them?!" the man asked, not taking his eyes or smile off them. His short blue hair jumped a bit as he approached his guests. "I'm Darius. It's *so* nice to meet you. This is incredible!" He shook their hands, unsure if they were ready for a more intimate embrace.

"Your great-grandparents," Ishmael said.

Despite already shaking their hands, Darius decided to give them a bear hug. A great deal of warm energy shifted from the man into the couple.

"It's not every day you get to meet your great-grandparents who were brought back to life," Darius said.

"I'm Catalina," the woman said, gluing her eyes to the two. "I cannot believe I am meeting my great-grandparents-in-law. Amazing!"

"Ishmael told us a few minutes ago that you had agreed to come," Darius said. "Months ago, we were told you two were brought back to life but were still undergoing medical tests. It sounds so strange to say that out loud! Ishmael said you might be a little shy at first, but we're so grateful to meet you."

"Maybe I'll get to meet *my* great-grandparents," Catalina said, smiling and nodding her head to Ishmael.

He shook his head in subtle disagreement.

"Oh. Bummer," Catalina said.

"What are you guys working on?" Sebastian asked.

"Oh, come," Catalina said. "You must see."

The hosts showed the couple a new species they were creating that wouldn't need oxygen to live. It could someday help them explore unknown areas of space. Afterward, they were told stories about how their hosts had met in a study abroad program on the moon. Then they started a conversation about possibly having a baby. It was explained that in these days, people were more inclined to have children since they were genetically engineered and much easier to raise with all the technology and resources available. With the extremely high fertility rates, the governments of the world had launched massive jobs-building programs. Despite this population boom, clone-producing programs were established to fill in foreseen gaps in the job markets. Most gaps in the workforce were in military and other dangerous job fields. There were countless babies born, and due to advances in science and technology, people were also living for as long as they wanted to. Not many people died, and therefore, those living now who were born from the 1990s to the 2070s were nicknamed the Last Generation, mainly because they were all born naturally, and babies now were born through genetic engineering and incubation. Ishmael, Sebastian and Giselle were part of this Last Generation. Darius and Catalina were both genetically engineered.

"We were both born in the year 2082," Catalina said. "That makes us seventeen over twenty-five years old."

"What does that mean?" Sebastian asked.

"It means we have been on this planet for seventeen years, but our bodies' ages are twenty-five," Darius filled in.

"And that's how our bodies' ages are going to stay," Catalina chimed in. "Frankly, most people stop their body's aging once in their twenties. We have science to thank for stopping our aging."

"Ishmael is forty over thirty," Darius informed. "How old are you two?"

"Well, Giselle and Sebastian were born in the year 2012 and 2010, respectively, so that would make them eighty-seven and eighty-nine," Ishmael said. "And since they are in their younger forms, they would be eighty-seven over twenty-one years old and eighty-nine over twenty-one years old."

Shivers went through Sebastian and Giselle as they found out how old they truly were. It was not made obvious through their youthful bodies. They knew they were from an earlier time, but to come to terms with the fact that they were about to hit the century mark was startling.

"Weren't we around thirty years old when we supposedly died?" Sebastian asked.

"Yes, but we start everyone's bodies at twenty-one years old," Ishmael said.

"Why is that?" Giselle asked.

Ishmael changed the conversation, and after a long talk about children, the hosts brought up that they wanted to have their own kid, admitting they felt a sudden "primitive urge," as they playfully tried to bite each other. What they meant, of course, was they wanted to have their first baby.

"What would we name him or her?" Catalina asked. "Maybe after a place we visited?"

"Well we've been to the moon and back, so let's call her Moon, or Luna," Darius suggested. "I honestly prefer a girl."

"I'm still undecided about boy or girl, but a girl, why not?" Catalina exclaimed.

"What about a color?" Ishmael asked.

"Giselle, what is your favorite color?" Catalina asked.

"Purple," Giselle said without hesitation.

"A name variation of purple would be?" Catalina pondered. "Violet!? Orchid!? Magenta!?"

"What about Amethyst?" Giselle recommended. The couple looked at her as if she had said something earth-shattering.

"Yes!" Catalina agreed. "That is perfect! Amethyst. Amethyst. Amethyst. Amethyst!"

"So, it's settled," Darius said. "We are having a girl and her name shall be Amethyst."

"We interrupt this broadcast for breaking news," a woman said, as a hologram appeared in front of the group. "The president of the United States of North America has been assassinated. She was killed moments ago by her aide here in Los Angeles. We have been notified by Police Chief Vanessa..."

It came as a shock to Sebastian and Giselle, not because they weren't expecting it—indeed they were—but because they weren't sure *when* the president's aide was going to complete the task. It was no secret to their institution that their team had gone on this mission to hack the president's aide, but Catalina and Darius knew nothing about the covert peacekeepers and their work. They reacted as if they, personally, were under attack. Given the president's security, something like that shouldn't have happened, they thought.

"The vice president is being sworn in underground," the reporter continued. "As of now, there is no information as to why this unfortunate event has taken place."

"Oh no," Catalina said with tears in her eyes.

"I voted for her," Darius sighed.

"We should be going," Ishmael said, remaining calm but serious. "Given what happened, I'm not sure what might occur next. Giselle and Sebastian will return with me. You two stay safe."

"Yes, you too," Darius said sadly. "All of you. I hope to see you two again."

"Please come for the birth of our child," Catalina said, lighting up the mood. "We'll let you know when we facilitate the incubation."

"Facilitate the incubation?" Giselle questioned.

"Oh, right, you might not know," Catalina said. "That's the term for when we genetically modify the babies in an incubator. It can take five minutes or several hours, depending on how picky the parents are about their babies' genetics. You do, after all, have to choose the hair color, eye color, height and on and on."

"That's fascinating," Giselle marveled. "Please keep us updated."

"It was so great to meet you," Catalina said quietly. "I'm loving the hair color, Ishmael."

Catalina immediately moved in for a fierce farewell hug. They said their goodbyes and were soon back at the institution discussing their day with their closest teammates and Arthur, who they had now grown closer to.

CHAPTER 22 – PALACE INTO DUST

The endless commotion about the recent assassination turned to applause and cheer as Sebastian, Rosa and Ryan entered the auditorium, and a path was cleared so they could make their way to the front. Charles and Citlali were at the stage, clapping their hands as well. There was one less socioeconomic criminal in the world.

"Who needs a president anyway?!" one man cheered.

"Yeah! Politics is so outdated!" a woman shouted.

"If anyone should run our nation, it should be an artificial intelligence like Citlali."

"Why isn't she in control of everything? She can manage things much better than any human being, given the fact that she is everywhere at once."

"Because people still don't trust an A.I."

"Why? Why can't they trust her? Because she isn't human? She's an amazing person. How could people not trust her? That's kind of racist, to be honest."

The commotion soon settled as Ishmael made his way to the center stage.

"First, I would like to congratulate Rosa, Ryan and Sebastian on a job well done," Ishmael said as another wave of applause commenced. "As you all know, they were the ones involved in this assassination. We now have one less problem in this world, and it's time to tackle the next one. We've recently discovered that one of the socioeconomic criminals has positioned himself in the South Pacific Alliance, a peacekeeper nation. He will be visiting the secluded Presidential Palace of the now-deceased president.

The public still does not know the president was a socioeconomic criminal, nor do they know our next target is one as well. We cannot let the public discover this secret, otherwise we will alarm our other targets and make it harder to track and terminate them. After the tournament results, we have registered those who will be going on the mission to the Presidential Palace. Everyone else will be put on reconnaissance operations. We are much closer to our final stage of invading the Orderkeeper nations. All your hard work is greatly appreciated." He paused, and after scanning the room to find Sebastian and Giselle, continued: "Good luck to you all."

As everyone was dismissed, Sebastian took Giselle to the end of the hallway to be alone.

"Before we go I think we should talk," Sebastian started, staring into her silent eyes and then cushioning his hands on her cheeks. "We've been through a lot. I know we haven't talked much about the past. We already lost each other once before, and if I don't say something now then I might not be able to in the future."

"Shhh!" she said with two of her fingers on his lips and then placed her hands on the sides of his head. "Don't talk like that. We are going to be fine! You hear me!? We are going to be fine. Life wasn't great then, but look at everything there is now. It's a great day to be alive, Sebastian. Don't you ever forget that."

Their lips got closer than their hearts. With their eyes still closed they parted. They opened their eyes to look at each other again. She knew exactly how to help him. Just like in the past, she still found ways to reach his soul. She took him to catch up with their teams. Sebastian and Giselle's teams were led together through a series of brightly lit arrows. At the end of a corridor were Ishmael, Charles and Citlali.

"The six of you still haven't undergone your specialty evaluations," Charles said. "Your specialty will decide your main job in this program. It can be infantry or intelligence focused to name just two areas. Your next mission will decide what your specialties are and truly test your capabilities as peacekeepers. Because of your success at the tournament, your two teams have been chosen to go on this vital mission. Once again you have to drop everything you're doing for the good of humanity."

"Your mission will be to infiltrate the Presidential Palace and eliminate the newly-discovered socioeconomic criminal," Citlali started. The surprised peacekeepers stayed still and quiet out of discipline. Sebastian's team was now again going to play a part in taking down a major target. Despite being a new team, they instantly noticed they were getting the high-ranking missions and felt fortunate. "We have information that a prominent member of the South Pacific Peacekeeper Alliance will be making his way there. His name is Typhus. Here is the thing: If you fail, we may not get another chance to kill him. Unbeknownst to anyone outside the covert peacekeeper initiative, this person has recently come into possession of a weapon from the Celestial Weapons Chest that gives him the power to shapeshift. So, once they find out we are trying to kill him, he will go into hiding. Here is an image of what he looks like without a disguise, beard, bald head, retro glasses and all. Of course, he may not look like this all the time."

"The coordinates have already been downloaded into your bracelets," Ishmael said. "But be careful. The palace is an incredibly dangerous place for intruders. With the president confirmed dead, the palace will consider everyone who enters it a threat, except of course warkeepers and socioeconomic criminals. But we've given you fake warkeeper identities. This place will come close to what it is like to fight in *their* territory, so be vigilant! We're not sure how the president went as long as she did without us knowing about her being a socioeconomic criminal. It makes you wonder who else might be our enemy. We have Underground, Air and Space warfare units standing by, though you might only need the Air Force if it comes to that. They'll be situated far from sight though, so no one— not even yourselves—will see them." Ishmael looked hard at the peacekeepers, his stare more focused on Sebastian and Giselle than the others. "I don't know what else to say," he concluded somberly. "I'll see you all soon."

***

Their clothes now consisted of Orderkeeper uniforms of the same black-and-red style they had when attempting to retrieve the Celestial Weapons Chest. They hovered downward into the underground along the elevator path, then sideways and up again. It brought the six operatives aboveground and into a grassy marsh in the middle of nowhere, the perfect place to deal in Orderkeeper activities far from any U-ITS-operated city. Through their zoomed-in contact lenses, the palace looked more like an abandoned fortress with its pointy towers, tall stone walls, and charcoal iron gates. What could be more fitting for a malevolent being's hideout? It was as if no one was there, but they knew at least one socioeconomic criminal lurked inside. But doing what? Possibly destroying evidence of the president being a socioeconomic criminal. Maybe collecting weapons and intelligence the president had left behind. The operatives speculated but didn't know. They only knew someone who committed atrocious acts was there.

"We will enter and scout the palace for the target," Sebastian started. "We'll send a distress signal through these microscopic transponders if anything happens."

They placed the transponders under their tongues or in their shoes. The six moved through the tall grass and cool wind toward their destination.

"Must be nice to be president," Ryan said sarcastically. "You can have your own evil fortress in the middle of nowhere and everybody will think it's your vacation home."

"I still can't believe there's a human for president," Arthur said. "I'm from the past and even *I* think a human president is outdated."

"Citlali for president 2100," Rosa said.

"She has my vote," Arthur smiled.

When they made it to the stone gates, they held up their bracelets to be scanned. Because of the fake Orderkeeper identification downloaded on their bracelets, they were allowed access into the palace. The gates moved on their own but made a loud metal sound that might as well have been an announcement to those inside.

"Who are you?" a thin, well-dressed hologram with dark eyes said, slowly appearing and hovering over them.

"We are Orderkeepers from the Central American Pact," Sebastian said, sticking to the cover provided on his contact lenses.

"Why are you here?" he asked, scratching his neck curiously.

"The same reason everyone else is here," Sebastian continued.

"And what is that?"

"To make sure the Orderkeeper operations continue successfully," Sebastian said vaguely. "Can you take me to see the representative from the South Pacific Alliance?"

"He is not seeing anyone right now."

"It's important."

"He might be available later."

"Then you don't mind if we look around, do you?"

"Do as you wish. I will remove myself from sight but will keep an eye on you all. You won't be able to see me, but I'll be able to see you. And no reanimation bars. I'll take those!" the hologram said, reaching out an impatient hand, collecting the bars, and disappearing into the distance.

They would have to be careful of the hologram's prying ears. From here on out the operatives would have to vaguely discuss their actions as they looked for the socioeconomic criminal. They continued down the stone path into the palace's self-opening colossal doors. They split up into their usual two teams. Sebastian, Rosa and Ryan went straight into the dining hall together, while Giselle, Arthur and Ramon crept up the spiraling stairs. It was quiet, and because of the size of the area they didn't know where to start. Every turn or walk down a hall resulted in rooms with openings into other hallways that also contained rooms. They soon realized the palace was constantly changing. They turned around after walking into a living room they had passed through and saw it was now an indoor garden. The next hall they went through was now a dead-end library. Even with the furniture and tokens changing in the palace, everything was quiet. Still, they carried on their search for the enemy in this bizarre home that seemed to have a mind of its own.

"Take a look," Rosa said, intentionally vague in case the hologram was listening in. She was the first to enter what looked like a weaponry room. It had items ranging from simple stone clubs to advanced weapons such as ray machine guns. Basically, they were looking at a collection of how weapons had evolved since the dawn of time. They walked out of the room, and when they turned around, it was now a two-story reading room. They continued walking until they reached what looked like a room dedicated to the president that showed pictures of when she was a known socioeconomic criminal. She was a political lobbyist and former president of a well-known chemical disposal corporation that dumped a small portion of used chemicals into waters close to where many people lived. Unfortunately, it was never considered a big enough issue to tackle a corporation controlled by hundreds of powerful people. This enormous room was a clear parallel to the president's ego. Video played about her accomplishments. The ego of the now-deceased leader caused the operatives to cringe. This was enough to set off an alarm.

"Why do you quail!?" the hologram shouted, materializing over them. "Are you not aware of what this great person has done? You're not Orderkeepers, are you?"

"It's not that," Sebastian said. "All of this caused by one person? We're impressed."

"I thought so," the hologram said, disappearing again. The three knew they had to be extra careful not to express any more emotions. The next room was dedicated to monitoring people in peril and despair, showing screens of people living in Orderkeeper nations. It was enough to make the three immediately leave the room, but because of the building, they were thrown into an endless loop of identical rooms like this. It was clear the hologram was in control of the palace and wanted to find out if they were Orderkeepers. Realizing this, the operatives decided to play along as best as they could. They began slowing down and glancing at the screens. It was horrifying to say the least. There were kids being indoctrinated into the Orderkeeper army. Many people were living in shacks being patrolled by holograms and genetically engineered animals and humans. There was obviously a large amount of sophisticated technology being used, yet most of the people were still living in undesirable circumstances. Finally, it was as if they were let go and allowed to explore different kinds of rooms. The next area was a club that was at least four stories high. It had holographic women and men dancing and chatting. The operatives were ignored by the holograms as they made their way up a two-story ramp. The ramp led them to a marble hallway fit for giants where they bumped into Giselle and her team. Sebastian shook his head "no" and Giselle responded the same. They had been unsuccessful in their search.

"Can we see the man I spoke of earlier?" Sebastian said out loud.

The hologram appeared again, this time not saying anything right away.

"Why are you so eager to see him?" the hologram asked.

"We have business with him," Arthur said.

"And what is that, exactly?" the hologram pondered, feeling the back of his hand with his chin.

"We are trying to find out how we should proceed in our operations," Sebastian said. "And due to recent events, we are in a rush."

"There are backup plans already in place for nearly every possible scenario. Our central artificial intelligence can without a doubt outsmart this nation's central artificial intelligence! What's this nation's A.I. called? Citlali? Ha! She doesn't stand a chance!" the hologram sensed a few of the peacekeepers' disdain at his comment and began growing bigger. "Why are you really here? You are being suspicious. Fine. If you want to see him, then—" He paused for a second, looking away and then back at Sebastian. "You have your wish," the hologram said with a rough voice as the lights dimmed around him.

A roaring sound rang throughout the hallway as vines of concrete broke through the floor and walls. Before they could react, the vines began wrapping themselves around the operatives, consuming everything but their heads and pulling them back against the walls. Their nanotech suits ruptured and sprinkled into the air. Not even Sebastian's ESP device could warn him in time to evade the rapid vines. The trapped warriors struggled to free themselves but were tightly gripped and unable to move.

"What is this?" Arthur struggled to ask through the choking green vines.

"Well, you wanted to see him," the hologram said. "Now I am taking you to him."

The hallway incinerated, revealing a dark stadium with rusted metal walls and black sandy dirt. The vines of concrete released their victims. A loud roar ensued as the peacekeepers looked around at the holographic audience from afar. On one side of the venue was a viewing booth that held a small group of individuals, including the hologram. One of the men at the booth sat in a throne-like golden chair. Another man waited at the seated person's side. Even from a distance it was obvious he was a giant. He raised his arms and the audience grew quiet.

"I hope you are all in for a treat!" the man said, shaking his head violently. The contact lenses of the peacekeeper operatives identified him as Mal. He was the known right-hand man of their South Pacific Alliance target. "This is proof that the peacekeepers have been launching a secret offensive on us! The time to act is now! We will strike back ferociously, starting with these peacekeepers before us!"

The crowd again began to roar. The operatives were quite not sure what to do. They hoped this was a test, and they were not made as peacekeepers. Their nerves tempted them to run scenarios on how to escape, but without their reanimation bars it would be nearly impossible. An Orderkeeper was guided onto a reanimation platform in front of the operatives. Silver highlights shined on the ends of his red clothes, and his black beret matched the bits of coal that dominated the arena floor. He was a giant with rock-hard muscles that appeared to be forged by steel. His hideous body was not made of skin, but of actual red diamonds.

"Our first contest will begin with the infamous Orderkeeper Hell's Savant!" Mal yelled, then pointed at one of the peacekeepers. "Against Arthur the peacekeeper."

Now they knew their covers were blown. It was either fight or flight. They could not stay where they were. They needed to move. Sebastian and Arthur immediately took out their transponders from under their tongues to send a warning signal to the military for backup.

"What are you doing?" Mal asked, looking at Sebastian. "It doesn't matter, we will kill anyone you send. No one will save you now. There is no hope for any of you!"

Everyone except Arthur was pushed far back against the coliseum wall by reanimation crystals. They dropped to the floor as jail cages fell on each of them, trapping them in separate cells. Arthur, with fists clenched, kept his focus on the Orderkeeper.

"Before we begin, our powerful leader would like to say a few words," Mal said, waving his arms toward the man in the throne chair. "Please welcome Typhus, the leader of the South Pacific Alliance!"

An applause commenced as a man stood up. A man even taller than Mal. He had on colorful robes and every bit of jewelry imaginable. A gold crown with gems sat on his head, and a gold cane nestled between his fingers. A ruby necklace with gold pendants attached to it hung over his chest. Maybe one of these accessories was the celestial weapon he was known to carry. He matched the exact description shown to them: bald head with a beard and retro glasses.

"Ladies and gentlemen, thank you for taking the time out of your busy lives to witness this turning point," Typhus said. "This is the start of the war we've all been waiting for. We will end every single one of these peacekeepers and send their heads to the steps of their headquarters. The peacekeepers have always thought they had the advantage, but it was us that were always steps ahead. We already control their politics and resources and they don't even know it. They are the ones under *our* leadership! They are the ones who will lose!"

The crowd roared with laughter. The peacekeepers tried to break free from the cell bars, but it was useless. They could not use reanimation technology to break out. They could only watch Arthur helplessly.

"Now, let us begin!" Typhus concluded.

"The rules are simple," Mal yelled. "Last man standing! Fight!"

Immediately the Orderkeeper charged at Arthur, throwing a jab and cross. Arthur dodged them both, dropping himself to the ground, slipping one leg behind the beast's knees and placing the other leg against his chest in an attempt to push him down. It did not work. The Orderkeeper picked up Arthur with one hand and threw him across the arena. Arthur rolled and rolled, stopping only when he hit the wall. He coughed blood out of his mouth as he struggled to get up.

"We have to do something!" Giselle yelled.

"Let me fight!" Sebastian yelled.

Arthur moved away from the wall as the beast approached again. He struggled to move at first and found himself on his knees again. The crowd laughed mockingly. Eventually, he stood up once more and moved away from the approaching beast.

"That's it? That's all these peacekeepers can do?" Mal said as Arthur limped under his booth. Sebastian wanted to give Arthur his ESP bracelet but didn't want the Orderkeepers to see they were in possession of a celestial grade weapon. The hideous Orderkeeper charged Arthur and knocked him to the ground. Arthur could not keep up with his opponent. He stood up and punched the diamond-skinned Orderkeeper in the chest, only to have the bones in his hand shatter. The Orderkeeper pulled Arthur's head down exposing his back. He then elbowed Arthur's back twice each time causing Arthur to yelp in pain. Arthur was picked up by the neck and lifted far from the ground. What could they do? Ryan coached Arthur to keep his distance and see if the Orderkeeper got tired. Rosa and Ramon continued to use their Orderkeeper uniforms to pull apart the bars to make a gap big enough to pass through. Giselle looked around, both for a possible escape route and for a sign of hope that the military might already be among the crowd and hatching a plan to free them all. Sebastian kept thinking of how he could get his ESP bracelet to Arthur. As Arthur's face turned blue his eyes turned red; he struggled between breathing and pain until he struggled no more. Their hope died then with their loving friend Arthur.

The giant threw Arthur's body to the ground. Sebastian's cell door opened itself next. It was Sebastian's turn to take on this beast. He said nothing and instead charged at Hell's Savant.

"Sebastian!" Giselle and the others cried out.

Sebastian's fierce face matched his speed. The ESP bracelet jolted a premonition into his head. He knew what to do. He jumped close to the being's eyes. Slicing the air as his hands moved, he was able to claw at its eyes, pulling them out and crushing them. He then retreated as the monster screamed in agony, grabbed hold of its face and stepped back. Sebastian then went for the giant's fingernail. It barely budged half an inch, but it was enough to make the being howl in more pain. The monster grabbed hold of Sebastian by the torso. Sebastian wheezed in pain as the giant began squeezing him. Sebastian dug his hands into the enormous now-empty eye sockets of the beast grabbing the brain. The monster let out one last violent movement before collapsing onto the ground. It was over. The crowd was silent. Sebastian had won the contest.

"This is unexpected," Mal said. "You killed an elite Orderkeeper. No one ever gets this close—"

"Enough of this," Typhus said, getting up from his seat. "We don't have time for this. I will finish him."

He descended toward Sebastian on a floating platform, vibrating the black sandy dirt under him as he drew nearer. Typhus was at least twice as tall as Sebastian. Sebastian glared at him in astonishment, wondering if all Orderkeepers were this monstrous.

"Are you ready, peacekeeper?" Typhus said, leaning over him. Sebastian had no choice but to get in his fighting stance and pray his ESP bracelet would give him the premonitions to save himself. Everyone looked up. Explosions were heard coming from outside.

"Is that our backup?" Ryan whispered.

"Whoever it is, they won't get to you in time," Typhus said. "Find out what is going on outside and take care of it. We are almost finished here."

The hologram at the booth agreed yet remained where he was, presumably because he was already simultaneously fighting off the threat from outside. More explosions erupted from outside, causing dust and small bits of debris to lightly hail down on the crowd. Without taking a step, Typhus was able to reach Sebastian's face with a punch that smacked him to the ground. The imprisoned peacekeepers shouted back in anger.

"So, you're the one they sent to kill me?" Typhus taunted. "I'm offended."

"How long do you all think you will continue to get away with this?" Sebastian asked, getting back up in his boxing stance. "Hasn't someone told you yet? Your species is coming to an end."

"Who is going to stop me? You?"

"Me, my teammates, all peacekeepers," Sebastian said, stalling for the backup team. "It's only a matter of time. You're no match for us."

"Wrong. It's only a matter of time before your people are condemned to extinction. And no match, you say? I don't think you can even grasp the capabilities of those working alongside us. It is you who are outmatched."

Sebastian studied Typhus to see if he could notice any jewelry that might be a celestial weapon. It was a nearly impossible task since Typhus had on so much jewelry. Maybe if Sebastian could grab all of it, surely one would be a celestial weapon. Sebastian snatched away at the necklace, but Typhus moved out of the way before Sebastian could come close to the precious metals.

"Don't even bother," Typhus cackled. "You'll never get it."

With more explosions, patches of the ceiling began collapsing all over the stadium.

"It looks like your world is collapsing," Sebastian said, letting out a sly smile. "Metaphoric, isn't it?"

"It is your world that will come to an end," Typhus responded angrily with another punch. This time Sebastian dodged it. Sebastian's counter kick to his knee also missed as Typhus morphed his leg to move away. They continued to exchange punches that only caught the air. Typhus kept using his celestial weapon to shapeshift his body parts to dodge every punch Sebastian threw. Sebastian was able to dodge every punch with his own celestial weapon as it continued to give him premonitions of where he was going to be hit. They were evenly matched.

"Let's have some fun, shall we?" Typhus said. He shapeshifted himself from the tall being into Arthur. They exchanged more punches and kicks but landed none of them.

"You're twisted!" Rosa shouted. "You know that?!"

"Don't worry, Sebastian!" Ramon called out. "That's not him!"

210

Debris continued to fall, missing the two. Then they heard screams coming from the jail cells where Sebastian's friends were being held. Debris had fallen onto everyone, but most of it landed in Ramon and Giselle's cell. Ramon was hit hard on the head, causing blood to pour out onto his face. He sat on the ground with his hands on his wound. Giselle was knocked to the ground with her leg trapped beneath the fallen rocks. She struggled to get the rocks off, but the cell was too small, and the bars too narrowly spaced to push them out. Another explosion led to more debris falling, this time landing onto sections of the stands, erasing where the Orderkeeper holograms once were.

"No!" Sebastian said, running to her with a desperate cry. He slid to his knees and tried to grab the rocks, but it was no use.

"I see you care for her very much," Typhus said in Arthur's voice. "If you want to save her, you'll have to defeat me first."

Sebastian turned around angrily but was caught off guard by what he saw. Typhus had shapeshifted himself into Giselle's figure. He was going to force Sebastian to fight the very image of the woman he loved.

"It's okay, Sebastian," Giselle said as she struggled to breathe with a stream of blood sliding down her face. "That's not me. You can beat him."

Typhus now as Giselle charged Sebastian, his clothes changing to match the Orderkeeper outfits they had on, but still wearing all the original jewelry he had on. Again they exchanged punches, and instead of dodging them this time, they blocked, their blows echoing throughout an arena filled with the bloodthirsty Orderkeeper holograms. Sebastian grabbed Typhus' fist as it was about to hit his cheek and bent his wrist, pushing him to the ground.

"*Now* what are you going to do?" Sebastian's opponent said in Giselle's voice.

"Shut up already!" Sebastian yelled, frustrated. "I know you feel pain! You must feel some sort of pain! Everybody feels pain!"

Sebastian straightened out Typhus' arm and laid a strike upward to the elbow, dislocating it. Seeing Giselle's form cry out in pain hurt Sebastian to hear, but the sudden laughter brought Sebastian to the reality that he wasn't fighting Giselle.

"I'm only joking," he said as his elbow instantly went back into place. "Yes, I feel pain, but barely. Let me get serious now. You know being in this body makes me much faster than you."

211

He pushed Sebastian back, throwing several punches to his arms to weaken his arm muscles. Sebastian moved back and massaged his biceps with his hands. The shapeshifter moved forward and again threw a barrage of punches, this time to his neck and face. For a moment Sebastian struggled to breathe and see clearly. He went back into his fighting stance, wondering why his ESP bracelet did not warn him before. Maybe he was too quick for Sebastian, but this wasn't the time to have doubts. He knew he had to focus. The lives of his friends were on the line.

Large parts of the ceiling began collapsing, exposing sunlight and two blue airships. The peacekeeper reinforcements were here. The holograms of Orderkeepers began disappearing one by one. This caught Typhus off guard, which gave Sebastian the chance to grab some dirt in one hand and attempt several hard punches to the chin with the other. When the first punch landed, Typhus brought up his hands to protect his chin. In pain, Typhus morphed to his original self. Sebastian threw the dirt into his eyes. When he brought his hands to his eyes to remove the dirt, Sebastian landed a second punch to the chin, knocking him flat onto the ground. He jumped onto his fallen opponent, using the front of Typhus' shirt as a grip to lift his upper body off the ground. He landed one more punch to the chin that caused the back of Typhus' head to hit the ground and knock him out. He had finished it. Sebastian turned around and looked over at the cells. An airship had made its way to it and began shooting beams of light, dismantling the cell bars and turning them to dust. Everyone began moving the rocks off the real Giselle. Sebastian and Rosa carefully picked her up while Ryan and a newly joined Jaime ran to Arthur's body. A wounded Ramon was escorted by Paula, who had just come off the ship, as the rest of the team brought Giselle and Arthur to the ship, where Alice helped them onto the aircraft.

"To the institution!" Alice said, as she looked over at the wounded peacekeepers.

When they thought they were saved, a bullet hit the side of the ship where they were entering to evacuate. It came from a newly animated gun in Typhus' hand.

"I'm not through with you," Typhus said, landing another shot squarely on his intended target: Giselle's heart. She was instantly silenced. "Mal! Hack his brain! I want to know who else he cares about!"

The shaken peacekeepers looked at Giselle. They knew if they didn't get her medical treatment as soon as possible, this would be it for her.

"Get her out of here, now!" Sebastian ordered while looking at Typhus. "I'm going to end this."

"I'm with you," Jaime said, handing a thick reanimation bar to Sebastian.

The airship carrying the remaining peacekeepers shot up into the air and took off. The other airship remained, waiting for the two. They used their reanimation bars to create see-through shields that allowed them to get past the bombardment of bullets coming from Typhus, who was still lying on the ground. Mal moved his hands around, trying to hack Sebastian's mind. Jaime immediately stepped in and started using his skills in human hacking to do the same to Mal.

"You can hack someone from outside Citlali's system?" Sebastian asked as blood silently streamed from his nose.

"Yeah, as long as they're in the global peacekeeper system I can hack them," Jaime reassured him.

Sebastian heard a loud screeching noise accompanied by the sound of a motorcycle engine revving in his ears as the enemy human hacker started making his way through Sebastian's mind. Sebastian fell to his knees with a hand against his head. Blood dripped from his eyes. Still, with the other hand he kept up his shield to protect his comrade.

"Take ... a look ... at this," Mal said with great difficulty as Jaime hacked his mind. Mal held up a small screen to Typhus whispering something to him.

"Perfect," Typhus said as Mal's head exploded in front of him. Blood and brains splattered all over an unsympathetic Typhus.

"Don't do that to Typhus," Sebastian said, now free from the hacker. He placed both hands on the shield. "He is mine."

"Fine, but if I have to I'm stepping in," Jaime said.

"Fine," Sebastian said as he ran toward Typhus. "If you're so bad then stand up and face me."

"How about something better?" Typhus shapeshifted again this time, into someone even smaller. Sebastian paused as the shapeshifter transformed into Sebastian's deceased son. A confused and angry Sebastian began pacing himself around the injured, resting boy. Around this haunting ghost. What kind of monster would think to do this?

"That's it, I'm stepping in!" Jaime said.

"No!" Sebastian yelled. The kid looked exactly as Sebastian last remembered seeing him. Unexpectedly, all the guilt he had been trying to suppress swept across his thoughts. Like a raging river, all the shame swept through him from that life-changing car crash. He had failed his son and Giselle through that accident, which led to Giselle and Sebastian being brought back to life many decades later while leaving behind their son all alone in the world. Sebastian was torn. He looked at the shapeshifter who was lying still. A confused Sebastian attempted to restart the boy's heart, pushing on the small chest in an attempt to save the boy's life. It worked. Sebastian was then again brought back to the realization that this wasn't his kid. With tears rolling down his cheeks, he got up again and let out a yell.

"It looks like you beat me here, but we'll meet again," Typhus said, shapeshifting back to his original body. A red ship reanimated around the injured Typhus and lifted him up. It burrowed into the ground escorted by a dozen other newly animated red airships. The stadium shook but became steadier when the ships disappeared into the ground leaving behind cracks.

"How dare he run off," Sebastian said now kneeling with his hands clenching his hair, looking at where the ship was a moment ago.

"Sebastian. Look around," Jaime said, eyeing the collapsing arena and tapping on the holographic palace on his satellite bracelet. "The building is destroying itself, possibly to get rid of any evidence that there was any warkeeper activity here. Come on, we need to go!"

The remaining blue airship came down to retrieve the two.

"Don't think you're going to get away that easily," said the well-dressed hologram from before. The collapsing debris redefined itself into reanimation technology. Streams of it hurtled itself at the ship, pushing it away from their escape route and into a series of rooms.

"Hold on!" said the peacekeeper pilot. They were immediately hit by numerous whips. Sebastian took off his ESP bracelet and gave it to the pilot.

"Don't question it. Trust it and yourself for now," Sebastian said, hoping the pilot would understand right away. In every room they maneuvered through, the place set itself on fire around the peacekeepers. It wasn't long before the pilot found a new escape route through the palace main entrance. They flew over the once-beautiful garden and away from the deteriorating fortress. Once the team was far away from the palace, they looked back and saw that it was nothing more than a burned-out stain on the face of the planet. Like Sebastian's past, it could only be brought back in memory.

CHAPTER 23 – THE START AND END OF LOVE

Before the airship even landed on the institution's rooftop, Sebastian had jumped off. He used reanimation crystals to create a descending platform to bring him down onto the courtyard. He rushed into the medical unit's waiting room and saw his friends huddled quietly.

"How is she?" Sebastian asked, nervously looking at Ryan and Rosa.

"She is going to be fine," Rosa said, shooting a worried glance at Sebastian.

"But there's something you should know," Ryan said.

"Sebastian," Citlali said, walking into the lobby with Charles, "please come with us."

The two led him into one of the private operating rooms. Sebastian looked through the one-way glass window at an unconscious Giselle. She was lying on a hospital bed clothed in a long patient shirt surrounded by metallic robots giving her medical tests.

"What's going on?" Sebastian asked. "Why does it look like the tests I was first given?"

"She is going to be all right," Charles reassured. "But you need to know that she will need some time to recover."

"What is going on?" Sebastian pleaded to know.

"Because of the critical state she was in she needed to be ... revived," Citlali said. "She will have to get all her memories back like before. She will remember you so long as you give her the time she needs to retrieve her memories."

"She is alive, Sebastian," Charles whispered. "That's more than we can say about Arthur."

216

"But why didn't he make it also?" Sebastian asked.

"If Arthur was given medical treatment right away, there might have been a chance to save him," Citlali said. "Giselle was fortunate that she made it here in time. We're sorry we didn't save him as well."

"So he's gone, just like that!?" Sebastian paused bringing down his tone. "After everything he's been through."

A moment of silence ensued as Giselle began opening her eyes.

"She's waking up," Sebastian said.

"We have to give her time to adapt to her settings before we introduce her to others," Citlali said.

"I understand," Sebastian whispered.

"Subject is coming close to shock," one of the metallic robots said.

A trembling Sebastian placed his head against the glass window with a fist covering his mouth.

"Initiating tranquilization for the patient," said another robot.

"Let's go, Sebastian," Citlali said, putting her hand on his shoulder. He shook his head and turned toward the exit, keeping his eyes closed most of the time. They walked back out into the waiting room to a group of concerned friends.

"What do you want me to do until then?" Sebastian said, containing himself.

"You have your peacekeeper graduation in a few days," Ishmael said, entering the lobby. "It'll be at the California Peacekeeper Headquarters in San Francisco. You, as well as those who were with you, have completed the mission."

"But we didn't eliminate our target, Typhus," Sebastian said, defeated.

"No, but thanks to Jaime's hacking success we know his routines, the places he stays at, and those he works closest with," Ishmael said. "We will take care of him soon. Until then, you have all been classified into your new units."

"New?" Rosa asked.

"Yes, although you three worked well together you have all shown varying qualities that fit you well with others," Ishmael said. "Don't worry, you three can still see each other, but many of your future missions will be with new peacekeepers. From time to time you will be placed in separate institutions and bases."

The three looked at each other. They had grown comfortable working together. They had lived together, faced this new world together, and now they were to be separated. Although now they would become peacekeepers, they were met with a realization that they would not always be able to look after each other. It was bittersweet to say the least.

A few afternoons later and with the sun as high as everyone's spirits, the peacekeeper initiation began. They lined up in the large spaces afforded to them at the headquarters, once again wearing their black slacks and dark-blue stand-collar button-down shirts with a navy-blue-and-white blazer over them. Blue bandannas tied themselves around their necks, and blue berets appeared on their heads.

"Repeat after me," Ishmael said. "I (state your name), do solemnly accept the responsibilities and dedication required to complete my humble work."

Everyone repeated together with their white-gloved right hands over their hearts.

"I will, to the best of my ability, preserve, protect and defend the people of our civilization."

After repeating this last bit of the Peacekeeper Oath, Ishmael let out a smile.

"Congratulations, you are now full members of the Peacekeeper Order," Ishmael said as a roaring of clapping and cheering followed. It was now time for each of them to walk onto the stage and be inducted into their new military fields.

"There are many specialties in our line of work, but after evaluating your past successes you each have been carefully chosen to represent select groups," Charles announced. "The first trio to successfully complete their basic training in this cohort, please come up."

Alice went up first, receiving the psychological warfare patch on her shoulder. Paula followed behind and received a communications patch. Jaime went up next to collect the cyber operations insignia. His new position would put him in a special intelligence unit that would use offensive psychological tactics through human hacking the masses. The three were made to stay on stage in formation while they waited for the remaining newly initiated peacekeepers. More peacekeepers walked onto the stage to claim artillery, combat engineering and environmental warfare badges, among others.

"The next three have made quite a reputation for themselves," Charles continued. "We expect a great deal from them, as we do all our peacekeepers."

Rosa went up first, receiving a reaper squad insignia. Peacekeepers who were made into reapers were expected to carry out assassinations. Ryan followed to receive his commando badge and was to be placed in the rebel training unit. He would play a crucial role in training foreign rebel groups to fight against their Orderkeeper dictatorships. A reluctant Sebastian went up next and received a skull patch that was only given to those who had eliminated an elite Orderkeeper. He was placed in the psychological warfare unit, the same specialty as Alice. In this unit, they were expected to administer offensive tactics by collaborating with locals in whichever territory they were assigned. It would be their jobs to recruit the locals to work with and be trained by peacekeepers. The trio was still standing at the front of the stage when Charles brought forward three silver medals with the words 'Peace and Prosperity Will Prevail' inscribed on them. Ishmael faced Charles and picked up a medal. He then turned to Ryan and ceremonially placed the medal over his head, before moving on to Rosa and Sebastian.

"We present these medals to you three for your efforts in defeating a socioeconomic criminal," Ishmael said as the crowd clapped.

Sebastian looked out in the crowd and saw the familiar faces of Patricio, Jaylyn, Chloe, Liam, Lydia, Ezekiel, Abigail, Gabriel and even the former Orderkeeper Angel in the crowd. It had been days since he last saw Giselle. He scanned the audience in hopes of catching a glimpse of her among the peacekeepers before it dawned on him that she was still recovering. Despite being surrounded by people he had trusted all these months, her absence added to his feeling of solitude. But he was hopeful he would see her soon and that she would recollect her memories of him and they would be back together. At that moment, he wanted nothing more than to wrap his arms around her and run his fingers through her silky hair. His mind jumped around as he came to the realization that she would have to relive all her flashbacks and recall the terrible world they once lived in. She would have to relive the tragic loss of their son. He remembered Citlali telling him to keep some distance from Giselle until she adjusted to her situation of being resurrected. Would he be around to comfort her when she had her memories restored? Or would he be out on a mission? Still on stage, Sebastian managed to suppress his tears and frustration. He tried to focus on something else. He looked around at the graduation ceremony. Ramon was next.

"We have been tasked to work in this field by chance," Ishmael said, taking the podium. "You are all here because chance would have it that your body and consciousness were preserved so you could help people in the future. And then there are dangers out there that we have chosen to take on. Many of us here know of a peacekeeper, ally and friend who has been taken from us. Recently, we had someone else taken from us. Please join me in a moment of silence for Arthur Alvares."

A moment of silence followed. Everyone was deeply saddened by the loss of their friend. Even the first peacekeepers, such as Thomas and Daniela, were saddened. The room became silent for everyone except Sebastian. For him everything was anything but silent as he fell into another flashback.

***

As darkness settled they put out the fire with the limitless dirt around them to avoid detection from enemy guerilla soldiers. It was time for the squad to go to sleep. Arthur would take the first shift to keep watch. Everyone else except Sebastian fell asleep. Sebastian continued looking into the star-filled sky.

"You should go to sleep, Sebastian," Arthur whispered, walking toward him.

"You know I have trouble sleeping," Sebastian replied. "With this war going on here and this world going to ruin, I don't know how anyone could sleep so soundly."

"I'm sure the world won't always be like this," Arthur responded.

"Then I'm sorry, but you are naïve."

"What makes you say that? Troubled times come and go."

"They do, but this time it's different."

"Oh? How? Because of climate catastrophes displacing millions of people every year? Because of all the crime happening in the United States and pretty much everywhere else? Do you seriously believe it is the end of humans? I say it's a test."

"A test? Who is testing us?"

"Well I know you don't believe in God, but I do believe we are being tested by a higher power. I mean, look at all those stars above and how incredible they are. In this darkness, they light the way."

"What do you mean?"

"One day, everyone will realize there is something more to life than conquering in the name of religion, race or resources. People need to look up and they'll see that there is something great out there waiting to be embraced."

"I still don't follow. People look at the sky all the time and they see stars they'll never reach. A universe they'll never understand."

"I will make this prediction right now: the world will have to get over your kind of pessimism before appreciating the positive motivation the dark sky above provides. One day we as humanity will realize we need to be at one with the universe. We will see past our petty differences and strive to be great."

"You're too optimistic. Maybe if everyone tried to make the world a better place, we wouldn't be here."

"That's why I have this tattoo," Arthur said, raising his sleeve to reveal *John 12:24*. "It's to remind me that people have always been giving their lives for the betterment of this world. Not Mars. Not Jupiter. Earth. This world we humans have been on for tens of thousands of years. Their sacrifices have inspired others to live their lives for good. It's true that not everyone is striving to make the world a better place, but sometimes it only takes a few people. Sometimes it only takes one person."

"I get where you're coming from, Arthur, I really do, but don't you think it's a little too late for the world?"

"I am optimistic, but I'm also a realist. I am not blind. I know what is going on in this world. But if you don't have hope, what's the point of doing anything? Why are you doing what you're doing? Fighting people you don't want to fight? Eating two meals a day and getting five hours of sleep a day—if you're lucky. Why are you doing any of this if you don't have hope? The answer is there's hope in those thoughts of yours. You have hope that one day you'll be back in the states enjoying another juicy steak with a beer on the side. See? Look at that smile! It's small, but it's there! You have hope that things *will* get better and that others will be able to enjoy the things they enjoy most in life. I know you have hope, it's hiding behind all that negativity."

Maybe Arthur was right. Maybe Sebastian did have hope. He got up from his back and decided to sit against the tree.

"Maybe I just want to see how the world ends," Sebastian said.

"Or maybe you want to see if the world *doesn't* end," Arthur responded.

Sebastian thought for a moment before changing the conversation. "What do you want to do when you get back to the states?" he asked.

"Like I said, I have hope," Arthur said, trying to relate back to the conversation they were having. "I will have kids because I know things will get better."

"Are you sure about that?"

"Yes."

"I wanted kids, but in this messed up world I don't think I'll have any."

"I know when you let your hope shine in that darkness, you too will come to terms with having kids."

"It would have to be one strong woman to have kids with someone as broken as me."

Sebastian returned to his sulky silence as Arthur knelt next to him and threw a hand onto his shoulders.

"Hey, we're going back to the States alive. Life will get better. You're going to be hopeful one day, and you're going to have kids with a strong woman. Mark my words. We're going to pull through."

Sebastian looked one more time into the starry sky. This time, a strange feeling stirred within him. It was like a light, calm energy flooded his body. What was it about that night sky that made him feel that way? Sebastian might never know. His mood had changed, and now all he knew was that everything would be all right.

***

Still on stage, Sebastian returned to the present. No one seem to have noticed he had a flashback. Everyone had finished their moment of silence. Ramon was to be placed in the same commando field as Ryan. The patch was placed warmly on him by Citlali.

"Peace and prosperity will not come easily," Ishmael said. "The sacrifices we make are for the future of our people. Losing someone close to you is never easy, but we will continue to prevail in our work and make sure no one dies in vain."

A round of applause followed. Sebastian clasped his hands, still recovering from the whirlwind of emotions about Giselle and the flashback about Arthur. He wondered how much longer he could hold himself together.

"And with that, I would like you to congratulate our new peacekeepers!" Ishmael said, managing a terrific smile.

After an endless series of white-gloved handshakes, the peacekeepers went to the saloon to celebrate. When given the chance, Sebastian slipped from his friends in the crowd and dashed around one of the corners. His satellite bracelet led him to a secluded courtyard. He received a notification from Catalina through his contact lenses but muted it. He couldn't hold it in anymore and needed to be alone. His tears dripped left and right, splattering onto the soil and flowers.

"Let it out," said a soft voice. Citlali had appeared to comfort him. She hugged him as his tears fell onto her shoulder. She was a hologram, but he could feel every bit of her flesh and warmth. Her feelings were programmed but her concern and emotions were genuine. She was an artificial intelligence, yes, but she was real and she cared. Although his head was tucked into her chest, his pleading cries still drifted out. The slow steps of Ishmael soon accompanied them.

"I was the one who caused the car crash," Sebastian wept. "I drove the car off the road. I had a flashback when we were driving, but..." he wiped away tears as more took their place on his already soaked face.

"You could never control those flashbacks," Citlali said. "Not then. Not now. It's not your fault."

"...a messed-up man like me should not have been driving," he continued, not hearing her. "It's my fault we're not with our son. It's my fault we're here. She shouldn't be in the hospital. We should have been with our son on our way to California to make a new home. We left him because of me. There were so many things I wanted to say to her. So many things we missed out on with our son. Because of me!"

Ishmael and Citlali didn't know what to say. They waited, praying for him to feel well.

"She will get better," Ishmael finally said. "Like her, I know you will need to take some time off."

"She will be better," Sebastian replied, drying his face with a handkerchief. "We still have a lot of work to do, and I still want to do my part."

"Hold on. All in good time, Sebastian," Citlali said. "The peacekeeper missions will be there when you're ready."

"You will be back soon," Ishmael said. "But for now, use your time to recollect your thoughts. I know something that might take your mind off everything."

Sebastian looked curiously up at Ishmael, and then at Citlali, who was gently swinging her arms back and forth as if rocking a baby. Sebastian then remembered that Catalina and Darius were going to have a baby. That must have been what the notification from Catalina was about. Since babies were genetically engineered and incubated, there was no need for a woman to become pregnant and wait nine months to give birth. The baby would be created right before everyone's eyes.

This was going to be the birth of his great-great-granddaughter, and he would not miss it for the world. Giselle certainly wouldn't want him to miss such a day. Sebastian's clothes changed from the peacekeeper attire to a casual civilian look. An excited Sebastian, Citlali and Ishmael rushed into an approaching hover car and dashed off into the sky to the birth center of the city.

"Where are you guys?!" Catalina gasped as she got ahold of Ishmael through the satellite bracelet.

"We're on our way," Ishmael said, looking at a map and a hologram of her on his bracelet.

"Well, hurry up! We're next in line!" she said excitedly. "I tried contacting Sebastian and Giselle."

"Don't worry, Sebastian is with us," Ishmael said, smiling. "Giselle can't make it because of an injury, but she's all right!"

The hover car deposited the three in front of the massive rainbow of a building. They ran through the glass entrance and followed the arrows and holographic map past the lobby filled with other excited soon-to-be parents. After a few turns, they heard someone call out to them.

"Over here!" Darius shouted through his bright smile, waving them over. "Just in time!"

"Come on, we're next!" Catalina said, locking arms with Ishmael.

They passed through the glossy gold double doors and were greeted by the genetic engineering designer and a room filled with mainly Catalina's family. Their cousins, nieces, nephews, aunts, uncles and grandparents warmly greeted Sebastian. The genetic engineering designer's tucked-in white collared shirt and black tie were covered by a red-and-black vest. Her red beret went well with her gold skin and yellow eyes. Her long dark skirt and stockings only added to her stunning attractiveness.

"Hi, I'm Aurelia," she said, her smile as big as the rainbow-colored building. "Are you ready?"

And so the process began. They all sat down in front of a massive metallic wall that was alive with buzzing and flickering lights. Aurelia swiped the incoming holographic projections, setting all the modifications for the incubator according to what the couple wanted for their child. "Name: Amethyst. Sex: female. Career interest: genetic engineering. Energy levels: above average. Hair color and type: amethyst and curly. Eye color: pink. Strength: max according to athletic body type...."

"Genetic engineering," Aurelia smiled. The attributes listed on the screen looked endless. "Looks like she might be a student of mine some day!"

They waited eagerly as the incubator did its job. The side of the machine was no longer opaque. A baby appeared in the middle of the water tank with a small cord connected to her belly while cradling in a seat no bigger than her.

"Look at her!" Catalina said, bursting into tears of joy. Darius placed his arm around her as the family around her gazed in awe. "That's her."

"In a few moments you'll be able to hold her," Aurelia said, examining a series of charts on the monitor. The tank began to drain, and once the last drop of water disappeared, the tank's glass dissolved into the air. Aurelia brought Amethyst out of the tank and placed her in Catalina's arms. "Here is your daughter, Amethyst."

Instantly everyone, including Sebastian, was filled with such overwhelming happiness. A new life and love was brought to them. Their hearts pounded warmly. Their eyes were hypnotized by Amethyst. Even through their tears, the couple could see she was the most beautiful miracle they had ever laid their eyes on.

A new member entered on this autumn day. The couple caressed the snuggled baby all the way back home, careful to keep Earth's newest member as close to them as possible. The family rode along with them in the flying limousine, chatting about the baby.

"Hey, where is Giselle?" Catalina whispered to Sebastian.

"She couldn't make it," Citlali interjected. "She had a minor accident, but don't worry, she'll be fine. She'll recover in time."

"I'm so sorry to hear that," Catalina said. "I'm so sorry, Sebastian."

"It's fine," Sebastian said. "She's the strongest person I know. She'll get better."

"Well, I can't wait until she gets to meet Amethyst," Catalina smiled, puppeteering Amethysts arms as if she were about to hug someone. At the new parents' apartment, Sebastian noticed Ishmael watching him from the balcony.

"What is it?" Sebastian asked, walking over to him.

"You got to meet you great-great-granddaughter," Ishmael said. "How do you feel about that?"

"I feel great," Sebastian said. "Really I do. Thanks for bringing me along."

"Of course I was going to bring you," Ishmael said, pausing. "You should go back to the ceremony though. In the meantime, I'll go check in on Giselle. Go have fun. She would have wanted you to."

"She would have, wouldn't she?"

"Go have fun, Sebastian."

"Yeah, Sebastian," Citlali said, walking up behind them. "Let's go have some fun!"

She locked arms with Sebastian and turned to the new parents.

"Congratulations on becoming mom and dad, Catalina and Darius!" Citlali said, pinching the newborn baby's soft little cheek. "We'll leave you two with your new daughter! And as nobody needs me here, take care all!"

"Take care, Citlali!" the family cheered as one of the kids ran up to Citlali and hugged her, letting go and returning to be with her parents.

"Thank you, Citlali," the new parents said.

"Congratulations," Sebastian began, but before he could say any more, Citlali dragged him onto the balcony and into the hover car. The two went back to the celebration at the headquarters, where the party was still in full swing. Music and laughter blasted well into the hallways.

"Got to love a party where people can keep it going!" Citlali said, her legs and hands breaking into small dance movements. Ryan, Rosa and the other peacekeepers Sebastian came to care for spotted the two newcomers. Sebastian's casual clothing changed to match the suits some of them had on. Citlali turned around and looked at Sebastian, throwing an imaginary rope around him and pretending to pull. "Come on, Sebastian!"

It was no use resisting; Citlali always got her way. He played along, shuffling closer to Citlali as if dragged by the imaginary lasso. After all they had gone through, they could at least let loose and enjoy themselves. The floor heated up as Citlali and Sebastian's feet moved closer and closer, their friendly spins around each other encouraging the others to pair up and compete in dance against the two. Jaylyn approached the two.

"My turn to dance with the single man," Jaylyn said, wrapping her arms over his shoulders.

"Single?" Sebastian said. "I am not."

"I'm only joking," she insisted. The two took turns tilting their bodies over one another and swinging each other around. Rosa and Ryan danced intimately nearby, staring at each other and speaking only with their adoring eyes. "She'll get better."

"I know," Sebastian said.

"She'll be back to her old self," Jaylyn said. "Until then, we're going to do what we can to get those warkeepers."

"She'll be back."

"And when she's back we'll celebrate fiestas together. Have you and Giselle celebrated Day of the Dead yet? That is something to look forward to as well."

Patricio had Paula in his arms. They appeared on the side and danced in a full circle around Sebastian and Jaylyn. Although there was no official dance contest taking place, there was for sure an air of competition going around the group of friends. Patricio picked Paula up and tilted her back, revealing her chest and neck. Paula then winked at Jaylyn as Patricio threw her into the air, catching her as she came down and neatly placing her onto her feet.

Sebastian and Jaylyn obviously had to counter this. The two linked right hands and made a sort of bow. Standing up, the two stomped a foot and pointed it down, shaking that leg. Sebastian bent his leg as Jaylyn got on top of it, placing her hands on one of his shoulders and sliding her hands to the other end seductively. She jumped down to the floor and they kicked their feet in the air touching each other's shoe ends. She gave Paula a 'were you watching' look. Then she glided to the side, as he twirled her in front of his body. Swiftly, the two began swinging each other back and forth. They continued to dance as an impressed Patricio and Paula danced away.

Alice and another man danced their way toward Sebastian and Jaylyn. She looked playfully at Sebastian, moving her hips from side to side while waving a scarf in the air. The man looked appreciative of her body as he moved around her, exploring every inch he could. Still though, Alice was gazing at Sebastian. She moved behind him and started dancing. Jaylyn moved closer to Sebastian, trying to grab his attention back. Alice pushed Jaylyn toward the man and began dancing with Sebastian. She led him away from Jaylyn and continued her dance with him.

"You're mine now," Alice said giving a sympathetic smile. "How are you feeling, Sebastian?"

"Amazing. I'm feeling much better now," Sebastian said, swinging Alice around. "By the way, do you know when the memory incursions are supposed to stop?"

"Oh, Sebastian," Alice said frowning. "They should have stopped for you by now."

"I was only wondering," he said thinking about the recent flashback he had at the ceremony. "I think mine have stopped. I'm remembering my memories without the incursions now."

"If you ever want to talk about them with me let me know."

"Thanks. I will keep that mind."

"Good," she said. "So, what's your next plan?"

"Next plan? Well, I was told I should take a break from peacekeeping for a while. I wish I could see Giselle, but she is still recovering. I would like to continue my work as a peacekeeper; it would help to take my mind off the last mission."

"I'm sorry we couldn't get to you guys in time. We had just finished our mission when Charles told us to go to the site of your mission. I'm not too sure why they needed my team but apparently the military was having a hard time forcing themselves into the palace. I'm going to question their incompetence later. I still can't believe they escaped, but we'll get them."

"Don't worry. It was a well-guarded building."

"You know I was told to take some time off, too. Many others were as well. Apparently, we're laying low for the time being."

"Why?"

"It looks as if a lot of warkeepers inside our nation went into hiding after our last mission. Until they make themselves known again, there won't be much work."

"Sounds like a retreat for now. That's good news"

"*For now.*"

"What are we expected to do until then?"

"Now that we are done with basic training and have been given our specialties, we're going to begin our psychological warfare training. It's more advanced training, but we're also given more free days to ourselves. We're going to be meeting other covert peacekeepers across the globe."

"Wait. We'll be traveling the world?"

"Yes, sir," she said widening her eyes. "Aren't you excited to see what the world has to offer?"

"Yeah," Sebastian sighed.

"Oh, the food! The music! The people we are going to meet!"

"I really wish I could have seen the world with Giselle," he said, musing about her warm eyes. He knew he needed something to get her off his mind. "If I have to travel for training then I will. She will recover. When that happens, she and I are going on a trip around the world. Just me and her."

The emptiness that haunted him before from not being with Giselle now remained closer to him than his shadow, ready to take his place in his body. His mind began to tip over the needle that marked the border between his soul and hollowness. He needed to find something to distract himself. It came to him what he would result to. Only until Giselle got back her memories, Sebastian thought, looking over Alice's shoulder then at her again. The emptiness began to take its toll on his heart.

"Okay, I can't wait," Sebastian said at last in a now monotone voice.

"Are you all right?" Alice asked, studying every part of his face, knowing that he wasn't.

"I look forward to our training sessions," Sebastian said, walking away beginning to sweat. "I'll be in my dorm."

Despite Sebastian's slow exit, nearly everyone was still lost in the glittering lights. Ryan, Rosa, Ramon, Chloe and Lydia hugged and patted Sebastian as he left the party. The group looked on worryingly as Sebastian commented that he would be all right and wanted to go to his room to sleep. The only one who followed was Citlali, who continued to keep an invisible watchful eye on him via U-ITS. A hover car brought him back to the institution. He made his way through the empty halls to his dorm. She secretly watched as he began his lonely descent into a world of happiness through a stimulant patch. He lay quietly on his bed dozing off. Once he was unconscious, Citlali entered the room in her hologram form, carrying the serape scarf, which she had taken from Giselle's room.

"It's best you hold on to this until Giselle gets her memories back," Citlali said, placing the folded scarf on the nightstand. She ran her fingers through his hair and kissed him on his forehead. Simultaneously she appeared by Giselle on her hospital bed and did the same. Giselle was unconscious as well, still recovering from her recent resurrection.

"Everyone will need you two," Citlali said. "You two are more special than you know. You'll see that soon enough. With these hands and these plans, you both will help to restore these lands."

She wondered if changing her holographic form into Giselle's appearance would bother or comfort him. She thought the same about changing into Sebastian's form with Giselle. She changed from her original form into Giselle's shape and body. She lay in front and faced him, hoping to help him feel something more than the stimulant he was on.

"You were doing so well, Sebastian," she whispered to him in Giselle's voice, looking into his closed eyes. "Hang in there. You two will need each other now more than ever."

While with Giselle, Citlali changed her appearance into that of Sebastian.

"I can't wait for you two to be with each other again," Citlali whispered in Sebastian's voice to the real Giselle.

Back in his dorm, though still asleep, the real Sebastian smiled and rubbed his hand against the waist of Citlali's hologram of Giselle. Citlali mimicked this gentle gesture through her hologram of Sebastian on the hospital bed. The real Giselle let out a faint giggle that echoed back to the real Sebastian. With a gentle smile, Giselle and Sebastian affectionately touched their foreheads together in tender defiance of what they so desperately wanted most. Love. Something everyone needs, especially in a time like this.

www.ingramcontent.com/pod-product-compliance
Lightning Source LLC
Chambersburg PA
CBHW060134130626
46556CB00006B/2343